# SEXY DEVIL

Books By Sasha White

PURE SEX

THE COP

LUSH

SEXY DEVIL

Published by Kensington Publishing Corporation

# SEXY DEVIL

## SASHA WHITE

APHRODISIA

KENSINGTON BOOKS
http://www.kensingtonbooks.com

APHRODISIA are published by

Kensington Publishing Corp.
850 Third Avenue
New York, NY 10022

All Kensington Titles, Imprints and Distributed Lines are available at special quantity discounts for bulk purchases for sales promotions, premiums, fund-raising, and educational or institutional use.

Special book excerpts or customized printings can also be created to fit specific needs. For details, write or phone the office of the Kensington special sales manager: Kensington Publishing Corp., 850 Third Avenue, New York, NY 10022, attn: Special Sales Department, Phone: 1-800-221-2647.

Aphrodisia and the A logo Reg. U.S. Pat & TM Off.

ISBN-13: 978-0-7582-1990-9
ISBN-10: 0-7582-1990-3

First Kensington Trade Paperback Printing: December 2007

10  9  8  7  6  5  4  3  2  1

Printed in the United States of America

# Acknowledgments

So many people helped me stay sane while writing this book, my first real trip with psychic and supernatural characters.

First off, thank you to John Scognamiglio, my wonderful editor who let me take the story where the characters wanted it to go and has patience with me when they get away from me.

For Vanessa Jaye, for being there for me, always. And Beth, JJ, Frauke, and Erin, for being my friends.

And to the Allure Authors, Cathryn Fox, Delilah Devlin, Myla Jackson, Lisa Renee Jones, Sylvia Day, and Vivi Anna, for all that you do.

# Contents

# THE DEVIL INSIDE

# PROLOGUE

She couldn't look away.

He had her wrists above her head, pinned against the mattress, and his eyes locked on hers as his hips thrust forward to slide gently into her body. Her pulse raced and she wrapped her legs around his waist, holding him tight. His rhythm picked up speed and she whimpered; her sex tightening around him, her body trembling with the strength of her approaching orgasm. Her heavy eyelids drooped, but she couldn't let them fall, couldn't look away from the well of emotions overflowing from his eyes.

"I love you, Gina," he whispered.

Joy filled her and she cried out, every fiber within her strung taut as she squeezed him between her thighs. She squeezed harder and thrust her hips again—and felt nothing but emptiness. He was gone. Her thighs pressed only against each other.

A growl of frustration echoed through Gina Devlin's empty bedroom as she opened her eyes and pressed a hand against her heated forehead.

Another dream. Another faceless lover with eyes that looked deep into her soul and filled her heart while he filled her body.

Flopping over onto her back in the queen-size bed, Gina kicked at the tangled sheets and let the cool air dance across her over-heated skin.

She was used to dreams waking her up. When she was a little girl, all her premonitions had come in the form of dreams. But as she grew, so had her skill at manipulating and controlling her gift. Now she could use touch, smell, and sometimes, strength of will, to bring forth a vision if she needed to.

And normally she could block them with equal ease.

She'd had to learn how to block the random psychic vibrations that floated around people or she wouldn't have been able to live a normal life. But at night, when she sought peace in sleep, sometimes the dreams still came.

The dream with the faceless lover declaring his love had been with her for years, and she wondered if it really was a premonition or just wishful thinking on her part.

She'd longed for a man to love her as she was for so long, it was more fantasy than dream.

Closing her eyes once more, Gina Devlin trailed a hand over her belly and past the small patch of tight curls. Trying to forget the familiar ache of loneliness in her heart, she concentrated on easing the ache of emptiness between her thighs.

# 1

Caleb Mann strode through the heavy glass doors of Fusion Cafe and continued straight to the service counter without looking left or right. The air-conditioning inside the café was a welcome relief from the humid heat of mid May in Pearson, British Columbia. It also took the edge off his nerves.

Mug of strong, black coffee firmly in hand, Caleb stepped to the side of the counter, and scanned the room carefully.

The sunlight bounced off the surface of Pearson Lake, directly across the street, brightening the small café. Colorful paintings on the walls and mismatched furniture gave it a funky, comfortable feel that was reflected in the diverse clientele. A slick-looking businessman stood a couple of feet away, impatiently ordering a fluffy latte from the frowning counter girl. An older lady and a girl who was probably her granddaughter sat with a coloring book in front of them.

None were who he was looking for.

He disregarded the twentysomething male engrossed in a novel nearby and briefly considered the woman by the window. Well dressed, with long dark hair, she sat ramrod straight as she watched people come and go. She was pretty, but Caleb didn't think she was the type of woman his brother would be friends with. Uncertain, he let his gaze slide away.

Then he saw *her*.

Removing his sunglasses, he gave the woman a slow perusal. She'd isolated herself by sitting at a small corner table, head bent over a notepad of some kind. Yet she still seemed approachable. The invisible wall that emanated from most people when they wanted to be left alone wasn't there.

She was dressed casually in a short camouflage skirt and a tight black tank top that made it impossible to ignore her pert breasts. If for some unknown reason he hadn't noticed her mouth-watering cleavage, he'd certainly have given the length of tanned flesh exposed by the short skirt a second glance. It had to be her.

Caleb had expected nothing less from his little brother than to set him up with a real looker. What he hadn't expected was his own primal reaction to her—the way his blood heated and his stomach clenched when he looked at her—or the way her inky black hair, which was full of vivid red streaks and skimmed across her pale shoulders, made his fingers itch with the urge to touch . . . to brush it aside so he could nibble on her tender flesh.

His reaction surprised him, but for once he didn't try to contain or control it. After all, if she was a friend of his "work hard–play harder" younger brother, chances were she was also a party girl—a bad girl.

*Oh, yeah*, he thought to himself. The total opposite of what he normally looked for in the fairer sex, and exactly what he *needed*.

Detail-oriented guy that he was, Caleb leaned against the

counter and studied her for a minute. Skimpy clothes flaunted bare limbs, bright purple polish sparkled on her fingertips, and silver jewelry flashed when she shifted in the filtered sunlight. There was also a tattoo on the inside of her wrist—very . . . exciting. He willed her to lift her head so he could see her face clearly, only to have his breath catch in his throat when she did so.

Flawless skin smoothed over high cheekbones, tiny white teeth nibbled at a full pink lip, dark eyebrows flared over almond-shaped eyes. He couldn't see their color from where he was, but it didn't matter. Her classic beauty and outrageous sex appeal called to him unlike anything, or anyone, ever had.

He wanted her, instantly and unequivocally.

Shrugging his suddenly tense shoulders, Caleb pushed off from the counter. *You're not here to find your soul mate*, he reminded himself, *just someone to let loose with*.

He was tired of everyone ragging on him for being a workaholic. Hell, if he hadn't worked so hard for the past ten years, Gabe wouldn't have been able to go to college. Someone had had to pay the bills after their parents died. Plus, his work was satisfying in a way his player of a brother would never understand, so the nagging hadn't really bothered him.

Until his last girlfriend dumped him because he was too "old and settled" for her, that is. *Then* he'd felt a bit of a sting. He was only thirty-three, for God's sake!

Even then her comments hadn't really hurt him. Not until she'd turned the sting into a downright festering burn by adding that his good looks couldn't compensate for his lack of imagination in the romance department, let alone the bedroom.

Anger, and a twist of uncertainty, burned a hole in his gut. That had been hitting below the belt, literally.

Lack of imagination? He had plenty of imagination. And the wild-child woman his little brother had set him up with was going to help him prove it.

Halting next to her table, he pasted a winning smile on his face and opened his mouth.

"Excuse me. Christina?"

When Gina Devlin realized the question was directed at her, she huffed out a grateful breath and tossed aside her charcoal pencil. Normally she didn't welcome interruptions when she was working, but her temperamental muse had deserted her, taking any semblance of artistic talent along with him. That made it pretty damn hard to get the sketches for her new commission down.

Eager for a distraction, Gina leaned back in the spindly chair and looked over the wall of muscle standing next to her corner table with a big grin on his gorgeous face. And her skin immediately began to itch from the inside out.

He was her favorite type of distraction—big and male.

The buttoned-up shirt and pressed jeans he wore did nothing to detract from the wide shoulders and slim hips they covered. But, in her mind, they did label him a stickler for the rules, and that made him totally not her type. Only a real stick-in-the-mud irons his *jeans*.

Not being her type didn't stop her eyes from continuing to skim appreciatively over his trim hips—and the impressive package between them, too. And of course she couldn't stop there, so she mentally drooled over his muscled thighs for a long moment before raising her gaze to meet his.

A steady gaze that was vaguely familiar.

Shaking off that thought, she realized he'd called her Christina.

The little devil inside her strained at the leash she'd kept him on for the last six months. Poking her with his pointy tail, he screamed, "Do it! Do it!"

Before she could think twice, her lips parted, and the words tumbled out. "I prefer Tina." *It's closer to Gina.*

# 2

In a voice that was so smooth and deep it sent shivers down her spine, Mr. Gorgeous stick-in-the-mud introduced himself. "I'm Caleb—Gabe's brother." He held out a large hand to her.

Gina leaned forward, slipping her hand into his. Long fingers wrapped gently around hers; the heat of him soaked through her skin and inched its way up her arm. Her palm tingled sharply, and images of open mouths, sweaty bodies, and tangled sheets filled her mind.

*Whoa!* She pulled back in surprise.

To cover up her sudden disquiet over the vision, she waved blithely at the empty seat across from her. "Have a seat, Caleb."

What was she thinking? Or better yet, what the hell was she doing? She had a deadline; she didn't have time to waste on a man, no matter how good-looking he was. Of course, it *was* rare for her to get a psychic flash just from shaking hands with a stranger—especially if she hadn't deliberately opened herself up and searched for one.

Rarer still for the vision to be one that made her whole body flush with arousal.

Gina eyed Caleb from under her lashes as he deposited his coffee mug gently on the table and settled his large body into the tiny iron chair. Despite his good looks and awesome body, this guy was here to meet someone else. Maybe she should've reined in her little devil and let him move on.

Then again, there was no such thing as a coincidence. Right? Which she could take to mean . . . he was meant to meet *her*.

She'd been struggling with her new collection of sketches anyway. Her muse had given up and run away to have some fun. She should do the same. She couldn't remember the last time she'd forgotten about everything but having a good time. And if the vision—of hot, sweaty bodies rolling around together— she'd had when they touched was any indication, this man could show her a *really* good time.

With a mental shrug, she smiled flirtatiously at her table-mate, and the hunk smiled back, blue eyes twinkling playfully.

There was a brief silence while they openly checked one another out. Gina shifted in her seat and crossed her legs, getting comfortable. His eyes followed her movements, and she fought back a wicked grin. Even dressed as she was, in casual just-off-work clothes, she knew she looked good. Then they both spoke at once.

"How do you—"

"So what do you—"

They laughed together, and the tension eased. Caleb settled back in his chair, spreading his hands wide. "Ladies first," he said with a crooked smile.

Relishing the jump in her pulse at his smile, she leaned forward, giving him a clear view of her cleavage, and arched an eyebrow at him. "I was just going to ask what you liked to do for fun?"

Heat warmed his gaze, but Gina was pleased to see that while he glanced at the offered view, he didn't stare down her top crudely. Instead he locked eyes with hers and showed off perfectly white teeth in a sardonic smile before answering softly. "I haven't made much time for fun lately. In fact, just the other day I was accused of being old and stodgy."

"You?" She chuckled softly. "You look like you might be a little uptight. But definitely not old, and, well ... stodgy we can fix."

His eyebrows jumped, a little taken aback by her bluntness maybe, but he didn't run away. He got points for that.

"That's good to hear. I will admit I've let business and various responsibilities take over a large chunk of my life in the past. My construction company is doing well now, and I've decided it's time for a change. Time to stop making work the focus of my life." He stared at her with earnest blue eyes. "That's why I agreed to this blind date. It's time to try new things and remember how to have a good time."

He got even more points for such an open answer. Gina understood the demands of starting and running one's own business. Her artwork was a business for her, a part-time one, but still a business. However, she also knew that sometimes a body just had to ignore business and concentrate on the pursuit of pleasure.

A quick scan of the room and her conscience was soothed when she didn't see a single woman alone anywhere. Caleb's date had either missed him or pulled a no-show. It was time to kick things up a notch.

"Do you have anything specific in mind for fun, or are you open to pretty much anything?"

The flickering flames in his baby blues burned hotter at her challenge, and his smile turned wolfish. "I'm ready for anything."

She fought the urge to crow in delight. So he wasn't as uptight as she'd thought. He might put business before pleasure, but a sense of responsibility wasn't really a *bad* thing in a man. And this man definitely had bad-boy potential. She could sense it.

Adrenaline pumped through her veins, and her inner bad girl roared to life, ready and willing to face all challenges. Suddenly very awake, Gina was fully energized for the first time in longer than she could remember.

It was time to play.

She grinned at Caleb. "I think I can help you out," she said with cocky confidence. With one last lingering look at her sketch pad, she shoved it into her canvas tote bag and gestured toward the door. "Let's go somewhere with a bit more action and see what happens."

# 3

She'd surprised him.

Not many people could do that.

Caleb wasn't sure what he'd expected when they left the coffee shop, but this wasn't it. When he watched her swing a slender leg over the seat of a sexy little crotch-rocket of a motorcycle, leaving her thighs almost completely bare, it had never entered his mind that they would end up in a gay bar.

Not that he minded. He didn't judge people by their sexual preference. It just wasn't somewhere he would've thought to take a woman he hoped to get intimate with.

A quick glance around the dark room made him reconsider. It was early, and the bar wasn't full, but it was busy enough. Yet no one bothered them. No one even gave them a second look.

Couples, of all combinations, lounged on the various sofas surrounding the room's perimeter. A small group of young guys were stationed in front of the bar, and a male couple was on the dance floor, swaying back and forth in each other's arms.

He thought about it, and excitement pushed past his apprehension. It was the perfect place to get to know someone. Everyone there was so intent on doing his or her own thing no one paid them any mind. He wasn't the boss or the big brother to anyone in that bar, and that was surprisingly freeing.

Especially considering where his thoughts were taking him. With his back to the wall, he had a clear view of the room and of Tina's antics. They'd been playing pool for almost two hours, and despite the fact that he'd been in a constant state of semi-arousal through it all, he'd learned some pretty interesting things about her.

In fact, she fascinated him.

"You mean to tell me that you work at the coffee shop, making sandwiches and lattes for people every day, when you could easily support yourself with your illustrations?" It didn't make sense to him. He could tell by the tone of her voice when she talked about her art that she loved it, so why would she want to work in a café when she could make a living doing what she loved?

A lush breast brushed against his arm as she reached past him for the cube of chalk on the edge of the table, heating his blood another degree. Was she deliberately trying to drive him insane with lust?

She continued to stroll around the table, looking for her next shot as she talked. "My artwork pays nicely, but if I devoted myself to it entirely, I could easily become a hermit. Working in the café lets me deal with real people without getting too close to them."

"You don't like getting close to people?"

"I love getting close to the right people," she said in a husky voice that made his cock swell. She bent over to take her shot, and he got an eyeful of plump womanly flesh cupped lovingly in fire-engine-red satin.

Swallowing hard, he dragged his gaze from her cleavage to her delicate face. The devilish glint in her dark eyes left no doubt in his mind that if he played his cards right, he could be one of the lucky ones. One of the ones she got *real* close to.

Tina was different than any other woman he'd ever gone out with. No, not different—*more*. More sexual, more flirtatious, and more unpredictable.

More *woman*.

Flirting was one of those things he'd just never gotten the hang of. It was too much of an iffy thing, a gray area that was always open to interpretation. He preferred to deal in things that were solid . . . black and white only.

Unsure of how to handle such blatant flirting without being a complete idiot, he ignored it. "Aspects of construction are like that, too. I deal with clients if I have to, but I prefer to leave that side of things to my brother. He's the smooth-talking salesman of the family."

Tina's lips twitched up on one side, but she didn't say anything about his lack of response to her flirting. She just let the conversation move on, and continued to kick his ass at pool.

It wasn't surprising she was winning. Watching her bend and stretch over the green felt that somehow reminded him of his bed was much more distracting than playing with one of the guys. Yet he felt like he was getting to know her better than he ever could sitting across from her at a dinner table.

"So you enjoy working with your hands then?" she asked in reference to his last comment about preferring to work with his crew instead of just supervising. The comment itself wasn't sexual, but to his fogged brain, everything she said and did had sexual connotations. He was having a hard time being the gentleman he'd always prided himself on being.

Thoughts of getting to know her better in any way but the physical disappeared as she stretched a bit farther to line up another shot, and her skirt rose another inch. Half an inch more and he'd know what color her panties were—if she even had any on.

Which he didn't think she did.

In his mind's eye, he undid the zipper of his jeans and stepped up behind her. Lifting her skirt that final bit, he'd thrust into her from behind. She'd grip the edge of the pool table and push back against him. If they were quiet, no one would even notice.

Ungluing his gaze from her legs and the temptation they represented, he shifted his stance. He glanced around the bar in an effort to distract his mind and keep his zipper from splitting, but it didn't help much.

What the hell? He'd never had a problem with control before. Tina's body was calling out to the caveman in him, and his baser urges were fast erasing his common sense. Along with his ability to hold a decent conversation. What *had* they been talking about?

He watched the cue stick slide through her purple-tipped fingers and bit back a groan. Hands—she'd asked if he liked to work with his hands. "Yeah." He tried desperately to get his mind back on topic. "There are few things as satisfying as looking at a completed project and knowing you built it with your own two hands."

He'd never fantasized about sex in public before. Hell, he'd never even had sex anywhere other than in a bed. He and his brother had been raised to treat women like ladies. He wined and dined them if he wanted to get to know them. And unlike his brother, Gabriel, he always got to know them before going to bed with them.

A lightning bolt of realization hit him between the eyes, and he groaned softly. His head fell back, thunking against the wall, and his eyes slid closed in misery.

He *was* a boring lover.

"What's wrong?"

Her small hand burned through his shirt, leaving an imprint right over his pounding heart. He straightened up and looked down at the sex kitten standing in front of him. A party girl, his wild younger brother had set him up with. What the hell had he been thinking? He couldn't please her!

Tina cocked her head to the side and studied him for a minute. A flame flickered to life in the depths of her dark eyes, her full lips slowly tilting into a naughty smile.

Without another word, she stepped closer, her body brushing against his as her breath danced across his chin. His pulse jumped, and regret fought with desire as her hand slid around his neck and pulled his head down. She didn't know what sort of a letdown she was setting herself up for.

Her tongue darted out, and he watched it teasingly wet her lips before they pressed softly against his and all thought ceased. She leaned her body against him fully, nudging his lips apart with the tip of her tongue. Determined to shake his insecurities, he thrust his hands into her silky hair and dove wholeheartedly into the kiss.

He needed this. Needed to feel the hot eagerness of a woman against him, sighing in pleasure and wanting only him. Tongues tangled, and heat burned through veins.

A deep groan formed in his chest, and he tore his mouth away as she boldly rubbed against him. Burying his face in the curve of her neck, he nipped at the soft skin there and tasted her flavor as his hands roamed greedily over her curves.

He spread his thighs, pulled her tight against him, and she pressed against the ache of his confined cock. Unfortunately the eager gyrating of her hips only encouraged him to lose control.

The abundance of her rounded ass filled his hands while he held her still and thrust against her soft warmth. Her sharp teeth nipped his earlobe just before he trailed his lips across her collarbone and down to the swell of her breasts. He couldn't get enough.

Closer, he needed to get closer. Her clothing was in the way. He inhaled deeply of her sweet scent before nudging aside the hem of her shirt in search of bare flesh.

A distinct pain bit into his skull, and his head was pulled back sharply.

"Down, boy, we don't want to get arrested now, do we?"

Tina's husky voice brought him back to reality with a shudder. She was breathing as heavily as he was, and her fingers stroked soothingly through the hair at the nape of his neck—the same hair she'd pulled to get him to back off.

A groan escaped, and he closed his eyes against the truth of it all. If she hadn't stopped him, he didn't think he would've stopped. How was he ever going to make her pant and beg and call out his name if he couldn't even control himself in public?

# 4

Confusion filled Caleb's eyes before his gaze slid away from Gina's. Her heart dropped into her stomach, and she hesitated. She wasn't sure when it had happened, or how it happened so fast, but Caleb had managed to get past her defenses. Not only was she attracted to him—she actually liked him.

It didn't matter that they were total opposites. Him with his settled life, career, and family; her, a military brat, with a life she could stuff into her backpack and move on a whim, just as she always had.

He'd been so open and accepting as they'd gotten to know each other she'd started to fall for him. She'd been having such a great time that when she'd caught a glimpse of vulnerability in him earlier, she couldn't stop from reaching out to him.

It was rare she reached out to anyone. Sure, she was friendly, but she didn't have any real friends. Moving from army base to army base while she was growing up had taught her to be self-reliant in many ways she was grateful for, but it also made keeping her protective walls in place a natural thing.

What had started as a teasing kiss, a way to distract him from his thoughts, had quickly burned out of control. Caleb's mouth on hers, his lips devouring hers greedily, his hands running over her body hungrily—had fired her up so much her blood was still racing through her veins at the memory of his taste. Liquid heat pooled between her thighs, and her heart felt like it was about to burst from her chest.

He had tasted like home.

Hell, she didn't have a clue what home tasted or felt like. She just knew it was something she craved on a soul-deep level. A level she rarely let herself acknowledge.

Gina gave Caleb a closer look. He was as turned on as she was . . . the evidence of that was still hard and undeniable between them. But the regret, and the hint of anger brimming from the bright blueness of his eyes, tainted her newfound revelations.

Pulling away from him, she tried to keep her expression playful but gave up that idea almost immediately. She wasn't one to hide her feelings normally, and she wasn't going to change now just to make things easy on him.

Besides that, she did like him.

And even though she wouldn't admit it to anyone, least of all herself, the vision she'd had earlier had planted the seed in the back of her mind that he could be *The One*. She'd never had a vision like that before.

"OK, Caleb. What's going on?" Taking a stand, she planted her hands on her hips and waited for illumination.

He straightened up from the wall. "What do you mean? You're the one who started that."

*Men.* She huffed out a frustrated breath. *And they say women are incapable of giving a straight answer.*

"I'm not talking about that little bit of petting. I'm talking about in your head. I know you're hiding something, something that concerns me, or at least this attraction between us, and I want to know what it is."

"I'm not hiding anything."

Her silence was louder than any words could be.

"You're imagining things." His lips tilted in a halfhearted smile.

Gina relaxed her stance, not wanting to seem antagonistic. "Caleb, sometimes I just know things. And I *know* you're hiding something from me. Something about why you wanted to go out with me specifically tonight."

His eyebrows rose a fraction. "What do you mean 'you just know things'?"

Not wanting to get distracted, she waved a dismissive hand. "It's a gift, forget about it. We're talking about you here. What are you hiding from me?"

"It's nothing," he stated firmly.

The words sounded good, but he still wouldn't meet her gaze. An ugly idea popped into her head, and her insides churned.

Wrapping her arms across her stomach, she took another step back, bracing herself. "Are you married?"

"What? No!" His eyes shot straight to hers, completely open now. "I'm not married. How could you even think that?"

"Your energy is all . . . wacky." *Good work, Gina, now he's going to think you're all wacky.* "Look, I know you're attracted to me." She dropped her eyes to his groin meaningfully. "But the vibes you're putting off are all mixed up. It's clear your body wants me, but the look in your eyes says you don't. So until you fess up, this is where the evening ends."

"You tell him, sugar."

Gina glanced over her shoulder to see an audience of two guys openly eavesdropping from the other side of the pool table. They were obviously a couple, the taller of the two draped over the smaller, more effeminate one with a "You go, girl!" look on his handsome face.

Ducking her head, Gina stifled a giggle while she waited to see how Caleb would react to the intrusion. When he reached for her hands and pulled her back toward him, she realized he was going to ignore it. Looking into his earnest eyes, she couldn't help but ignore the couple as well. Heat seeped in through her fingertips, and she tried to focus on what he was saying.

"I swear I'm not married, Tina. Do you really think Gabe would have set us up if I were?"

Shit! She'd forgotten all about that!

Maybe now was a good time to tell him she didn't know his brother and she wasn't actually his date. No. The timing was all wrong. If she told him now he might walk away, and she wasn't quite ready for that to happen.

"You're right, Caleb. I should know better." She ignored the irony of the situation and forged ahead. "But my radar is telling me you're hiding something. Something I should know."

He glanced over her shoulder, and emotions flickered across his face. His full lips firmed, and he looked at her meaningfully. Tugging her closer, he leaned in until his lips brushed the shell of her ear and his husky voice made shivers skip down her spine. "There's a place, and a time, to talk about things. And this isn't it."

He was right about that.

Unable to stop herself she nipped at his neck before she pulled back. Keeping hold of one of his hands, she turned to leave the bar with him trailing her, their audience of two left behind.

When a waspish voice called out to her not to let him get away with keeping secrets, she stopped and faced the couple with a wicked grin.

"Don't you worry about me, honey. I think turning him over my knee for a little spanking will go a long way to making him talk."

They exited the club with hoots and hollers still echoing in Gina's ears. She was feeling pretty confident until they got to the parking lot. Then she noticed Caleb's silence.

She bumped her hip against him playfully as they crossed the dark parking lot. "Why so quiet?"

"You're not really into spanking and stuff, are you?"

A laugh jumped loudly from her lips before she could control it, and she slapped a hand across her mouth briefly. Sometimes she was embarrassed by her own lack of inhibitions. Clamping her lips together tightly, she stopped next to her bike and turned to Caleb.

"Spanking doesn't really appeal to me. I just said that to lighten things up." Her hands had a mind of their own, and the one that wasn't trapped in Caleb's fist reached for his belt and pulled him against her once again. "What about you? What appeals to you?"

He lifted his hand and slowly stroked a rough fingertip over her cheek and across her bottom lip. "You appeal to me."

His gentleness caused her heartbeat to trip, and something akin to fear shot through her. His touch was so tender, almost . . . loving.

Gina took a steadying breath. She could almost feel her inner walls crumbling to dust—walls that no one had been able to break through since she was a kid. Her gut was telling her that Caleb was special. She'd felt an instant connection with him—that had to mean something.

She sucked in a deep breath and flashed him a brave smile. It was time to do what she did best. Take a chance.

"So what are you going to do about it?"

# 5

Adrenaline made her almost giddy. She was going for it. There was a reason he approached *her* table, and this was it.

"What am I going to do about it?" Caleb looked at her and grinned. "Well, while I enjoyed our little foray into exhibitionism in there, all I really want right now is to get you out of those skimpy clothes and into my bed."

It hurt more than it should've, those words that told her she was wrong about him.

Disappointment made her shoulders heavy as she realized he hadn't been able to see past the easygoing facade she lived behind. Like many men, he'd approached her because she looked good, not because of some instinctive connection.

With a deep breath, she forced herself to pull her hands away from his solid heat. Stuffing them into her pockets, she struggled to keep her inner balance and bury her disillusionment.

Even the solid, good men of the world wanted only sex from her. She should just accept it, and the night, for what it was. A brief escape from loneliness.

Stiffening her spine, Gina looked Caleb over and issued her ultimatum. She had to get it out before she was tempted to let it slide, to just go home with him and lose herself in mindless lust.

"I'm attracted to you, Caleb. You're tall, you're gorgeous, and you have a body I would love to run my tongue all over, but that'll never happen unless you tell me what you're hiding."

Caleb's gaze dropped to her lips, and his cock twitched at the thought of that mouth all over his body. He took in her stance and the determination on her face.

Stalemate.

No way was he going to tell her he sucked in bed, and not necessarily in a good way. If she walked away, she walked away. There were plenty of women out there, and he was good-looking enough that he could find another one to work with, to explore with. He was sure of it.

But he wanted this one. He wanted her with a hunger and a certainty he didn't understand.

He crossed his arms in front of his chest and eyed her. "I've been told recently that I'm a boring lover."

She laughed! She actually laughed!

Humiliation burned a hole in his chest, but he straightened his spine and turned to walk away.

"Wait!" Her small hand latched on to his arm and wouldn't let go. With a deep breath he faced her once again, waiting.

Big, dark eyes full of compassion, she smiled softly. "I'm sorry. I shouldn't have laughed. But, honey, if you believe the idiot that told you that, then you're not as smart as I thought you were."

She trailed her fingers up his arm and over his shoulder. Cupping the back of his head, she leaned in to kiss and nibble her way up his neck, making it hard for him to think straight. She nipped his earlobe sharply and whispered, "I have no doubts that you can rock my world, and if that's what you want to do, I promise to return the favor. All I ask is that you be honest with me."

Caleb parked his truck and climbed out quickly. Tina wasn't far behind him, and saliva pooled in his mouth as he watched her pull up and park at the curb in front of his house. When he realized he was bouncing up and down on his toes, he stopped instantly and gave himself a mental shake.

*Christ, relax, would you? It's not as if you're a virgin.*

He may not have been the most adventurous lover in the past, but he was starting to believe that wasn't all his fault.

With a couple of long strides, he was next to Tina as she put the kickstand down and turned off the rumbling engine of the bike. He looked at her sitting astride her sexy little motorcycle—her skirt stretched tight against her thighs, toes just touching the pavement—and his heart started to pound.

He ignored the tightness building in his chest and concentrated on the fact that he was going to soon be naked with, and buried deep inside, the sexiest woman he'd ever met.

Caleb grinned in anticipation as Tina pulled off the ebony safety helmet she'd worn. She brushed her hair out of her eyes and winked at him flirtatiously. "Enjoying the view?"

Her outrageous openness made him even more determined to be everything she could possibly dream of in a lover. He wanted to see that naughty smile of hers melt into a satisfied one as she drifted off into an exhausted slumber in his bed. In order to accomplish that, he needed to loosen up. To be just as open as she was.

Taking a deep breath, he told her the truth. "How could I not be? Although I do admit to being a bit jealous."

"Jealous?" She cocked her head to the side. "Of what?"

"Of the time that motorcycle gets to spend between your legs."

A flush bloomed on her cheeks, and he felt a touch of smugness when she appeared speechless. With a husky laugh, she climbed off the bike to stand directly in front of him. Looking up with unreadable eyes, she didn't back down. "I'm ready for you to take its place whenever you are."

Turning abruptly, he grabbed her hand and strode up the walkway to his door. He shoved the key into the lock and turned the doorknob just as a hand cupped his ass and squeezed gently, causing him to stumble slightly when he stepped over the threshold.

He pulled her into the house behind him and closed the door, shaking his head at her in mock exasperation. "You're a naughty one, aren't you? What *am* I going to do with you?"

Normally he'd invite a date to sit in the front room. He'd turn on some music, crack open a bottle of wine, and slowly set about making her comfortable. After a bit of kissing and caressing on the sofa, he'd lead her to the bedroom where they'd make love. Then again, normally he wasn't fighting the urge to take the woman against the door the minute they walked through it. And normally he was confident in his ability to please her.

As though sensing his uncertainty, she locked eyes with him and inched closer until their bodies were mere centimeters apart. The air thick and hot between them, she slid her hands up his chest to his shoulders, and he felt the caress throughout his body.

Balancing herself carefully, she kept their bodies that tantalizing distance apart while she whispered in his ear. "Fuck me."

Her words cut the leash that had been holding him back as pure animal lust slammed through him. He thrust his hands into her hair, bringing his mouth down on hers. Her lips opened, and he tasted heaven as her tongue danced with his, their bodies straining to get closer. Her fingers dug into his shoulders, her lithe body undulating against him boldly.

Fighting for control, he tugged her head back and dragged his lips across her cheek to a delicate earlobe. He sucked it into his mouth, nipped at the exposed skin of her neck, and let his hands roam the body that curved and dipped in all the right places.

He reached under her skirt and filled his hands with the firm roundness of her ass. Aside from the minuscule scrap of cloth bisecting her plump cheeks, she was naked. With a guttural moan, he lifted, and her strong legs wrapped around his waist. The heat of her desire burned through the material between them as he mindlessly thrust against her.

Soft whimpers and heavy breathing echoed in the hollow foyer, reminding him of where they were . . . what he was doing . . . what he *wanted* to do.

Unwilling to let her go, he stood rooted to the spot and dropped his head onto her shoulder. Her scent enveloped him, and he fought desperately to regain some semblance of control. He didn't want to lose it the way he had in the bar. He wanted to make her lose it instead.

"The bedroom," he muttered. Tightening his arms around her waist, he lifted her so that her legs wrapped tight around him; he focused on the doorway at the end of the hall and began to walk. Her breath skimmed across his neck as she playfully spread kisses wherever she could reach, her fingers tangling in the hair at the nape of his neck. Teeth clenched tight, he tried desperately to ignore the way her hot softness bumped against him with every step.

Just as he was about to enter the bedroom, she planted her

lips on the sensitive skin directly behind his earlobe and sucked. Hard.

His knees buckled at the sensation, and he fell back against the wall. A determined hand pulled his head down to hers, and she planted her lips on his, murmuring encouragement against his as their mouths ate at each other.

"That's it, Caleb. Don't think, just go with it. Play with me."

He turned, pinning her to the wall with his body firmly between her legs. His hips thrust against her, rubbing his hard-on against her soft core while his hands skimmed roughly over her rib cage and her legs drifted away from his waist.

Powerless to stop the wild hunger whipping through his body, he nipped and bit at her neck and shoulders. He tugged down the neckline of her shirt, dipped his head, and ate at the soft flesh spilling over the cups of her bra before nudging the lace out of the way. Cupping a handful of plump flesh, he pulled a rigid nipple into his mouth and suckled at one nipple while the fingers of his other hand tugged and pinched the other.

Her panting sighs turned to whimpers, and her body arched against him. With one foot on the floor, she still had the other leg hooked around his waist as she shamelessly ground against him. "More, Caleb, more. I love it."

Slipping a hand beneath her skirt, he shoved aside the tiny scrap of material keeping him from her naked flesh. Her hot, wet, slick, naked flesh. He thrust a stiff finger into her with ease, his groan mingling with her primal cry of satisfaction. Sharp fingertips dug into his shoulders, scraping down his back as she moved against his hand.

"Yesss," she hissed eagerly, her husky voice filling his head. "Right there. Oooh."

God, she was wet. A flash of pride hit him as her inner muscles clenched around his fingers. This is what *he* did to her. She wanted *him*.

She placed her lips against his and panted into his mouth. Demanding more. Every spare ounce of blood filled his cock and made him harder than he'd ever been. Her fingers wrapped in his hair, and she pulled his head back.

"I want you inside me." She nipped at his bottom lip before thrusting her tongue deep into his mouth. Their hands tangled, both of them reaching for the button on his jeans. Finally the button gave, and she shoved his jeans and shorts down just enough so that her hand could wrap around him and squeeze gently.

Caleb sucked air deep into his lungs and fought to keep from coming.

"Condom." He pushed out a puff of air as her hand continued to stroke him. He reached deep into his side pocket and with trembling fingers found the condom he'd put there earlier. Gripping her wrist with one hand, he ripped the packet open with his teeth and spit the brightly colored foil aside before rolling it down his length.

Their gazes locked briefly before their lips met again in a hungry, eating kiss. He reached around, gripped her bare ass cheeks, and lifted her so that her legs were once again wrapped around his waist. But this time nothing separated them.

Tina reached between their bodies and guided him to her entrance, and with one quick thrust he was wrapped in her hot tightness, and any hope for control was shattered. His hips pumped hard and fast, his hands holding her still as she moaned and whimpered against his mouth. Her insides clenched greedily around his cock, and the pressure built at the base of his cock. He swelled even more, the throbbing of blood pulsing through him the only thing he felt until he couldn't hold back any longer. He thrust deep and ground against the hard knob of her clit as his body jerked and he ripped his mouth away from hers. A primal groan of satisfaction roared up from deep inside and echoed through the house, mixing with her sharp cries as her sex spasmed, milking him for all he had.

Dropping his head to her shoulder, Caleb tried to catch his breath. Her hands fell limply to her sides, and he kissed her neck softly. A minute later her legs unwrapped from around his waist and dropped slowly down to the floor while he prayed he hadn't hurt her with his roughness.

He'd never lost control like that before.

Jesus! They still had all their clothes on, and he'd never even made it to the bedroom, let alone the bed!

He pulled back to look into her face. Her head was tilted back against the wall, her eyes closed and lips parted as she breathed deeply. He raised a hand and gently stroked a finger over a delicately arched eyebrow.

"Tina?" She stiffened in his arms, and his heart dropped to his stomach. "Tina, sweetheart, I'm sorry."

Her eyes snapped open, but she refused to meet his gaze. "Sorry?" She gave a rusty chuckle and skimmed a hand over his chest. "Why are you sorry?"

He pressed his forehead against hers, kissing the tip of her nose. "For being so rough, so impatient. For losing control. I didn't hurt you, did I?"

Her lips parted in a smile, and Caleb watched as a laugh bubbled out from between them.

"Oh, Caleb," she said and finally met his gaze head-on, eyes gleaming with sassy satisfaction. "You weren't the only one who was impatient and lost control. I was literally begging for that, and you gave me just what I asked for. You certainly didn't hurt me."

Relief swept through him, and he hugged her to him for a long moment as he remembered her begging him, demanding him, for more.

He hitched up his jeans, zipped the fly, and lifted her against his chest. With her cradled in his arms, he carried her swiftly into the bedroom, where he planned to make her beg again.

Only this time he would do it his way. Slowly and methodically, with attention to *every* detail.

# 6

Gina thrilled at being lifted and held against Caleb's chest, but he was headed in the wrong direction.

"Where are you going?" she asked, running her fingers over his collarbone.

He stopped just inside the bedroom door and looked down at her, a small crease between his brows. "Don't you want to spend the night?"

"Oh, yeah. And for an all-nighter, we're going to need sustenance." When he raised his eyebrows and stayed where he was, she giggled like a schoolgirl. "To the kitchen, man. I'm hungry."

Caleb reversed directions and headed for the kitchen, where he pulled a chair out from the table with his foot and set Gina down in it. He executed a courtly bow, grinned at her, and asked, "What is the lady hungry for?"

Gina swiped her tongue across her lips and tried to keep a straight face. She wondered briefly what he would do if she told him what she was *really* hungry for. She smiled wickedly and replied, "Whatever you feel like feeding me."

He blushed! A slow flush crawled up over the big built

blond's neck and over his cheekbones. Gina watched wide-eyed as he turned away quickly without meeting her eyes.

"Oh, my God, Caleb! Are you blushing?"

"What? No, of course not." He went to the fridge and pulled it open. Standing in the cool air, he looked like he was just searching for something to eat, but she was beyond curious and couldn't let him get away with hiding from her.

They'd been doing so well in the communication department, despite the fact that she still hadn't told him her real name, that Gina decided she couldn't let him get away with holding back now. If they were only going to have this one night together, she wanted it to be a night he'd never forget.

He didn't need to prove it to her, but she knew he wanted to prove to himself that he wasn't a boring lover, and in order to do that she had to help him open up. If that meant not letting him blush and hold back, then she was up for the challenge.

Rising from her seat, she went to stand in front of him and block his view into the fridge.

He tried to look around her, but she shifted so he couldn't see. Arms folded across her chest, she waited until he finally lifted his gaze to hers.

"What did I tell you in the parking lot?" she asked. He didn't answer right away, and she continued in a gentle but firm voice. "I told you all I wanted from you was honesty. If we can't be honest about what we're feeling, or what we want from each other, how are we going to get it?"

Caleb rolled his head back and shrugged his shoulders as if he were getting ready to tackle an opponent on the football field. He let out a long sigh and met her gaze once again.

"I'm not like you, Tina. I'm not as open or adventurous, and when you say things like that it just brings the point home."

"Things like what?" she squeaked. "That I expect you to be honest?"

He shook his head and chuckled. "No, not that. When you look at me with that gleam in your eyes and tell me to feed you whatever I want. I admit it, it shocks me, and I'm just not quite sure what to do."

Finally getting a clear picture of what was going on, the devil inside Gina leaped to attention for the second time that night and strained at his leash. Figuring it had gotten her this far with Caleb, she undid the leash and gave it free rein.

Stepping closer to him so that the tips of her breasts brushed against his chest, she infused as much heat into her gaze as she could and licked her lips provocatively.

"Just what is it that shocks you? What do you want to feed me, Caleb?"

His eyes darkened until the blue was almost black; his mouth moved, but no words came out. His big body was tense, and in her peripheral vision she saw his fingers flex at his sides.

But he didn't make a move toward her.

Loving her ability to shake him up and wanting to shock him even more, she placed her hands on his chest and began to unbutton his shirt. "Your cock? Is that what you want to feed me, Caleb?"

Gina pressed a damp kiss amongst the dusting of hair on the center of his chest and worked her way upward until she nibbled along his jaw to his ear. After sucking the lobe between her teeth for a brief moment, she continued to tease him.

"Do you look at my mouth and wonder what it would feel like to have my lips wrapped around your cock? To have my tongue stroking you, my teeth grazing the sensitive underside as I make my way to your balls?" The thought of suiting action to words had her own insides heating and softening again.

She leaned into his muscled frame, flattening her body against his from knees to shoulders. His hard-on pressed against her belly, and his hands gripped her hips. She nestled her head into the crook of his neck and inhaled the scent of musky man before swiping her tongue over the skin there, eliciting a low growl from him.

When she looked deep into his eyes and brushed her lips across his, the desire she saw there fed hers. Letting her tongue dart out, she teased him some more until, finally, their lips met in a hungry openmouthed kiss, their eyes speaking to each other the whole time.

Arousal swamped her, and Gina tore her mouth away from his to start a trail down his naked chest.

She could feel his heart pound beneath his chest as she drew damp circles around a flat male nipple. Closing her lips around it, she sucked, and this time she actually felt his groan while she worried the hard tip between her teeth gently. Replacing her mouth with her fingers, she moved on his other nipple.

Heat flashed through her at the feel of him, the taste of him filling her mouth. He was salty and manly and all things that made her primal side take over. She hungered to feel him thick and throbbing and hitting the back of her throat. Bending her knees, she slid down his body, trailing kisses as she went.

"Stop," Caleb whispered, his hands grasping her shoulders and pulling her back up, hugging her tight to his chest. "You're driving me crazy here."

Gina wrapped her arms around his waist, unsure of what to think. Didn't he want this? Wasn't the night supposed to be about pleasure, about him being more adventurous? Her going down on him in the kitchen wasn't exactly sedate.

As if reading her mind, he continued to talk, his voice raspy in the quiet kitchen. "I won't deny that I want your mouth on me. Hell, oral sex is a huge fantasy for me. But right now, I want more than your mouth."

With that, Caleb lowered his head and took charge, his hands cradling her head, his lips firm and determined on hers. One of his hands swept over her rib cage and cupped a breast through her top. With a low growl, he reached for the hem of her shirt and pulled it roughly over her head, his hands going for the snap on her skirt. "I want you naked this time. I want to see all of you."

Lust swamped Gina. She *needed* this. It didn't matter that her original intent had been to shock him. The need to be with Caleb burned through her veins, shocking *her*.

She needed to feel him against her, his heart pounding in time with hers, his body moving to the same rhythm. She pushed his shirt off his shoulders and gloried in the feel of the muscles that jumped and twitched beneath her fingertips. Trying to get closer still, she hooked a leg over his hip and ground against him, practically climbing his body, but his hands working at her clothes kept her from getting as close as she wanted.

When he finally had her skirt pushed down off her hips, her panties going with them, he palmed her naked butt and lifted her into his arms. He stepped away from the fridge, turned, and sat her down right on the kitchen table.

"You're so beautiful," he whispered, something like awe thick in his voice.

The heat of his hands seared her naked body everywhere he touched. With a flick of his wrist, her bra disappeared and they were skin against skin. The dusting of hair on his chest rasped against her nipples as he lowered his head and claimed her lips again.

Gina pulled him closer, her fingers tangled in his silky hair, her legs wrapped around his hips. His denim-encased hard-on pressed firmly against her core, shifting and rubbing, turning her into a wild woman.

"Fuck, Caleb," she panted, tearing her mouth away from his. "Who's driving who crazy here?"

Caleb's only response was to bury his hand in her hair and

tug her head back. He bit her neck sharply and then suckled it until she whimpered and her nails dug into his arms.

"Please," she begged. Her body was burning up from the inside out. Moving her hands from his arms to his hips, pulling him closer to her, her body jerked against him, her sex aching to be filled. "I need you inside me."

Pleasure ripped through Caleb at Tina's words. She wanted him. She *needed* him.

Determined to maintain his control this time, he stepped back, pulling Tina with him until her feet touched the floor, her body clinging to his. With one sharp movement he turned her around and bent her over the table.

A firm hand in the center of her back kept her there while he fought for breath. His control was paper-thin already, and he knew if she kept touching him with her hot little hands and sharp nails he'd lose it again, and he wasn't going to let that happen.

He leaned forward, licking and nibbling at her shoulders and the back of her neck while his hands made quick work of his zipper. "You want me inside you?" he murmured against her soft skin. Cool air flowed over his cock for a brief moment before he thrust it between her thighs, her slick heat welcoming him as he rubbed his length along her crease.

"Yes." Gina's voice was breathless, her body shifting restlessly between him and the table. "Please . . . now . . . I need you now!"

He fumbled for his wallet and searched for the second condom he'd tucked away when planning for tonight. He found it, ripped it open, and sheathed himself quicker than ever. Gripping her hips, he bent his knees slightly and placed the head of his cock at her entrance. "Your wish," he grunted, thrusting hard, "is my command."

Her cries of pleasure were music to his ears as he pumped

his hips, sliding in and out of her wet heat. Tina braced herself on the table, and he gritted his teeth, a hiss of satisfaction escaping when she thrust back against him. Despite the fact that he'd come a short time ago, he knew he wouldn't last long. Tina's cunt was milking him with every stroke, and his balls were tight and full.

"Come on, Tina," he coaxed. One hand left her hip and reached underneath them, searching for the magic button of her clit. He needed to hurry her orgasm along because he was already on the edge. Finding it, he rolled it gently between his fingertips. "Come for me, baby."

Her body bucked against him, her cries getting sharper and louder. "Yes, again. Do it again, Caleb!"

Feeling his control start to slip, his hips pumped faster, his belly slapping against her ass; he pinched her clit harder, and her whole body tensed a split second before her scream of pleasure echoed through the kitchen. With a grunt of his own, he relaxed his control and thrust deep, every cell of his body focused on the pleasure spewing from his cock.

Drained but content, he curved his body over hers and held on while he caught his breath.

# 7

The sun was just peeping over the rooftops, promising a beautiful summer day, when Gina rolled into her parking spot the next morning, but she was too distracted to notice. Helmet in one hand, keys in the other, she climbed the stairs to her apartment on autopilot.

She'd just had the best night of her life with a man who didn't even know her name. And the worst thing about it was she wasn't sure what to do about it. Running out on him while he was still asleep had been a cowardly thing to do, but she'd had to get out.

Shoving her key into the lock, Gina twisted it and entered her tiny studio apartment. Her *empty* tiny studio apartment. She loved her little haven. She'd done her best to make *a home* for herself there, but it was hard when she'd never really had a home. Her mother had died when she was young, and her father, being a military man, wasn't always as nurturing as a young girl needed.

One thing he had done, though, was make sure she knew how to take care of herself. Between her father and her older brother, she'd learned to think more like a man than a woman and to protect herself, too—physically and emotionally.

Sex was all about pleasure, and she'd never been ashamed of seeking out pleasure when she wanted it. She liked being single and independent—most of the time. But lately she'd been longing for something more . . . for someone special.

There were times when she laid in bed at night and wondered if she'd ever find a man who wanted her for more than a good time. She tried not to think about the way Caleb had been both confident and vulnerable with her, because it made her heart yearn.

She set her helmet on the couch and walked slowly toward her bedroom, trying not to think of the way he'd taken charge of her body and mind, by bending her over the kitchen table and then cooking a midnight breakfast for her. Or the slow and thorough way he'd seduced her one last time before falling asleep with his arms wrapped around her, holding her tight to his body.

She stopped at the foot of her bed, staring at the pillows and tangled sheets, and remembered the way he'd made her *feel*. The way he'd looked at her when he'd slid into her body that final time. Her knees turned to water, and she dropped onto the bed finally acknowledging the way her heart had soared when she realized she had seen Caleb's face above hers before.

Gina wiped at the tears trickling silently down her cheeks and tried not to think about the fact that she'd just walked away from the man of her dreams.

Literally.

# 8

Caleb wasn't sure how he felt when he woke up the next morning alone in his big bed. If it hadn't been for the empty foil packets littering the floor in the hall and by the bed, and the scent of sex still lingering in the air, he would've thought it had all been a dream. But the proof was there. It *had* been a fantasy, but it was a fantasy come true.

The clock said nine A.M. when he rolled over, and it surprised him. He was usually awake by seven, no matter what. Then his eyes caught sight of the heavy piece of paper next to the clock. Suddenly more alert, he opened the note quickly. A feminine scrawl filled the space.

*Hey sexy,*
  *When you're winning on the basketball court today, know that you also won in the bedroom last night. You rocked my world, just like I knew you could.*

No name—as if he didn't know who it was from—and no phone number.

Pride and disappointment fought for the space in his head. He understood where the pride came from but not the disappointment. With a shake of his head, he stepped into the shower and acknowledged that Tina had just about worn him out.

She'd been just what he'd needed. There was no reason to feel let down because she was gone, because she'd left without leaving so much as a phone number. He knew she worked at the coffee shop. If he really wanted to see her again he could drop by there sometime, but why would he want to do that? They'd had a good time. That was all he'd been looking for, and that was what she'd given him. His first one-night stand.

Then why was he so dissatisfied?

She'd certainly helped him to realize that it wasn't where you made love that made it exciting, it was who you were with.

"Forget about it," he told himself. "Forget about her." Yet, when he stepped out of the shower, his mind ignored the order and searched for a plausible reason to look up her up again.

He rushed through his morning routine, completely distracted by thoughts of Tina. If he didn't hurry, he'd be late for his Saturday morning pickup basketball game, another first for him. And how did she know he played basketball on Saturdays, anyway? It must've been one of the things Gabe told her to get her to agree to a date with him.

A loud pounding sounded at his door, and he grabbed a hand towel from the counter. Wiping the last dregs of shaving cream off his jaw, he started out of the bathroom in time to hear a key slide into the lock. It had to be Gabe; his brother was the only person who had a key to his house.

"Caleb? Anybody home?"

"In the bedroom," he called back.

Cursing softly, he tossed the damp towel into the laundry bin and reached for a clean T-shirt. The one time in his life

Gabriel was on time and it had to be when Caleb was running late.

He heard Gabe's footsteps coming down the hall and pulled the shirt over his head quickly. "You're early, for a change," he greeted his little brother.

"I thought it was worth the effort to find out why you asked me to set you up with someone if you were just going to stand her up?"

"What? I didn't stand her up, I met her at the coffee shop and we went to a—" He stopped himself before saying too much. "We went out and had a good time."

Gabe crossed his arms and leaned against the doorjamb, shaking his head. "I don't know who you went out with, but it wasn't Tina."

Unease tickled the back of his neck. "Short, supersexy, brunette with red streaks in her hair, and an amazing body. Rides a motorcycle?"

"If I knew the girl you just described I wouldn't be setting her up with you, bro. I'd have her tied to my own bed." Gabe chuckled. "But now I see why you ditched Tina."

"I didn't ditch her! I thought that *was* her."

Caleb watched as Gabe shook his head, an annoying grin firmly in place.

Who the hell had he spent the night with? He shook his head. "She said she was Tina. Why would she lie to me?"

# 9

"Gina!" Sally's shrill voice called out over the noisy din in the coffee shop. "The computer's frozen again."

It was Monday morning, and the business crowd was lined up at the cash register impatiently waiting for their morning cappuccinos. With a muttered curse and a sharp twist of her wrist, Gina shut off the steamer and deftly poured piping-hot milk into the waiting cup of espresso. She topped it off with a scoop of foam and handed it to the scowling customer with a huge fake smile and a cheerful "Have a nice day!"

Of course the register froze up—they were busy. Things could never go south during a slow afternoon.

"Ginaaa!" Sally whined again from beside the till.

Gina turned her fake smile on her young coworker. "Just reboot it, Sally," she said clearly, trying to keep her irritation from her voice. The day had all the signs of a classic Monday from hell, and it wasn't fair to take it out on Sally. Not when it was herself she was really mad at.

"Press the little white button on the bottom right of the till and hold it down until the screen flickers off and back on. It'll take only a minute to restart." She ignored the impatient look on the customer's face and went back to filling the orders that were already rung up.

Monday mornings were always hectic at the coffee shop. Gina, who was good under pressure, usually handled the till and the customers. But this particular Monday she'd woken up on the wrong side of the bed, alone, mad at herself, and not wanting to deal with people at all. So she'd asked Sally to take the till so she could work the back counter.

It probably wasn't the best idea, considering Sally's lack of knowledge where cash registers were concerned, but it was too late to change now.

Gina turned back to the espresso machine, focusing on getting the rest of the orders made as fast as possible. The good thing about the busy pace was that she didn't have time to think. However, a short hour later, the last of the morning rush was gone, Sally was on a break, and Gina was on autopilot.

Cleaning and restocking so things would be ready for the next rush didn't take much brainpower, and her mind wandered back to its new favorite topic. Caleb.

Confusion reigned when she remembered the way things had gone on Friday night. Confusion heavily laced with self-recrimination.

What had made her lie to Caleb and go out with him? She never lied. It was bad karma. Yet when she'd looked up at his smiling face on Friday night, something inside her had taken over. The next thing she knew she was sitting across from the man and answering to someone else's name.

If that wasn't bad enough, she'd let the whole night pass without telling him the truth. And then she'd run out on him.

Mental head slap. She was such an idiot!

Panic was an extremely unusual reaction for her. She didn't enjoy confrontations, but she'd never run from one before either. It was clear to her now that she'd gone with him because part of her had recognized him from her dreams, just as she knew that not all her premonitions were absolutes.

Just because she'd dreamed that he loved her didn't mean he would. Despite the fact that he'd gone to a gay bar with her, and that he'd surprised her with his willingness to open up and let her know where he was vulnerable, he still wasn't the type to accept her for who she was.

A construction worker, business owner, workaholic who pressed his jeans. Not the type of guy to accept—let alone love—a psychic.

He'd wanted someone for one night, someone to stroke his ego, among other things, and she'd had a good time doing just that. That's all there was to it. Sometimes a dream was just a dream, nothing more.

Then why couldn't she stop thinking about him?

"Excuse me?"

Gina shook her head to clear it and turned to see a woman in a business suit leaning over the counter by the till. "What can I get for you?"

"I'd kill for an almond-flavored latte with real cream right about now," she replied with a harried smile.

"Tough morning?" Gina asked as she started on the order.

"A true Monday morning. You know, the kind when everything that can go wrong will?" The woman looked up from digging in her purse.

"Yeah, I know the kind you're talking about." The women shared a silent look, and Gina finished up the drink.

She rang up the order, and knowing that the end of her own shift was near, handed the coffee over to the woman with a sincere wish for a great day.

"Thank you." She smiled gratefully, dropped some change in the tip jar on the counter, and dashed away in a hurry.

After she closed the cash register, Gina turned to the back counter again, this time with a small smile on her face. It was nice to know some things never changed. A smile could still be contagious.

The smile faded gently from her face as she resumed her restocking and her thought pattern. She'd cried herself to sleep shortly after walking in her door Saturday morning. All over the silly dream of Caleb being The One for her. When she woke up from her impromptu nap, the dark purple birthmark on her wrist was tingling and itching like crazy.

Most people assumed the perfect crescent moon on her inner wrist was a tattoo, and she didn't bother to correct them. The fact that it was a birthmark, and that her older brother, Angelo, had the exact same one on the inner biceps of his left arm, was no one's business.

It was also no one's business that the birthmarks acted like some sort of psychic beacon for the siblings.

The strong burning in her wrist Saturday made Gina realize that Angelo had sensed her upset over Caleb and was worried about her. She'd tried to call him and tell him she was fine, but he didn't answer his cell phone, and it wasn't dire enough for her to try the emergency number he'd given her.

Getting a hold of him nowadays was harder than when he'd been in the military. It was easier to just calm herself down and concentrate on sending out positive vibes for him to pick up. It hadn't taken long after that for the burning and itching at her wrist to fade.

The heaviness in her chest had taken a while longer. She was pissed at herself. Partly for letting Caleb get so close to her so fast, but mostly for doing it while pretending to be someone else.

It had been a crazy thing to do. There was no way she and

Caleb could ever have a future together, no matter what sort of premonitions she'd had, not when it had all started as a lark.

Even if they did get past that, they were totally wrong for each other; he was a straight-laced, average, Monday-to-Friday business owner; she was a carefree military brat who had never been able to conform to anything remotely "average." Caleb had a home, responsibilities, and stability. She had a sketch pad, a backpack, and itchy feet. He'd experienced lasting relationships. Her only lasting relationship was with her brother, and she wasn't even sure if he was currently in the country.

She and Caleb were just too different.

It would never work. Why was she even thinking about it? He'd been looking for a one-night stand. She'd scratched an itch and given it to him.

*Get over it already,* she chided herself. *Focus on something else.*

Like where the hell Angelo was. Normally it didn't bother her when she didn't hear from him for a long time, but he hadn't called when he'd sensed her upset, and she hadn't been able to get a hold of him through normal channels all weekend. Something was definitely up.

Then again, where Angelo was and what he was doing wasn't something she really wanted to think about *too* much. He'd been pretty blasé about leaving the army to work in private security, but she worried. Every time she asked about his job, or what exactly it was he did, he'd skirt the question with answers like bodyguard this guy or investigate that business, find this missing person. It sounded good, but something tweaked her radar. He was trying too hard to protect her, and that usually meant he was doing something dangerous.

Her stomach clenched at the thought of something happening to her brother. Maybe it *was* better to focus on work.

51

When her shift was done she'd go home and immerse herself in her artwork. Creating new scenes on a blank page always helped to clear her mind and put her in a happy place.

"Ahem."

The sound of a voice clearing behind her startled Gina, and she noticed that the container of cinnamon she'd been refilling had been full a long time ago. Her autopilot was malfunctioning, and she'd spilled all over the back counter.

"I'll be right there," she called out over her shoulder. She set about quickly sweeping the extra spice into the sink and putting the cap back on the spice shaker.

"Ahem!" Louder this time.

"Jeez, unknot your shorts for a second. I'm coming," Gina said again as she gave the lid a final twist and turned to the impatient customer.

"Caleb!" she gasped, her heart giving a little kick of recognition.

"Hello . . ." he looked pointedly at her name tag, "Gina."

Panic flashed across her pretty face, and Caleb tightened the leash on his emotions. He shouldn't care that he'd surprised her. She was the one who'd lied.

"What are you doing here?" she asked. Her smile started out weak but grew in strength. "Did you come looking for me?"

"Yes, *Gina*, I did. Can we talk?"

Pink crept up her neck to her cheeks. "I can explain."

"That would be good. When are you done with work? Unless you want to do it right here and now." He made a show of glancing at the man to his right who'd given up on his newspaper and was openly eavesdropping.

She didn't take her eyes off him. "Five minutes. Can I get you a coffee while you wait?"

He took a black coffee and stepped back from the counter.

Too restless to sit, he walked over and stood by the window and pretended to enjoy the view of the lake. But, really, he saw nothing.

Gabe had called him an idiot for wanting to go back to the café, but Caleb couldn't let it rest. One-night stands were just not his style, and he'd been kidding himself to think he'd let it go even before he knew she'd lied to him.

It didn't matter that she hadn't left her number or her name—either of them—on the note. All weekend he'd stewed over the situation until he'd decided he had to see her again. He'd had a damn good time with her, the best ever.

They might not have a traditional relationship, but he needed to find out why she'd gone out with him in the first place.

He was here. Oh, god, Caleb was here. He knew she'd lied about being his date on Friday night, and he'd come looking for her.

*Shit!*

Running her fingers through her hair one last time, Gina dredged up a confident smile for the reflection in the mirror. If she took any longer changing out of her uniform he might think she'd run out the back door and left before they had a chance to talk. She pulled open the staff-room door and headed into the coffee shop.

At first she didn't see him, and she cursed herself for taking the time to change. Then she spotted him—he'd left the window and was waiting at the same small corner table where she'd been sitting the night he'd walked into the café and approached her.

Dressed in jeans that hugged his thighs and a black dress shirt tucked in, he looked casual and manly with his back to the wall. Fate had been very kind to her when it had brought him to her on Friday, and she'd almost screwed that up. She noted his blank expression as he watched her approach and promised herself she wasn't going to screw it up again.

This was the man she'd been dreaming about for years, and she wasn't going to run from him.

She pressed a hand to her stomach in an effort to still the butterflies there. Her name was called out, but Gina just waved an absent hello to the two secretaries who had just entered the café and kept on moving. When she reached the table, Caleb stood, as if to pull out her chair for her, and she glimpsed the heat of anger in his eyes.

*Oh, boy. He's pissed.*

She spoke before he could. "Do you mind if we go somewhere else to talk?"

He glanced around the café at the thickening crowd. "Not at all," he answered swiftly. "Do you have somewhere in mind?"

"There's a small park at the end of the block with some benches. If you want, I can grab some biscotti or muffins and we can sit there."

"Are you hungry?" he asked.

"Not really. You?" Geez! This small talk was going to kill her!

He shook his head, his voice chillingly polite. "Why don't we just sit and talk then? It's a beautiful day."

She nodded okay and, trembling inside, led the way out the front door.

# 10

Outside in the bright sunshine, they started down the sidewalk in silence. Gina wanted to ask him why he was there, what he wanted, but she wasn't sure she truly wanted the answers just yet, so she kept her mouth shut.

They reached the small park within minutes, and she dropped her satchel on the grass as they settled onto a wooden bench. There were kids playing on a small jungle gym nearby, some mothers just watching, some helping the kids on the slide or the swing. A man in shorts jogged by with a large yellow dog panting at his side. It was a beautiful day, and she really hoped it was going to stay that way.

When Caleb didn't speak after a few minutes, Gina couldn't stand it anymore. "Are you angry?" she blurted out.

"About what in particular?" he asked in a clipped voice.

"About me pretending to be your blind date."

"It depends," he said, "on what else was pretend for you that night."

Reacting instinctively, she grabbed his arm, needing that physical connection with him. "Nothing else." She stared into his true-blue eyes and fervently wished she could read his mind. "I may have lied about my name, but that was it. Everything else I said to you ... did with you ... was true. It was real."

He nodded once, but his courteous mask was breaking. A flush was spreading across his cheekbones, and when he spoke, his anger was clear. "Then why did you run out and leave me to wake up to my brother demanding to know why I stood up his friend?"

She hesitated for a second before blurting out, "Maybe because you were only looking for someone to make you feel like a stud, and I figured I'd accomplished that, so it was time to go." She glanced away, unwilling to take the chance that he could read her emotions in her eyes. She wasn't ready for him to know just how much she cared or how much she wanted to be more than just a one-night stand.

"That can't be true." He raked a hand through his thick hair and blew out a sharp breath before he continued. "Not if you're being honest about everything else being real. If what you said, what we did ... my god, what we *felt* ... was real, then you have to know that there was more to it than that. My original plan may have been for only one night, but you blew that out of the water just by being you."

Gina could feel herself melting, softening at his romantic words. God, how she'd longed to hear words like that!

She struggled with her emotions for a minute, aware that he was watching her the whole time. Fear told her not to let him get any closer to her than he already had. Not when she *knew* he had the ability to hurt her. But when she looked into his handsome face, when she saw his strong features and felt the sincerity coming off him in waves, she couldn't deny that she wanted it all.

She wanted love, a real place she could call home with a man she could call hers. She wanted the happily-ever-after she'd refused to let herself believe in. When she looked at him, she wanted to open up . . . to take a chance.

Sucking in a deep breath, she let it out slowly before speaking. "To be honest with you, Caleb, the realness of it all sort of scares me. That's why I ran."

He gazed at her for a silent moment, and then a huge grin spread slowly across his face and they were past the rough patch. He chuckled and said, "There's no need to be scared of me. I'm the tame boring guy, remember?"

She rolled her eyes and giggled like a schoolgirl. "Tame boring guys don't pick up strange chicks in coffee shops and follow them to gay bars."

He shook his head at her, a smile flirting at his lips. "You have to remember, I didn't think I was picking up a strange chick. I thought I was going on a date with a friend of my brother. And I was just as surprised as you to find myself in a gay bar!"

Lighthearted and carefree, she grinned at him sassily. "Okay. I'll give you that. It was my fault that you strayed off the stodgy and boring path."

"You get credit for that, Gina, not blame." He reached for one of her hands and tangled his fingers with hers. "And I'm hoping you'll help me stay off that path for a while longer. But first . . . I would like to know why you let me believe you were Christina."

Why had she done it?

*It just seemed like the thing to do at the time* was too flip. But how would he handle the truth?

"It was a combination of things, really. Does it matter?"

"I'd like to know."

Gina swallowed a sigh. *Here goes nothing.* "My muse had taken off for parts unknown, and I was struggling with my latest commission when you interrupted me. And . . . when we shook hands, I had a vision of us in bed together. I figured everything happened for a reason, and it was about time for me to take a break from working so hard, to recharge and all that, so I went with it."

"You had a vision?" Doubt clouded his expressive eyes.

"Yeah."

"Do you . . . uh . . . have visions often?"

Gina tamped down the urge to laugh. He was so gracious in his disbelief. "Often enough. They usually come when I'm asleep, like dreams that really do come true. But sometimes, if a person's energy, or my connection to them, is strong enough, it can happen when I'm awake." She grinned at him. "And I promise you, I'm not crazy."

"I don't think you're crazy. It's just that I don't believe in that sort of stuff."

"What sort of 'stuff'?" She tried not to be offended. Normally people's disbelief, or even contempt, didn't bother her. But with Caleb, it tweaked her temper.

He shifted in his seat. "Psychics and witches and vampires. Any of that 'new age' stuff."

Since he was trying so hard to be benign, and because she liked him, she strove for patience. "It's not 'new age' to me. Psychic abilities are a gift that's been in my family for generations in one form or another. My mother was an empath, and my brother, Angelo, is telepathic. I'm precognitive; that means I get premonitions." She decided to leave the topic of her psychic emotional link to her brother for another time.

"Premonitions? You think you can see the future?"

"I know that sometimes I get a look at what *might* be the future. Nothing is ever set in stone—free will and all that. I've learned to accept the gift and even how to use it. It's part of who I am."

He nodded, staring out at the kids on the jungle gym.

Gina watched as his fingers wove together and his brow wrinkled. He was thinking, hard.

Finally he settled back on the bench and aimed a small smile at her. "Part of what makes you a successful artist, you mean. Okay . . . well . . . I did want to shake things up a bit for myself. What better way to do it than dating a self-proclaimed psychic?"

She sighed inwardly. He didn't believe in psychics or the paranormal. That was fine, for now; disbelief was nothing new to her. At least he wasn't calling for the men in white coats to come to get her.

They sat together on the park bench, enjoying the sunshine, chatting comfortably, neither in a hurry to leave. Caleb, very formally, asked if he could take her out to dinner the next night, and not bothering to try and hide the fact that she was grinning like an idiot, she accepted.

They were arguing about whether Creedence Clearwater was considered classic rock music or country rock when a shadow fell over them and a deep voice interrupted.

"Gina? I was hoping I'd find you here."

"Hey, Mac," Gina greeted the newcomer warmly. "How are you?"

"Not so good." The newcomer glanced at Caleb before continuing. "I need your help."

Remembering her manners, she introduced the two men while looking Mac over. A big blond bear of a man that normally radiated confidence, he looked tired. There was worry in his dark eyes, and his face was tight.

She didn't need to be psychic to see the negative energy that was hanging over him like a thundercloud. "Mac, this is a friend of mine, Caleb Mann. Caleb, this is Detective Mac Goodman."

The two men shook hands, checking each other out in the way two protective men always do.

After a minute she interrupted their posturing. "What can I do for you, Mac?"

His gaze lingered for a moment longer on Caleb before he faced her again. "If you have a bit of time, I need some help. The kind only you can give."

Almost a year earlier Gina had dreamed about a missing woman and ended up working with Mac on it. It had been the first hint that her gift was still growing. Her visions of the missing girl weren't the future but the present. She'd seen the missing woman at that moment. It had confused and confounded her, but it had also shown her just how helpful her gift could be.

Clairvoyance was a new aspect of her talent, but because of that dream, and that case with Mac, she'd really worked on strengthening it in the past year. Gina had discovered that if she concentrated, she could sometimes find missing or hidden people and objects.

At first Mac had been suspicious of her—he hadn't believed in psychics either—but she'd proven herself. Trust and mutual respect had grown on both sides. Now he sometimes came to her when he was stuck and needed a lead.

And Gina would never turn him away.

Not just because it had felt good to be able to help the police, to save the woman, but because Mac had become a friend. His respect and acceptance had made the loneliness that came with the gift more bearable.

Gina peeked at Caleb from under her lashes to see what he was making of the situation, only to see his polite mask firmly in place. With a mental shrug, she looked at Mac again. "You know I'll always help if I can."

Mac's lips pressed together, and he swallowed before he reached into his pocket and pulled out a photo and a plastic evidence bag with a gold locket inside. "It's another girl. This one is on the run, and I need to find her. Fast."

Before she could reach for the items, Caleb stood up hastily. "I think that's my cue to leave."

Panic flashed through Gina, and she reached for his hand. "No! It's okay if you're here. I don't mind."

He squeezed her hand briefly before releasing it. "I have to get back to work. I've been here longer than I planned already, so I'll just leave you two to your business."

He nodded to Mac, and Gina watched him walk away, her heart sinking.

What did he just get himself into? A relationship with a psychic? Caleb shook his head as he strode back to where he'd parked in front of the café.

No, that was wrong.

First off, he didn't believe in psychics, no matter what that cop thought. And secondly, he wasn't planning on having a serious "relationship" with Gina. He just wanted to spend more time with her. He felt good when he was with her. She was bright and funny and beautiful—and so sexy he could barely think when he was around her.

Relieved, he smiled to himself as he climbed into his truck. The connection he'd felt with her was real, but it wasn't a love connection. He was fine with that. He'd been looking for someone to let loose with when he'd stepped into the coffee shop Friday night, and he'd found her.

# 11

---

"Maybe we should take this somewhere else?" Mac asked gently, still holding the evidence bag.

"Yeah." Gina tore her gaze away from the departing Caleb and looked at the man in front of her. "Your car will work. Is it nearby?"

Mac pointed, and she stood to walk with him. "New boyfriend?"

"Maybe." She sighed. "I've never really had a real boyfriend, so I'm not exactly sure if that's what I'd classify Caleb as."

Mac opened the passenger door for her, and she got in, but before he closed the door he looked down at her. "I'm not psychic, but I am a guy, and I can tell you—that guy is not the type to be classified as anything less than a full-on boyfriend, and I got the distinct impression he has you in his sights."

Gina's heart skipped a beat. "Thank you," she said simply.

Mac smiled tightly, pushed his sunglasses up on his nose, and closed the door. By the time he settled in behind the wheel and handed over the evidence bag, Gina was in a much better frame of mind and eager to help.

Knowing the drill, Mac didn't speak; he sat there while Gina held the bag and concentrated. She closed her eyes and focused her attention inward. Deep breaths in through the nose and out through the mouth as she searched for the pinpoint of light in her mind.

She found it, but it was too small.

Without opening her eyes or asking permission, she opened the baggie and touched the gold locket.

The pinpoint grew, and a picture formed inside Gina's mind. She saw a dark-haired woman driving through the mountains in a beat-up blue Toyota truck. The woman's expression was calm, but Gina was picking up on a sense of panic or fear—maybe it was the overstuffed backpack in the passenger seat or the way the woman was chewing on her bottom lip.

With a deep breath Gina shifted her focus to the passing scenery just before the light went out and she was left staring down at the locket in her hands.

"Gina?" Mac's voice was barely a whisper.

She lifted her head and met his worried gaze. "I saw her in a small blue Toyota truck, driving through the mountains."

"Where in the mountains?"

Gina pressed her lips together and shook her head. "I don't know. I couldn't get that deep."

Mac slammed a fist against the steering wheel. "Damnit!"

Something in Mac's expression tugged at Gina's heart. "Is this a case, Mac? Or is it personal?"

"A bit of both." He glanced at her. "Her name is Nikki Marks, and she's an old friend who got into some trouble. But she won't let me help her. She doesn't think I can help her."

His frustration was clear in his voice, and beneath it, Gina could hear his hurt. He cared for this woman deeply.

"She's okay, Mac. She's unhurt and alone, but . . ."

"But what?"

63

"She's scared."

His eyes widened, and he stared at her, helpless frustration clear in his gaze.

"I'm sorry, Mac. That's all I got." Unwilling to give up so easily, Gina reached out a hand and covered his fist. "Do we have time for me to try again?"

He knew what she was asking. She'd done it for him before. Sometimes, if she could sleep, she could get more from an item.

His voice was strong and sure. "Definitely."

Gina reached for the side of the car seat and tilted it back. She shoved all lingering thoughts of Caleb away and closed her eyes. "We'll find her, Mac."

The next day Gina was massaging shampoo into her hair, deliberately focusing on the scenarios of teasing Caleb under the table in a fancy restaurant running through her head. While she sometimes got visions of not-so-nice things in life, she did damn good work, and she deserved some sexy fun.

Never mind that Caleb had walked away from the park pretty abruptly the day before, as though being faced with a cop coming to her for psychic help had freaked him out a little. It meant someone else believed in her ability, too. It wasn't just in *her* head.

It didn't really matter if he was freaked though, he needed to be shaken up a little, to realize that there was more to life than work and responsibilities. That was why he'd been attracted to her in the first place, right? And, really, if he couldn't deal with that, there was nothing she could do. She certainly wasn't going to tell Mac not to ask her for help when he needed it.

She'd dozed in Mac's car for a while, and when she'd woken up, she'd been able to give him details of where Nikki had finally stopped driving. Gina had seen a fast-running river and a small cabin. As soon as she'd mentioned the antlers above the cabin door, Mac had known where it was.

He'd dropped Gina off at the café and headed out, his shoulders set and determination clear in his every look and move.

Gina stuck her head under the sharp spray of water and decided it would be fun to see just how much it took to make him loosen up, in a naughty way, in public. She'd just stepped out of the shower and was toweling her hair dry when the phone rang.

She picked it up without looking at the caller I.D. "Hey, sexy."

"Gina? It's Caleb calling." He sounded a bit uncertain.

"I know." She laughed. "What's up?"

"I'm really sorry about this, but I have to cancel dinner tonight. My accountant was supposed to finish up the month-end invoices, but his wife went into labor a week early and he's at the hospital right now."

"And that means you have to do the paperwork," she concluded.

"Yes. I'm sorry. I was really looking forward to taking you out for a nice dinner, maybe some dancing."

Warmth flooded Gina's chest. He sounded truly disappointed. "Don't worry about it. You do what you have to do, and we can go out another night."

"I'd like that."

"So you're going to be in the office until late, huh?" A plan began to form in her mind.

"Most of the night, I'm sure. I'm sorry about this, Gina. I was really looking forward to seeing you tonight."

"Me, too, but I should go now. I'm standing here dripping all over the carpet."

They said their good-byes, and without missing a beat, Gina went back to getting ready. The sensations she'd been feeling in her wrist had stopped, so she figured all was well with Angelo and that he'd just been worried about her. Now that things were moving forward with Caleb, she probably wasn't putting out the angsty vibes she'd projected all weekend.

She used the blow-dryer to give her hair body, a fat curling iron to give it some style, and blue gel on some of the curls to give it attitude. Feeling daring, she used blue liquid eyeliner to give her eyes a seductive tilt and layered on the mascara. And because she knew it wasn't good to emphasize both the lips and the eyes, she used clear lip gloss for balance.

When she left the apartment, she was wearing a tight electric-blue spandex top that matched her colored curls and was covered partially by a black spine protector and elbow guards. Black cargo pants tucked into her biker boots completed the ensemble, making her look like a cross between a futuristic warrior and a cover model and feel a little like a dominatrix.

Tucking her curls up under her helmet, she climbed onto her bike and headed for a nearby pizza place. Forty minutes later when she stopped her bike in front of the trailer office at Mann's Construction, it was just starting to get dark.

A lone truck parked in the lot, and a single light was on in the trailer. She set her helmet on the seat of the bike and fluffed her hair out with her fingers before reaching for the pizza secured to the back of her bike. It had been a short ride on the highway to the construction site, and the pizza was probably cold, but cold pizza was a small price to pay for time spent speeding along the blacktop on her beloved Ninja.

Pizza in hand, she climbed the three steps to the office door and knocked sharply before twisting the knob. She stepped inside and saw a small desk with a silent computer on it and files neatly stacked at the corner. No one sat behind the desk, so she stepped past the worn-looking sofa to the right of it and into the open door behind the desk.

Caleb was seated behind a large cluttered desk, pencil poised in one hand, a coffee mug frozen in midair in the other.

"Gina?"

"Hey, sexy," she said and sauntered toward him. "Since you couldn't come out for dinner, I thought I'd bring dinner to you."

A genuine grin split his face, and Gina's heart jumped. God, he was gorgeous.

He stood and moved to stand beside the desk, gesturing her to come closer. He was wearing faded jeans and a tight blue T-shirt that molded to his muscles in a way that would make any woman's mouth water. On the first day they met she'd lied to him, slept with him, and run out on him. Yet there he stood, looking like the poster boy for a woman's fantasy calendar, pleased to see her show up uninvited at his office.

That said a lot.

Her heart clenched in her chest at his seemingly open acceptance of her and her actions.

"You brought me dinner?" He waited at the edge of his desk, a boyishly pleased look on his face. It was as though no one had ever thought to do something as simple as bring him dinner before.

"I did. I hope you like pepperoni and mushrooms." She sauntered closer. Remembering his fear of being a boring lover, and their pillow talk that night at his place, Gina knew what she really wanted to do.

Setting the pizza on the edge of his desk, she locked eyes with him and let her desire show. "I thought bringing dinner would be a nice treat for you, but now I think having you for dinner will be an even better treat for me."

Without giving him a chance to say anything, she leaned into his solid body. Tangling her fingers in the curls at the nape of his neck, she pulled his head down and kissed him hungrily. His hands gripped her hips as she nibbled at his lips. Her other hand rested on his chest with his speeding heartbeat beneath her palm.

Caleb tried to pull back, but she refused to let him. She held tight to his head and let her body surge into his so that he stumbled back a step until he was braced against the desk.

Heavy breathing filled the air as her tongue darted between his lips and she tasted his earthy flavor. Putting everything into the kiss, she knew the moment he gave in. His lips parted wider, and his tongue fenced with hers; his hands clutched her tighter against him, and his arousal poked firmly against her belly.

Her nimble fingers danced across his chest and belly to cup his hardness through faded denim. Gina felt the groan of pleasure that rumbled in his chest, and with a wicked grin, pulled back slightly and bent her knees. Slowly she dragged her breasts against his chest, his belly, his thighs, until she was kneeling in front of him, her face to his groin, her fingers quickly undoing his button fly. She tugged his jeans down to his knees and leaned forward, close enough to let her breath be felt through the material of his shorts.

Tilting her head back, she looked up, met his eyes, and saw the struggle in them. Desire warred with his innate sense of what was proper and what was not. Getting a blow job in his office was definitely *not* proper.

She licked her lips and winked up at him before pressing her open mouth against his cotton-encased cock. His head fell back, and excitement whipped through her. Desire had won the battle.

Running her hands up and down his bare thighs lightly, Gina nuzzled his groin and breathed in the musky smell of aroused male. The earthy scent filled her head and heated her blood. The minute trembling in Caleb's muscles, and the groan that rumbled from his throat when she bared his cock, made her completely aware of her feminine power.

That this conservative man desired her enough—that he trusted her enough—to let her seduce him in his office could've made her fall just a little bit in love, if she were the "falling in love" type. Which she wasn't. She had to remember that.

Determined to make this better than any fantasy he'd ever had, she teased him, and herself, by skimming her hands all over his nakedness. Her fingernails scraped over his hip and across the soft skin where thigh met groin. Her lips and tongue followed wherever her hands went, except where she knew he wanted it most.

When his ragged breathing filled the room, she reached for his cock and pulled it away from his belly. Slowly she licked up his length and swirled her tongue around the swollen red head before sucking him between her lips like a lollipop.

His loud moan echoed in the room as she relaxed her throat and took him deep. She reached between his legs and cupped his balls, fondling them gently while using her other hand in tandem with her mouth to stroke his cock. Using a slow, steady pace, she sucked him deep and then slid her lips all the way to the tip, where she could press her tongue against the sensitive underside.

Her body flushed, her breasts grew heavy, and her core heated and dampened in preparation. Pleasing him was pleasing her in a new way. Pride and power combined with her arousal, increasing the pleasure she derived in making one of his fantasies come true.

Humming her appreciation of his male beauty, she didn't stop when his hands tangled in her hair and he tried to gently pull her away. She gloried in the throbbing pulse against her tongue, the taste that told her he was close to coming.

"Gina." Her name was more groan than anything. "I can't take much more."

Ignoring his plea, she slid her hand deeper between his legs and rubbed her thumb lightly over his puckered entrance. His knees buckled, his fingers tightened in her hair, and his cock swelled enormously, throbbing against her tongue. A growl ripped through the air, and his juices filled her mouth to overflowing, dribbling down her chin as she struggled to breathe and swallow all he could give her at the same time.

His fingers loosened their hold in her hair about the same time it occurred to Gina that she'd let him come *in* her mouth. That she'd let him do something she'd never let another do, simply because she knew it would make it better for him.

She stayed on her knees, with him lovingly stroking her hair while they both fought to catch their breath. Finally he gripped her shoulders and tugged her to a standing position. Cradling her against his body, he tapped a finger under her chin until she met his eyes.

No words were needed. Gina could see tenderness, desire, and adoration all swirling in his eyes. She hoped he could read her just as easily, because she wasn't ready to put what she was feeling into words. Hell, she wasn't even sure what it was she was feeling.

Instead, she leaned forward, brushed a quick kiss across his lips, and stepped away.

"The pizza's probably cold by now," she said in a tone meant to lighten the mood. She gave the room a quick glance and gestured to the clear space in the middle of the room. "Why don't we just have a little picnic right here in your office?"

After a considering look, Caleb smiled and said, "Sure."

He retrieved two cans of Coke from a cooler he kept behind his desk, and minutes later they had the cushions from the worn sofa in the foyer spread out on the floor. Dining on the still slightly warm pizza, they talked about this and that, what had happened during their day.

They were keeping things light and fun until, suddenly, a dark curtain dropped over Gina's eyes, only to be pulled back so she could see a completely different room full of colorful images. Feeling herself get pulled into the vision, she reached out to Caleb instinctively.

"Gina!" Caleb's gut clenched when her body went rigid and her expression blank. It lasted less than a minute, not long at all, just long enough for him to start to panic. Then she was back to normal, relaxed and smiling at him across an empty pizza box. "Your accountant's wife—is she a redhead?"

"Yes." He paused, watching her carefully as his heart slowed to a normal rate. "Why?"

Her smile turned to a delighted grin. "She's going to have a healthy squalling baby boy by dawn!"

A tingle of unease ran through Caleb as he digested what she'd said. *She thinks she had a vision of Maria having the baby.* Unsure of how to deal with her delusion, he spoke gently but firmly. "Maria and Tom are having a baby girl, not a boy. They've known for months now."

"She's a redhead, right? And she's been in this office recently? It would've had to be *very* recent for me to pick up her energy, but she was here, probably on this sofa cushion, and she's in for a surprise if she's expecting a girl."

Was she crazy?

Gina was so confident in her affirmation, and Caleb's emotions were so twisted at that moment, he just couldn't argue with her. He pushed aside the empty pizza box, inched closer to her, and cupped her soft cheek in the palm of his hand. His thumb tested the suppleness of her seductive mouth, and he whispered, "It seems to be a night for surprises then, doesn't it?"

Her eyes softened, and Caleb's heart kicked in his chest. Lowering his lips to hers, all his confusion and unease slipped away at the rightness of her in his arms.

# 12

Gina rolled over and stretched before forcing her eyes open. Caleb's bed was warm and cozy, but it was also half empty. She watched through half-open eyes as her man bent over and pulled his jeans up over his glorious butt. "The sun isn't even up yet, Caleb. Come back to bed."

Over the last two weeks she'd spent many a night over at his place, and he was always an early riser. Even on weekends. She now knew firsthand that he was indeed a workaholic, but it didn't bother her. He worked hard, and he was honest, and when they were together she had *all* his attention.

She didn't need him to be with her constantly or to always be calling. She liked her own time as well, so what they had together worked very well, and Gina liked the way it was progressing.

Caleb shook his head and gave her a rueful look. "I'd love to, sweetheart, but this job has turned into a nightmare. The city's sending out an inspector today, and I can't afford any more problems."

"Is this the Marquettes' house?"

"Yeah, and after that mix-up with the electrical wiring, I had to get rid of the foreman, so it's going to be just Gabe and I running the job for the next week until John, the foreman on the Welsh job, is done, and then he can take over." He heaved a sigh and sat on the edge of the bed, his hand rubbing over the curve of her hip. "And as much as I love my brother, he's not much help when it comes to running a crew."

"There won't be any more problems," she said confidently. *Not aside from Gabe getting knocked down a notch.*

"No?"

"Nope." Gina reached up, weaving her fingers into his hair and tugging him down for a kiss. "In fact, I'd bet you money that Gabe is at the job site, hammer in hand, when you get there."

The muscle in Caleb's jaw twitched, and Gina bit back a sigh. If he didn't believe that, her warning was gonna be a hard pill to swallow. "But when you do see Gabe, hammer in hand, I need you to do me a favor."

His eyebrows went up at that. When Gabe had met her, he'd made it pretty clear he didn't think Gina was a good fit for his big brother. But Gina forgave him his rudeness; she was protective of her big brother, too. And she cared enough about Caleb to mention it.

"Make sure the wiring in the room he's boarding is okay or properly covered or whatever it is you do to protect it."

"Why?" He drew the word out slowly. They both knew why she was saying it, but Caleb had to ask.

"I had a dream that he hits something exposed and gets a bit of a shock."

"A bit of a shock?"

"Yup." And that was all she was going to say.

Caleb rubbed his forehead and spoke firmly. "We've already

been over it all twice so when the inspector comes in today, it's all good."

"Babe." Gina met his gaze dead-on. "You might not want to believe me, but what if I'm right and you *don't* check it out? Gabe's little shock could turn into something worse for another of the workers."

"I'll triple-check it. Just for you." He smiled, gave her one last lingering kiss and left the room.

Gina flopped onto the bed. She really hoped he did triple-check it. The shock wouldn't kill Gabe, but it would hurt him. And then what would Caleb do?

What would *she* do if he always doubted her? She kept mentioning small things that he could verify in hopes he'd start to believe, but it didn't seem to be happening.

Caleb hated to leave Gina in his bed when all he wanted was to crawl back in there. The worst thing about it all was he knew that when he got home from work, she wouldn't be there. He enjoyed having her spend the night, and he was starting to crave having her around more and more. Not just in his bed either. Which was something he really wasn't sure was so smart.

It certainly wasn't anything he had time to contemplate right now. The first stop when he got to the work site was the trailer. He made quick work of the must-be-done paperwork and then headed onto the site. The crew had already arrived, and Caleb wasn't really surprised when he found Gabe upstairs, joking around with the guys hanging Sheetrock, hammer in hand. After all, it *was* a construction site; carrying a hammer around was pretty much a given.

"You're late," Gabe called out to him with a smirk. "Is it hard to get out of bed in the morning, old man?"

Caleb shook his head at his brother. Gabe could be such a brat sometimes. "It is, but not because of my age."

"Oh, yeah, must be that hot new girlfriend that's wearing you out."

The crew hooted and nudged each other, but the men knew him well enough to not voice an opinion on Gina.

"Did it occur to you that I was in the trailer doing some work and that's why I wasn't here earlier?" He watched as Gabe finished on one wall and hefted another piece of Sheetrock. The men lined up the cutout for the electrical fixture, and Gabe held up his hammer, nail at the ready.

The hair on the back of Caleb's neck stood up, and before he could say anything, Gabe started hammering the nail in. Just as Caleb's muscles started to relax, a small spark burst from the wall, Gabe yelped, and his body shot back three feet to land flat on his back.

"Gabe!" Caleb raced across the room. When he knelt by his brother, Gabe was shaking his head and chuckling.

"Holy shit! What was that?"

"You must've nicked a wire. Are you okay?" Caleb's heart was pounding and his brain racing. Why hadn't he listened to Gina's warning? He didn't have to believe in psychics for that one. There was a reason they'd fired the electrician.

Caleb lifted his head and stared at the men surrounding them. "I want that wiring checked throughout *again.* Eyes open, everybody!"

"Don't worry, man," Gabe said as he stood, shaking his hands. "It was just a little kick in the ass. Nothing major. And the inspector will be here soon."

A little kick in the ass?

"I'll give you a kick in the ass. If the inspector had seen what just happened, we'd be shut down. He can't find anything like that." Caleb stepped closer, bracing his hands on his little brother's shoulders and looking him in the eye. "You sure you're all right?"

Gabe nodded and shrugged him off, but Caleb couldn't shake the heaviness in the pit of his gut all day. The inspector came and went, the wiring passed inspection, and everything was okay'd. Gabe laughed and joked as he continued to work with the men—everything good there, but Caleb had gotten a shock, too.

He didn't know what he'd do if anything happened to his little brother. They were all each other had. He should've listened to Gina's warning. Then again, he didn't need to believe in psychic visions to be cautious about safety.

# 13

Almost two weeks later Gina streaked through her tiny apartment with a damp towel clutched in one fist and nothing on. Between Caleb's crew hitting the home stretch on their job and him lining up two new ones, and her pushing to finish her last commission by deadline, she hadn't seen much of him outside the bedroom. So they were going to try the "real date" thing again.

She wasn't exactly sure what Caleb had in mind, but she figured they weren't going to shoot pool at a gay bar. Things were going great between them—no more cops dropping by for help or visions interrupting meals—and she was superexcited about the date.

Snatching a cold beer out of the near-empty fridge, Gina rushed back to the bathroom and set the bottle on the counter. She wrapped the towel around her still dripping hair and then twisted off the cap and took a long, soothing drink.

Her nerves were still strung taut, but the beer helped weigh down the butterflies that had taken up permanent residence in her stomach.

"Relax." She pointed at her reflection. "You are the queen of the five-minute makeovers. This'll be a snap."

After another sip of her beer, she set it down and started getting ready for her date with Caleb. She'd lost track of time when she was sketching out ideas for a new collection, and he was due any minute.

With that in mind, Gina pinned her hair back off her face and toned down her normal funky style by applying her makeup with subtle strokes. After swiping the mascara wand over her lashes one last time, she carried her beer into the bedroom. With a glance at the clock, she pulled a matching leopard-print bra and thong set from a drawer and started getting dressed.

Just because she was taming her makeup a little didn't mean she couldn't have a little fun with her underwear. She knew Caleb's reaction to it would be well worth keeping it under wraps for a while.

She'd wiggled into a short flirty skirt and was buttoning her blouse when the door buzzer sounded. Her time was up; she refused to make Caleb wait so she could primp. After rushing to the door, she glanced in the hall mirror as she was reaching for the doorknob and stopped dead in her tracks.

She'd forgotten about her hair.

"Shit," she muttered. She reached for the pins holding her hair back only to be interrupted by a brisk knock. She flicked a glance at the door and then at her reflection, and a laugh bubbled up in her throat. What the hell?

Winking at the image in the mirror, she undid the top three buttons on her blouse and reached for the door handle. Flash him a bit more cleavage and he'd never even notice her hair.

When Gina pulled the door open and beamed at Caleb in welcome, he felt the inexplicable pull of her hit him full force.

"Wow!" His breath left his lungs in a rush. "You look great."

Not only did his blood heat and his body tighten when he saw her, but he also felt an invisible weight lift off his shoulders. Somehow, just being near her made him feel better when he hadn't even been aware of feeling bad. If he didn't know better he'd think he was falling in love. Except, love wasn't an option with Gina.

She was his lover, the most open and erotic one he'd ever had, but he couldn't—he wouldn't—fall for a wild child who thought she got visions of the future. Even if she had been right about the sex of Tom's baby—and Gabe's little flirtation with electricity.

Those things had been nothing more than coincidence. She'd guessed about the baby, and she'd known they'd had a problem with the electrician. There was nothing mystical about her predictions; one was a lucky guess, the other was a logical deduction. She wasn't psychic, she was just observant . . . and damn sexy.

"Thanks. You look pretty yummy yourself." She reached out and tugged him into the apartment by his tie. Pleasure swept over him at the soft, brief kiss she planted on his lips before asking, "What's the plan for tonight?"

"Dinner at Sophia's, maybe some dancing." He owed her a nice evening out after the past couple of weeks of sporadic phone calls and nights in bed. He'd loved every second of the picnic in his office trailer, and even though she didn't seem to mind eating cold pizza on the floor, it was past time they had a normal date.

He watched, and tried not to drool, while she slipped into a pair of spiky high heels. When she placed one foot up on a step stool to do the straps up around her ankles, his whole body tensed with the need to touch her. To run his hands over her toned calves and up her legs . . . under that flimsy skirt.

She switched feet and started on the other shoe, and saliva

pooled in his mouth. *Normal date, idiot. That means a night out at a nice restaurant. Stop thinking with your dick!* With a mental grimace Caleb tore his eyes off her legs and glanced around her apartment. Since she'd always offered to come to his house, because his schedule was more rigid than hers, this was his first look at her private living space.

It was a tiny, basic, one-bedroom studio, white walls, beige carpets, and yellow appliances. Colored pillows were piled high on the sofa, paintings leaned against every available surface, and the warm scent of cinnamon gave it personality. But it was the clean laundry piled in one of the chairs and the paint-spattered smock tossed on the kitchen table next to the easel that made it lived in, almost homey. He wasn't sure what he'd expected from Gina, maybe lots of candles and a crystal ball? Whatever it was, this normality wasn't it.

"I don't have a crystal ball, if that's what you're looking for."

He turned and raised an eyebrow at Gina, ignoring the shiver that skipped down his spine. "You read minds, too?"

She laughed delightfully and pointed a brightly painted fingernail at him. "No, that's my brother's job. I can read faces though, and you should never play poker."

The sudden tenseness he'd felt fled. He did suck at poker; his construction crew could testify to that. Laughing at himself, he walked out the door and waited while she locked up. What the hell had he thought? No one could read minds; even Gina didn't claim that ability.

He ushered her toward his baby, the midnight-blue '65 Mustang GT Fastback he'd pulled out of the garage for their date. Gina whistled low and long when he reached for the door and opened it for her.

"Nice ride, baby."

"Thanks," he said, eyeing the way her skirt rose up when

she settled into the leather seat and crossed her legs. "I like them. I mean it . . . like it." Christ! Would he ever not be a drooling idiot with her?

This date was supposed to prove to her, and to him, that he'd loosened up in more than just the bedroom. That uptight and stodgy were things of the past. Dinner was traditional and normal, but like sex, it was the person that made things exciting, not the place or the action. He wanted to prove to Gina that he could be exciting and charming, no matter where they were.

It would be easier to prove if he didn't gawk and stutter at the tantalizing sight of her thighs though.

Although he wasn't sure why *that* mattered. What they had was a relationship based on sexual attraction. Why he should try to act as though there was more to it was something he preferred not to analyze.

He pulled open the driver's door and slid behind the wheel. When he glanced at Gina, she was smiling at him with a mischievous twinkle glittering in her eyes.

"It's okay, you know."

"What's okay?"

"That you like my legs. There's no need to be shy about what turns you on, Caleb. I thought we were past that."

He sighed. "We are . . . or we were . . . No, I mean we are. *Ugh!*" He groaned in frustration and let his head fall back against the seat. Would he ever get used to being so . . . open with a woman?

He felt the featherlight touch of her hand on his and opened his eyes. Turning to look at her, he laughed. What the hell? "Okay. I admit it. I love your legs. And your breasts and your ass. I love your body, and I get hard every time I think about what you look like naked."

Her eyes darkened with pleasure at his words, and she

chuckled softly. Cupping a hand behind her head, he pulled her close. After planting a quick, hard kiss on her soft lips, he reached for the ignition and spoke lightly. "You know, some women would take offense to what I just said and make some snide comment about the immaturity of men."

Gina just smiled her naughty smile and winked at him playfully. "I'm not 'some women.' "

As if there had ever been any doubt about *that*.

# 14

There was a line at Sophia's when they arrived, but Caleb had a reservation, so they were seated right away. The Spanish-style restaurant was large and open inside, with tables surrounding the hardwood dance floor at its center. Their table was perfect. Set a bit back from the dance floor and the band, the atmosphere was intimate, the food delicious, and the company supreme.

For the first time in her life, Gina felt comfortable enough with a man to stop playing the lighthearted good-time girl and be completely open about everything. They were talking about movies when Caleb let it slip that he didn't see what the fuss was about with *The Lord of the Rings* trilogy.

"It's magical, it's sweeping, it's epic. It's about good versus evil. What's not to like?" she asked.

"It's completely unrealistic."

"What do you mean unrealistic? Of course it's unrealistic, it's fantasy!"

He toyed with his fork for a minute before continuing. "I

know it's fantasy, but some people want to believe it's real. They get too into it, like that role-playing game with the dungeons and dragons or movies with magic or vampires. People get so into them they start to believe it's all real."

"You mean people like me." All her inner warmth disappeared at his words, and she sat back in her chair. "You still don't believe in my gift, do you?"

When he looked at her, his eyes were as gentle as his words. "I believe that *you* believe in it."

Was it enough?

Gina knew Caleb was the man she'd been dreaming about for years. She also knew that if she really wanted to prove herself, she could try opening herself up to him, try to get something from him that would be proof. The only trouble with that was that she could never pull visions from people she was close to. Something in the universe kept those from her.

Knowing that Caleb was the man of her dreams didn't really help. Her premonitions were only a *possible* outcome of the situation she saw. People had free will, and paths could change in a split second of time, but could a person's beliefs change? Could she have a happily-ever-after with a man who didn't believe in her?

"Gina?" His husky voice interrupted her thoughts.

Chest tight, she focused her gaze on him again, and her breath caught in her throat. He was the one for her. She knew it. She just needed to give him some time and he would know it, too. He *would* believe in her.

She shook off her momentary doubts and winked at Caleb. "If I'd ever had any doubts about there being magic in this world, they disappeared after spending a night in your bed."

Gina giggled like a schoolgirl when his mouth opened and

closed briefly but no words came out. It was too cute for words when he got all shy and flustered on her.

Unexpectedly he didn't let her change the subject. "But you said what you do, with the visions and stuff . . . it isn't magic."

She looked into his earnest eyes, and her heart rate picked up. He was willing to talk about it, to try to understand what she was. That must mean he was starting to believe . . . to accept.

"No, it isn't magic." She thought for a minute and then spoke softly. "Everybody has five senses, right? And some people believe in a sixth sense. Call it woman's intuition, a survival instinct, whatever. What I have is just like that . . . times a hundred."

When she saw that he wasn't laughing at her or looking derisive, that he was actually listening, she continued excitedly.

"Sometimes I get a feeling, a 'vibe,' for lack of a better term, and that feeling translates into a mental snapshot. It can be an image or a phrase. I think I'm just extrasensitive to the energy on a deeper surface." She shrugged. "I don't really have an explanation for how it works, just that it does."

He stretched his arm across the table and held her hand. The roughness of his workingman's hand made her feel small and delicate, the sincerity in his gaze only enhancing that "cared for" sensation.

"You said psychic abilities run in your family?" He was a bit hesitant, as if he were speaking to a wild animal, afraid to startle it and chase it away. "Does this mean you weren't surprised when you started . . . seeing things?"

"No, I don't think so. To be honest, I don't remember a time when I didn't have visions or, at the very least, very intense feelings about certain people without knowing why."

"You've been like this your whole life?"

"Yup. When I was a kid it was mostly dreams, like any other kid, only my dreams and nightmares usually came true." She shrugged, trying to make light of it. Before she could think twice, she forced a playful smile to her lips and told him everything. "So when I tell you you're my dream come true, I'm being completely honest."

His eyes widened, and he sat up straight, his hand abandoning hers. "You dreamt about me? Before we ever met?"

The loss of his touch ricocheted through her. Hoping he'd pulled back unintentionally, in surprise, she went for broke. "I did, many times."

Deep lines furrowed his brow, and clouds rolled into his beautiful eyes. The same eyes she'd seen search her soul and shine with love in her dreams.

"Is that really why you went out with me that first night? Not because you 'felt a connection' but because you'd seen me in your dreams and knew what was going to happen?" Anger started to creep into his tone. "Did you know about my ex calling me a bad lay before I told you? Did you make me say it just to humiliate me?"

"No! At first I just thought you looked familiar. In my dreams I never got a clear look at your face, just your eyes. And a very strong impression. An image of naked bodies and tangled sheets did flash into my mind when I shook your hand, but that was it. I didn't know anything about you personally or your past." Gina met his troubled gaze head-on and let him see everything she felt in her eyes. "I never knew who you were until later," she said softly.

There was a brief silence before he spoke again, the anger gone from his voice. "How much later?"

"After the last time we made love that night. That's why I left before you woke up." She shrugged. "I panicked."

He said nothing. Just sat there and digested everything she'd told him.

She waited for him to tell her that was it, that she was nuts. She waited, and when he finally met her gaze again, she was relieved to see no condemnation or recrimination in them. There was interest and attraction, but there was still no acceptance or love.

And maybe a tinge of panic.

Pain fluttered in Gina's chest, and she fought the urge to challenge him. She wanted to ask Caleb how he could possibly believe she would know what his ex had said about him if he didn't believe in psychics? He was contradicting what he said he believed.

Heart aching and head pounding, she didn't want to think about it anymore. That road led only to loneliness. In an effort to move on, she straightened her spine and gave him a small smile. "How did you get reservations in this place on such short notice? I hear they're booked up almost a month in advance."

"My crew did their renovations last year. Marc and Sophia always told me I could come in anytime. Although I've never taken them up on it until tonight."

The conversation changed smoothly, and she set about just enjoying her time with him and not thinking about if he would ever accept her for who she was or if it would always be just sex for him. One thing she'd learned long ago; enjoy the now of things because, even for her, the future was uncertain.

A short while later, she watched, hypnotized, as Caleb's tongue slowly licked icing off the spoon from their shared chocolate cake. Her body heated, and she pressed her thighs together to ease the sudden ache there. All of a sudden it didn't matter how good the conversation was, how intimate the atmosphere, or how much he believed in her. She wanted dinner to be over. She wanted to get him home, naked, and between her thighs. She wanted to *connect* with him in the only way she knew how.

Lifting her eyes to his, she saw that they were dark with a passion that matched her own. He'd been teasing her deliberately—she could see it in the way his lips tilted just the slightest bit.

He wanted to tease, did he? Two could play that game.

She swiped her finger across the dessert plate and lifted it to her mouth. Parting her lips slightly, she locked gazes with him and let her tongue slip out to sample the sweetness on her fingertip. When his gaze dropped from hers to watch what she was doing, she shaped her lips into a small O and sucked her finger all the way into her mouth, slowly.

Cheeks flushed and eyes burning, Caleb raised his hand to signal the waiter for the check, only to be brought up short when the lights dimmed and a voice spoke softly over the loudspeakers.

"Ladies and gentlemen, Sophia's is proud to start your night of dancing off with a short performance of a traditional Spanish dance, the zapateado! Please welcome Theresa!"

When the soft applause had died down, Caleb and Gina turned toward the center of the room to see a woman dressed in a crimson flared skirt and white off-the-shoulder peasant blouse tapping her feet in time with the band.

Seduction plans were shelved while Gina watched in awe as rhythmic tapping filled the room. The woman's dark curls tumbled down her back and around her barely moving shoulders as her feet tapped out a staccato beat. The crowd clapped, and soon the band picked up the beat quietly, not overwhelming the sound of the woman's tapping feet but accentuating it.

Halfway through the dance she started going from table to table, inviting others up onto the dance floor with her.

When she reached Gina and Caleb's table, Gina didn't hesitate.

Caleb watched Gina join the other women in the middle of the dance floor. It soon became clear to everyone who watched that while Gina could keep up with the dancer in the foot tapping, she couldn't stop her body from following the beat, too.

Her hips swiveled, and her breasts bounced enticingly as she tossed her head, her husky laugh echoing through the room. Her smile was wide, and her eyes glowed when they met Caleb's over everyone's heads. The joy of life shone clearly on her face, and Caleb's heart swelled as he watched her. She was beautiful, so vibrant and energetic.

Warmth flooded his body, radiating out from his heart as he realized it didn't matter that she was a bit kooky with the new-age stuff—he was falling in love with her. He'd done his best to keep her pigeonholed as nothing more than a lover, but it was hopeless. There was so much more to Gina Devlin than her open sexuality, and he was kidding himself if he thought he was immune to it or to her.

The music built to a crescendo, and she spun faster and faster and stopped with a sharp clap on the exact final beat. Immediately he reached into his wallet, tossed a hundred-dollar bill on the table, and stood, waiting for her to reach their table once again.

A knowing smile graced her lips as she strolled toward him, hips swinging. It was time to stop holding back with her. She might be slightly wild and crazy, but she was just what he needed in his life. Open, honest, and full of a zest for life he hadn't felt in himself for far too long.

He wrapped his fingers around hers and pulled her body flush against him. He bent his head and brushed his lips across hers and then across her cheek until he could nip her on the earlobe before whispering.

"Let's get out of here."

# 15

The drive back to Gina's place was thankfully short because Caleb was having a hard time keeping his mind on the road. All he could think about was how the woman next to him had come to be so important to him in such a short time. He refused to focus on the psychic thing and instead concentrated on how she made him feel when he was with her.

Over the years he hadn't even been aware of how shut off he'd become. How business, and Gabe, had taken over every aspect of his emotions. He no longer cared that he'd been called a boring lover, because he *had* been. How could someone who had shut off his emotions be anything but?

But Gina had changed that. She touched something inside of him and reminded him what it was like to care again, to feel.

For the first time in a long time, he felt . . . alive. His heart hammered, and his blood flowed hot through his veins. And it was more than the thought of getting under her skirt that did it to him. It was just being *with* her that did it. When he'd first set eyes on her his brain had stumbled and his body had picked up the slack. But now, not only had his brain caught up, but his . . . damnit!

His heart had caught up, too.

When he'd started to pull away from her earlier at dinner—when she'd told him about her dreams of him—he'd not only seen the flash of hurt in her eyes but felt it deep in his own gut. He'd felt the loss of something he wasn't aware they'd even built—a relationship.

A relationship that had begun with lust but turned into so much more. He'd never felt this open—he'd never *been* this open, or this passionate, with anyone before.

Caleb parked the car and dashed around to open her door. Her hand slid into his, and his heart thumped against his ribs as he helped her from the car.

"You're quiet," she said, placing a warm hand on his chest.

He kissed her. A slow, sensual promise of what was to come. "You're beautiful."

Her lips tilted in a slow smile, and a wicked gleam sparked in her eye. God, she was hot! From the deadly curves of her body to the wicked tilt of her lips, all it took was one look from those gleaming eyes and he was ready to get on his knees and do whatever she asked.

She started up the steps with him close behind her, her swinging hips filling his line of vision and making him wonder if she had underwear on. He didn't see any panty lines, and she was just naughty enough to go without. When they reached the top and her fingers trembled slightly as she wrestled the key into the lock, his cock hardened. She was just as affected by him as he was by her!

They stepped into the small apartment, and she closed the door behind him. When she faced him once again, he reached out and cupped her cheek. Her skin was so pale, so smooth and soft to the touch. He burned to touch her all over, to taste her, to fill her . . . to connect with her.

"Where's your bedroom?" he asked hoarsely.

He stepped aside to let her lead the way. Once in her room she moved to the lamp beside the bed and surprised him by turning it on. Facing him once again, she smiled naughtily and started to unbutton her blouse. Moving forward quickly, he grabbed her hands.

"Uh-uh," he said. "That's my job."

He lowered his head and took her lips in a hard kiss. The sweetness of the Spanish dessert lingered, blending with the uniqueness that was her personal flavor. Fire raced through his veins, replacing blood as his mouth ate at hers. The primitive need to make her his, to give her more pleasure than any other man ever had, vibrated through him. He worked at the small buttons quickly before he forced himself to slow down. He pulled back and sucked in some air. He wasn't going to lose control, not this time.

When the buttons were all undone, he tugged the shirt slowly down her arms and tossed it aside. He kissed her bare shoulder gently and nibbled his way up her neck to the soft spot behind her ear, making her shiver and grip him tighter.

*That's more like it.* He wanted her trembling and crying out his name. He wanted her to burn the same way he did.

The firm, round cheeks of her ass filled his hands, and he pulled her closer, reveling in their differences. Her softness against his hardness; her free-spirited, him solid and calm. But together, they sparked off each other, and both went up in flames.

He gripped the elastic waist of her skirt, pulled it down over her hips, and let it drop to the floor.

"Beautiful," he breathed at his first full look at Gina's semi-naked form. Standing there in nothing but a few tiny scraps of leopard-print material and black heels, she stole the breath from his lungs. Reaching out, he trailed his fingertips reverently across the swell of her breasts, down over her gently curved belly, and fought to find the right words to tell her what he saw. What he felt. "You're perfect."

Her eyes glowed with pleasure when he stepped forward, backing her up until her knees hit the edge of the bed, forcing her to sit. Dropping to his knees between her spread thighs, he leaned in and kissed her again.

Unable to be satisfied with just the taste of her mouth, he ran his hands over her silky skin, enjoying the play of supple muscles beneath as his hands circled her waist. With a sharp jerk he pulled her hips to the edge of the bed and settled himself between her thighs.

His shoulders kept her legs spread wide as he bent his head forward and inhaled her scent. Musky with a hint of spice. Unable to stop himself, he pressed his lips against the scrap of material still covering her.

A hungry moan filled the room, and he realized it came from her. Gina's fingers were tangled in his hair, and her hips jerked against his mouth. His tongue darted out only to be stopped from its goal by the taut silk of her panties. With a low growl he reached for the elastic at her hip and gave it a sharp tug, severing it. He repeated the movement at her other hip, and she was bared to him.

Awe spread through him at the view. She was so exquisite. Completely open to him. He glanced up at her and saw her looking down at him, passion and eagerness stamped on her features as she tickled his earlobe with her fingertip. When he didn't move, her hands left him and moved to unclasp the front catch of her bra. Her breasts spilled out into her own waiting hands, and she winked at him.

He grinned back at her and then focused on the bounty in front of him. Spreading her swollen pussy lips with his thumbs, he licked up her crease slowly, completely. The hard nub of her clit brushed against his tongue, and he sealed his lips around it, sucking as her flavor burst in his mouth. Flicking his tongue back and forth across the tiny nerve center, he rubbed his thumb at her opening, coating it with her juices. He slid it into her and felt her sex clutch at him greedily.

A rush of warm cream soaked his chin, her smell filling his head and driving him to invade her body deeper with his fingers. It wasn't enough; he wanted to claim more of her. All of her. Two fingers continued to thrust in and out of her grasping tunnel, and his thumb inched its way lower to tease her puckered anus.

"Oh, yes, Caleb. More."

Her words, accompanied by the grinding of her hips and the death grip she had on his hair, told him she wanted his exploration. Sucking her clit between his teeth, he pressed his thumb slowly into her hole and felt her insides clench rhythmically against his fingers as a series of low whimpers filled the room and her juices gushed onto his tongue.

When her grip on his head lessened and the trembling in her thighs subsided, he gently removed his hand and lapped at her one last time. Bracing his hands on the mattress, he pushed himself to his feet, quickly rid himself of his own clothes, and climbed onto the bed, sliding his naked length against hers. When they were knee to knee, chest to chest, she tried to wiggle her hands between their bodies, but he snatched them and pinned them to the bed beside her head. If she touched him now he'd lose it.

She didn't fight his grip on her wrists; she just wrapped her legs around his hips and gave him a languorous smile. The smile he'd wanted to see on her face since the night he met her.

Emotions swelled inside him as he read satisfaction, pride, and love in her expression.

*Love??*

Gina shifted her hips beneath him, and he settled in close, his cock nudging at her entrance. He locked eyes with her and felt his heart pound in a way that had nothing to do with the closeness of their bodies and everything to do with the rightness he felt at the thought of loving her back.

Holding her gaze, he thrust his hips forward and felt her wet heat surround his body at the same time her love surrounded him. His body caught onto the beat of his heart, and his rhythm picked up speed. Gina whimpered, her insides tightening around him until he shook with the effort of holding back. He could see the pleasure of her approaching orgasm clearly on her face, the way she bit her lip and panted his name with every breath. The emotions swirling about in her gaze matched the ones flooding his mind and body until he couldn't hold back any longer.

"I love you, Gina," he whispered and let go.

She cried out in joy, every muscle in her body taut, her thighs holding him tight to her, her hands clasping his with surprising strength, as he emptied his body into hers and their souls merged.

# 16

Gina turned and scooped the eggs out of the frying pan onto the plates waiting on the counter. They were supposed to be fried, but she'd messed them up, so . . . scrambled it was. Not that it mattered; nothing could bring her down from the cloud she was floating on.

Her dream had come true. Right down to the way Caleb had pinned her hands to the bed and the look in his eyes when he'd said he loved her. When she'd returned to earth from the massive orgasm his declaration had brought on, he was lying on top of her, breathing harshly. He'd tried to shift his weight off, but she'd held him tight, not letting go until they drifted off to sleep like that.

The gentle brush of his lips across hers had woken her a short time ago, but before she'd even opened her eyes, he'd patted her sharply on her naked bottom. "Go start breakfast, sexy. It's your turn to feed me," he'd said with a chuckle before disappearing into the bathroom.

She hadn't had a chance to say the words to him, but his confident and comfortable behavior told her he already knew she returned his declaration of love. With joy in her heart and a spring in her step, she'd floated into the kitchen to find them fuel, and she hadn't stepped off her cloud since.

"Is your tattoo bothering you?" Caleb asked as he walked into the kitchen, still buttoning his shirt.

Turning away from the toaster, Gina gave him a once-over as contentment seeped into her bones. Hands still on his buttons, he bent close and gave her a lingering kiss, the taste of minty freshness competing with the flavor of Caleb as their tongues slid against each other lazily.

"Hmmm?" she hummed dreamily when he pulled away, completely forgetting what he'd asked her. He smirked, and she glanced at the still bare expanse of his muscled chest and wondered briefly about pushing the shirt off his shoulders and showing him how easily *he* could be distracted by her tongue.

"Your tattoo," he pointed to her hands, bringing her attention back to the conversation. "Is it bothering you?"

She glanced down at her wrist and realized she'd been scratching at it subconsciously. Cupping her other hand over the burning spot on her wrist, she reached out with her mind, and a faint sense of well-being, tinged with impatience, settled over her.

She smiled. Angelo was very frustrated about something—something that had made him think of her—but he was okay.

"It's a birthmark, not a tattoo." She held her arm out to Caleb, palm up, so he could get a closer look.

Few people knew that the dark purple crescent moon on her wrist was identical to the birthmark her brother had on the inside of his arm. And even fewer knew that they acted like homing beacons for the siblings. But Caleb was her destiny, and she wanted him to know everything.

"So it is," he murmured, running a rough fingertip over the dark purple mark. "It's very unusual."

"My brother has an identical one on the inside of his biceps. Our birthmarks connect us, help us keep track of one another."

His eyebrows jumped and hid beneath his tousled locks for a moment. "Really?"

Ignoring the incredulous note infused in that one word, Gina continued. "Sometimes, like a few minutes ago, my birthmark will tingle or heat up, and I know Angelo is thinking about me. If he's thinking about me, or I him, and we reach out with our minds, we can get an impression of what the other is feeling at that moment in time. He can actually hear my thoughts, but me, well, I just get impressions."

Skepticism flashed in his eyes, and his lips pressed together, but he didn't say anything. Gina's heart sank to her stomach, and she tumbled off her cloud. "You don't believe me, do you?"

She struggled to keep her voice even. She should give him time to accept her, to believe in her, but he'd told her he loved her. There was love in his eyes last night, just as she'd seen it in her dreams for years. Somehow, when he'd said he loved her, she'd thought that meant they were past all the doubt and disbelief. Disappointment flooded her chest and spread in a slow burn that had nothing to do with her previous lustful thoughts.

"I didn't say that." He stepped closer, reaching for her hands. The bread popped out of the toaster, ready to be buttered and added to their plates, but they both ignored it.

She didn't have any men's cologne at her place, and the scent of pure Caleb invaded her senses so much she had to pull her hands from his and step back. She couldn't let him get that close; she wouldn't—she couldn't—put off this discussion any longer.

It was time to face reality.

"You didn't have to say the words—your expression said it for you."

"Do we have to get into this now?" He sighed, and for the first time since they'd met, Gina heard exasperation in his voice. "I told you I believe that you believe in that stuff, and that's good enough for me."

"Yeah, well, it's not good enough for me," she said, planting her hands on her hips and facing him head-on. If he didn't believe her—he couldn't truly love *her*.

Not the way she wanted to be loved. The way she deserved to be loved.

"What are you saying?" Caleb's brow furrowed, and his lips tightened into a thin line.

With her heart cracking down the middle, she took a deep breath and let it out slowly before meeting his gaze. "I'm saying I think we need to take a step back."

"Back?"

"Yes, from each other." *Breathe, Gina.*

"What? I thought we were just getting started? I love you, Gina. This is just the beginning." He took another step, reaching for her, but she stepped back.

"You don't love me, Caleb." She fought to keep her voice steady and calm, but they both heard the quiver in it. "You just love the way I make you feel."

"What's that supposed to mean?" A slow flush crept up his neck.

"It means you like the fact that I turn you on. Let's face it, Caleb, you don't love me . . . you just love that I make you feel like a stud in bed. I'm nothing more to you than an ego boost."

"That's not true, and it's not fair." The angry flush spread from his neck to high on his cheekbones. "If that was all I'd wanted from you I never would have set foot in that café again, but I did. And, yes, this thing between us *started* because of sexual attraction—hell, it even continued because of the great sex. But there's more to it than that now, and you know it!"

"That's just it!" she cried out, throwing her hands up in the air. "If all I wanted from you was a good fuck, this wouldn't be an issue, but I want more than that. I want it all, Caleb! I want your heart."

"You have my heart, Gina. I love you! You're beautiful and sexy and smart. . . ."

"And psychic."

That stopped him in his tracks. The hands that had been reaching for her dropped to his sides, his jaw clicked shut, and he glanced away.

"Don't you see?" Gina whispered into the silence. "You can't pick and choose only parts of me to love. I need you to accept—to love—all of me."

More silence, broken only by their harsh breathing.

Gina watched as Caleb's fists clenched at his sides and he faced her. Deep in his eyes she saw the tinge of doubt he refused to acknowledge. "We have a connection, you can't lie about that. You even dreamed of me!"

"I never lie!" Anger made her speak rashly. "Yeah, we have a connection." She swallowed her tears and forced the words through her lips. "But it's only physical. You were worried about being a bad lay, and now you think you love me because you can make me have screaming orgasms."

Caleb's spine straightened, and his shoulders went back. He looked exactly like the stiff, uptight, square guy she'd thought he was when she first saw him. The blaze in his eyes was the only thing that showed her just how affected he really was.

"I may have been looking for an ego boost when I agreed to let Gabe set me up on a blind date, but we both know there was more between us than sex from the start." His voice was even stiffer than his body language. "And you *did* lie to me that night."

An arrow of hurt pierced her anger. He was right. She had lied to him, and the situation they were in now was as much her fault as it was his.

Pressure built behind her eyes, and Gina fought to keep her tears at bay. After a slow, deep breath, she tried to explain it to him. To make him understand what she wanted, what she needed from him.

"You can't have it both ways, Caleb. You can't say I dreamt of you, if you don't believe in my abilities. *Your* inability to believe tells me you might have the face and the body of the man of my dreams but not the heart. Because the man of my dreams accepts me for who, and what, I am."

"I do accept you," he barked, frustration and anger clear in his tone. "When have I ever talked down to you or been snide? I respect your beliefs as part of who you are."

Her anger was gone, but a sad resignation had taken its place. She had to be strong. If she wanted it all, they had to deal with this now.

She looked at him steadily and spoke gently. "But you still think of them as beliefs, not abilities."

The flames of emotion in his eyes banked slightly at her words but didn't disappear. "And you, Gina? Do you truly love me? Because you're doing the exact thing you're accusing me of. You won't accept me, and you're turning me away because of something I believe, something that makes me who I am."

With a small sob, she walked over to him and cupped his cheek. Gina knew she was taking a huge chance, but she had to. She stroked her thumb over his full lips, silencing him and letting him see her heartbreak in the tears rolling down her cheeks. Gazing into the maelstrom of emotions clear in every feature on his handsome face, she stood on tiptoe and pressed her lips to his. With a shuddering breath, she said good-bye.

"I love you, Caleb, and I believe in you. I believe in us. But I refuse to settle for a man who doesn't believe in me." With that said, she walked across the apartment and into her bedroom, leaving him standing alone in the kitchen.

\* \* \*

*What the hell just happened?*

Caleb resisted the urge to slam the door behind him. Keys held tight in one hand, his suit jacket clutched in the other, he marched down the steps and to his car.

He climbed in and turned the car over, letting the sound and feel of the rumbling engine soothe him. Hands wrapped tight around the steering wheel, he leaned his head back, eyes closed, and breathed deep. His blood was flowing hot, his chest was tight, and every breath hurt.

She didn't think he loved her! She actually believed he was stupid enough to mistake lust for love.

After one last deep breath he straightened in his seat and shoved the car in gear. Forcing himself not to look up at her window and see if she was watching him, he pulled away from the curb. She'd run from him once, and he'd followed. Then, when he'd finally opened his eyes and his heart enough to see that she was the one for him . . . she'd shoved him out the door.

He should've known better than to think they could ever be more than lovers. They were too different, and this time he wasn't going to go after her.

# 17

Caleb wedged his truck into the last parking stall in the café's small lot and turned off the ignition. Why the lot was so full was beyond him, since the café looked empty inside. Through the plate-glass window he watched Gina hand some frothy coffee drink to a lone customer with a smile. She was still beautiful, and he missed her so much. It had been only a week since she'd walked away from him, but it felt like a year. A year in hell.

But it didn't matter how long they'd been apart, because he was about to remedy that. He was about to do something he never, ever would've thought he would do. He was going to marry a psychic.

Well, he was going to propose to one. And pray she said yes.

Hell, he'd never believed in the supernatural before, but he couldn't deny his heart any longer. The past week, without any contact whatsoever with Gina, had been a purgatory he didn't want to ever visit again. When Maria had visited Tom in the trailer office earlier that day, the sight of the gurgling baby boy had been like a knife to the chest, and he knew he couldn't deny it anymore.

Gina Devlin was psychic.

The note she'd left him after their first night together that mentioned him winning his basketball game, when he'd never even mentioned his plans to play; he'd assumed Gabe had said something to her about their regular games, but then it turned out she wasn't even the friend Gabe had set him up with. The way she'd known Tom and Maria's baby would be a boy. The electrical thing. Shit, she'd even known he was hiding something from her when they were playing pool. He'd kept denying she was exactly what she said, even when the evidence was right in front of his face.

The boy who had become a man grounded in the reality of his parents' death and the responsibility of looking out for his younger brother had stopped believing in anything remotely magical. It had just all sounded so far-fetched, like vampires, witches, and dragons. At least until he'd taken Gina in his arms and lost any semblance of control.

There was no denying the magic between them, and he now realized that deep down he'd believed in her abilities all along. But it had scared him, so he'd refused to let himself see her as more than an adventurous fling, until his heart wouldn't be ignored any longer. He wasn't ignoring it now, and he sure as hell wasn't going to let the woman he loved ignore *him* anymore.

He reached for the door handle of the truck, only to stop at the sight of two very large, dangerous-looking men dressed in all black heading through the doors of the café. The hair on the back of his neck stood up, and his hands fisted on the steering wheel instinctively. The sense that something big was about to happen hit him between the eyes a split second before he saw Gina turn toward the door.

When she spotted the two men she froze; the ceramic teapot

in her hands dropped to the floor, shattering on impact. Caleb was out of the truck and halfway across the parking lot by the time her face lit up and she ran around the counter—straight into the arms of the taller guy.

For a split second his heart stopped, but then it started back up, double-time. For a brief minute he'd feared he was too late, but he knew Gina. Whoever that guy was, he wasn't her dream man. Caleb was her dream man.

He leaned against the side of his truck, watched the show, and waited for the right time to make his next move.

Gina looked at the two men sitting at her kitchen table wolfing down bacon and eggs, the only real meal she could cook without fear of giving them food poisoning. When they'd walked into the café an hour earlier, she'd just about jumped out of her skin. It wasn't often her brother could sneak up on her, but she'd been so preoccupied with thoughts of Caleb for the past week she hadn't felt his presence until he'd stepped into the shop.

"Angelo!" she'd cried out as she ran across the café floor and leaped into her brother's arms. She'd wrapped her arms around his neck and closed her eyes as his strong arms hugged her tight to him.

"Shhh," he'd crooned into her ear, rocking her back and forth as if she were still the little girl who had always run to him to kiss her cuts and bruises. "It's okay, little sis. I'm here now. I've got you."

The comfort of hearing his voice in her ear had made her realize just how much she'd needed him. After chasing Caleb away, she needed to have someone around her who loved and believed in her, and he'd known it. He and Drake Wheeler, his teammate and best friend since boot camp, had both known it.

The minute Angelo had set her down and stepped back, she'd been wrapped up in Drake's brawny arms and twirled around.

Immensely cheered by their presence, she'd laughed loudly and demanded to be put down. Without a second's hesitation she'd dashed to the back office to tell Sally she was leaving early. She didn't feel guilty, because the café was empty and would likely stay that way until the after-work crowd hit, and by then Gina's replacement would be in.

They'd gone straight to her apartment, Drake taking the long way with Gina's motorcycle while Angelo drove them in a rented SUV. As soon as they were alone, Gina felt his psychic fingers poking around in her head, and she didn't try to block him. Instead she'd closed her eyes and let him see in.

The drive was short, and when they'd arrived at her place, Angelo had turned to her before getting out of the vehicle and reached for her hand. A warm sense of love and comfort, tinged with a protective anger, flowed into her, and she squeezed his hand tightly.

"Are you sure you did the right thing?" he'd asked after a moment.

She met his gaze without flinching. "Yes, I'm sure. He has to accept me as I am before we can go any further." She saw his eyes darken, mirroring the pain she knew was in hers.

"What if . . ."

She held up a hand and interrupted him. "If I'm wrong, I'm wrong. I'll live." Reaching out, she'd smoothed the angry frown from between his brows. "It's all right, Angelo; you can't protect me from everything."

Lord knew he tried, though. Their father had been killed in the line of duty, working for a private security company after he'd left the army—the same company Angelo now worked for. And while they'd said the murderer was caught and was in jail, Gina had always doubted it. Strange nightmares about her father's death haunted her. Nightmares that made no sense at all.

Angelo knew that, and it made him even more protective of her because he knew the one thing he could never protect her from was her visions—nightmarish or otherwise. She'd given him a quick hug and raced him up the steps to her apartment.

Now she looked at the two big men—seated at her table—so opposite from each other physically but so similar in other ways. They were bickering, as only those who truly know each other can, while they scraped their plates clean. Both of them were men of strength and honor; both of them were ex-military working for a security company so private even she didn't even know what they really did—just that it was . . . special. Both of them were men who would do anything to take away the pain in her heart if they'd had the power—Angelo because he was her big brother and he always tried to protect her; Drake because it wounded him to have the people he cared about hurting.

As an empath Drake had learned to block most people's feelings and emotions, but when it came to someone he was close to personally, his defenses were minimal.

Drake and Angelo played off each other in every way. While Angelo was all lazy, dark, and a smooth talker, Drake was big, blond, and quiet. They'd met in boot camp and had become instant brothers in spirit when they'd each recognized the other for what he was. Together they were a family.

Refusing to let her heartache keep her from enjoying what time she had with them, Gina snapped her dish towel at Angelo's hand when he pointed at something out the window for Drake to see before trying to snatch the last piece of bacon from Drake's plate.

"Hey!" Angelo cried in mock dismay. "You'd punish a starving man for trying to eat?"

"When you've already eaten two platefuls yourself? Yes!"

"Yeah, Devil, you ate all yours already. Back off." Drake smirked at Angelo as he popped the threatened meat into his mouth and chewed in slow exaggeration. Gina's body tensed as Angelo rose slowly from his seat and gave her a look she recognized well.

She twirled the dish towel menacingly and prepared to strike. "Don't even think about it, Angelo! I just fed you all the food I had in my kitchen."

The door buzzer sounded, and Drake rose from his seat to answer its summons, leaving them to do battle.

Angelo tore the dish towel out of her hand and lunged. She turned and dashed for the small living room; her only hope in stopping him was getting the couch between them. As she rounded the corner of it, he grabbed her from behind and threw her on the sofa. Putting his knee in her back, he started his fingertips digging into her sides, his low growls of menace mingling with her shrieks of laughter as she tried to wiggle out from under him.

"Devil!" Drake's intense voice cut through the noise, and they froze as they were. Gina turned her head and saw Caleb standing a few feet away, hands fisted at his sides.

"Caleb," she whispered. Her heart kicked in her chest, and her pulse throbbed in recognition of his nearness. "What are you doing here?"

He ignored her question and glared at Angelo. "Get off her," he demanded. "Now!"

Gina pushed up against Angelo's knee, scrambling to get off the couch. Angelo straightened first, all traces of the playful big brother disappearing as he morphed into the deadly and protective one.

He stepped in front of Gina and blocked her view of Caleb and Caleb's of her. When he spoke, his voice was soft with menace. "You have no say about what goes on here. You gave up that right when you walked out of here last week."

Gina tried to step around him, to go to Caleb, but Drake stopped her with a hand on her arm. He'd crossed the room so quietly she hadn't even seen him. She'd had eyes for only Caleb, standing in her living room.

"Just watch, Gina," Drake said in a voice only she could hear.

She widened her focus and took in the sight. There he stood, the uptight, conservative, quiet construction worker going face-to-face with her protective, lethal ex-military brother. Over her.

Meeting Angelo head-on, Caleb's voice held its own threat. "I didn't walk out of here." He didn't back down a millimeter, and she was so proud of him for it. "Gina threw me out, and since I won't let that happen again, I have every right to tell you to back off."

It was all she needed to see and hear.

"Angelo." She placed a firm hand on his arm. "Enough. Leave us alone, please."

Angelo stepped back, shooting Caleb a hard look before turning his back to them and heading for the kitchen, Drake a step behind him.

"Not many people stand up to my brother like that," Gina said softly.

"I'll stand up to anyone who tries to get between us." He stepped forward until they were only inches apart. He gave her a small smile. "Even you."

Her heart skipped a beat at the emotion shining in his eyes. But she wouldn't back down so easily. "What are you doing here, Caleb?"

"I went to the café this afternoon," he said. "I left the office early because I finally realized how stuck in a rut I truly was—mentally, that is—and I couldn't wait to tell you. But when I got there I saw you run and jump into another man's arms and . . . for a second, I just about died."

"Oh, Ca—"

He pressed a finger to her lips. "Shhhh. Let me say this." He paused and didn't speak again until she'd nodded her acceptance. "You see, I went to the coffee shop because I couldn't wait to tell you I loved you. I mean truly love and accept and *believe* in you and all your abilities. In fact, I've believed in them all along, right from that day in the park when you told me about them. The evidence was right in front of me—you pushing me to tell you about my ex, the note about the basketball game, Tom and Maria's baby . . . everything. And when I saw you with your brother, while I didn't know then that it *was* your brother, I did know he wasn't going to keep us apart . . . because you dreamed of me and you together, having it all." He smiled at her. "And I believe in your dreams. I knew in my heart you were for real; it just took a while for my head to accept it."

"I know you did," she said, smiling softly. "But I needed you to know it, too."

"You knew?" He wrapped his arms around her and pulled her tight to him. "You put me through hell this past week just to prove a point you already knew?"

"No." She pressed her lips against his quickly. "I did it because we couldn't have a future together until you knew it too. I—"

He dropped a quick, hard kiss to her lips, silencing her midsentence.

"I'm not done yet," he whispered. Holding her hands in his, he slowly went down on one knee. Looking up at her, his true-blue eyes filled with more love than she could've ever imagined, he offered her everything she'd ever wanted. "Gina Devlin, eccentric artist, coffee-shop clerk, and sexy psychic, will you marry me?"

"Yes!" she cried out, wrapping her arms around him and knocking him to the floor. She pelted his face with kisses until he laughingly grabbed her head and kissed her full on the mouth.

Their lips parted, tongues tangled and breath melded as they sealed the deal.

"Is it safe to come in there now?" Angelo's voice broke through the haze of passion forming around them. Gina pulled her head out of Caleb's hold and sat up, still astride him, to look over her shoulder at the two large men entering the living room.

"Come on in and celebrate. We're getting married!" she called out.

"I know," Angelo said smugly as he stepped into the room and flopped onto the sofa.

Caleb sat up with Gina still in his lap. "You know?"

Gina smiled into Caleb's scowling face. "He wasn't eavesdropping, baby. Remember, I told you? He can read minds. He probably knew what you were going to do the minute you walked into the room."

Caleb's scowl deepened, and he glared at Angelo over her shoulder. "If you knew what I intended to do, why the guard-dog act?"

"I had to make sure you knew that if you hurt her again, you'd have to answer to me." Angelo's drawl was lazy, his smile almost evil.

"Great!" Caleb gave her a mock disgruntled look. "I'm marrying a psychic with a mind reader for a brother."

"And an empath for a best friend." She nodded in Drake's direction, a sympathetic chuckle rumbling from her lips at Caleb's sincere look of horror. "Don't worry, babe. I'll teach you how to shield yourself from them."

She cupped his head in her hands and placed her lips on his. Feeling his muscled thighs beneath her and his strong arms encircling her, she was right where she'd always dreamed of being.

Surrounded by love and acceptance.

# DEVIL'S JEWEL

# PROLOGUE

---

*July 3*
*Bear Pond Campground, Pearson, BC*

The glare from the beat-up truck's headlights cut through the darkness as Jewel Kattalis made her way back to camp. The elders were going to be mad at her for being late. Again.

You'd think they'd know better than to send her into town for supplies, but they still did it. Rarely, though. In fact, even though Leon, the clan's elder, would never admit it, he'd probably sent her into town that night on purpose, knowing she'd find a pub and a game of cards.

Five years earlier, after twenty years in Canada, the clan had given up on keeping the traveling carnival going. Families didn't want the same life here they'd had back in Romania, so they were quick to settle in new towns once they found one they liked. Because of this, those that could took odd jobs or hustled cards to make a few bucks. But the clan was always running a little short on money lately, and more families kept peeling off.

It had been a smart move to send Jewel into town. She'd had

a good night. Hell, the five hundred dollars in her pocket said it had been a great night. The radio in the old truck had quit working earlier that day, but even that didn't bother her, since she always kept her iPod with her. She actually enjoyed singing when she wore the headphones because then she could hear the music but not herself. Jewel never sang along when she was in public though—she didn't want to be shot.

Turning off the rutted road, the headlights passed over the small group gathered in the middle of the campground. With a twist of her wrist she shut the truck off and jumped out of the truck. "Great. A welcoming committee," she muttered. It sucked to be twenty-eight years old and still explaining her time to an elder, but she stayed with the traveling clan because they offered an education for her little sister that couldn't be gotten elsewhere.

Ignoring the tension rising in her gut, she thumbed down the volume on her music and hefted a couple of bags of groceries from the back of the truck before moving forward. When Leon turned from the group to face her, his arms folded across his chest, she grinned. "C'mon, Leon, you didn't really expect me to just get supplies and come right back, did you? It's Saturday night, and I found a pub full of suckers."

"Jewel—"

She interrupted him with a wide smile and held up the food bags. "I made some good money."

"Jewel, listen to me."

Something in the elder's voice tweaked her brain, and she stopped dead in her tracks. A quick glance at the others showed solemn faces and concerned stares that sent a shiver skipping down her spine. "What?"

Leon stepped forward, his strong hands circling her bare arms, his dark eyes looking deep into hers. "Nadya's gone."

Her heart stopped and then kick-started again, pounding a mile a minute against her ribs. "What do you mean 'gone'?"

The crowd behind their leader parted, and Jewel saw what they'd been doing. Stretched out on two pallets next to the fire were Kaz and Jimmy, the guardians of the clan. Alive but unconscious.

Leon's hand landed heavily on her shoulder. "She was taken."

# 1

*July 4*
*Pearson, BC*

"We need your help."

Angelo Devlin was not a man who asked for help often, especially if he knew it could possibly put his little sister in danger. But this time he forced the words past his tight throat and made a mental promise to their dead father; he wouldn't let anything happen to Gina.

It didn't matter that he knew Gina Devlin could kick serious ass when needed. The only thing that mattered was that she was all the family he had. And by asking for her help in this, there was a good chance he was going to open up a whole new world to her—an evil one he'd done his damnedest to protect her from.

Gina looked at him, her big, dark eyes shining with happiness as she snuggled under her new fiancés shoulder. "Whatever you need. You know that, Angel."

Angel.

His chest tightened. She was the only one who could ever

get away with calling him that, the only person who saw him that way. Those who knew him better—the teammates he worked with, his best friend, and certainly the psychopaths and other evil beings he hunted—they all shortened his last name instead of his first and called him Devil.

It suited him a lot better. He'd sent plenty of things back to the hell from which they were born; he'd even sent some people there. He'd end up there himself eventually, but he'd do everything in his power to make sure his sister never even glimpsed it.

His gaze slid away from the couple in front of him to his partner. Big, blond, and silent, unless he had something specific to say, Drake Wheeler was also his closest friend since they'd met ten years ago in boot camp. And he knew how much Devil didn't want to drag Gina into their world.

*You have to, man. We're lost, and she can show us what we need.*

Drake's thoughts echoed through Angelo's mind, and he tensed. He knew Drake was right. They'd been over it again and again, but that didn't mean he liked what he was about to do.

Trying to hide his own thoughts, he turned to his sister. "We're looking for someone, and the trail has brought us this far, but we've hit a wall."

She knew immediately what he needed. "You have something for me to work with?"

"What's going on?" Caleb Mann's arm went around Gina and pulled her close, making Devil's insides warm. His sister had a big personality and an even bigger heart; she deserved someone to share her life with. And it was clear Caleb was the right man for her.

He knew it had been hard for Caleb to accept Gina's psychic talent, and he knew if things went the way he was expecting, his sister and her new fiancé could be in for some more ups and downs in their relationship. He swallowed a sigh.

*We need her.* Drake's second reminder was more gentle, but Devil still had the urge to hit him. Sometimes having an empath for a friend sucked.

Then again, he knew there were times when his buddy hated having a telepath for a friend, too.

Snatching up the backpack he'd dropped just inside the door, he waved his sister and her man to the sofa and settled into the overstuffed chair next to it, keeping the coffee table between them. "I'd love to say I'm here just to visit, but that's not the case. HPG was hired to find this guy, and we're stuck."

Caleb sat forward. "HPG?"

"Hunter Protection Group," Gina answered for him. "The private security company Angelo and Drake have worked for ever since they left the military. Everything from bodyguarding to private investigations, right?"

"Among other things, yes."

Caleb's eyebrows lifted. "Being a mind reader must be handy in that line of work."

Devil ignored the tinge of sarcasm and just smiled. "It can be."

"So who are you tracking in Pearson, and how can I help?" Gina asked.

"We have something you should be able to get a reading off, and we're hoping you can point us in the right direction."

Her brow puckered, and the light in her eyes dimmed. "There's more to it than that, though, isn't there?"

His gut clenched.

Gina was no fool, and now that her relationship with Caleb was on track, she was making it clear it was time to deal with Angelo. She'd sensed it when he was in trouble in South America a couple weeks back, the same way he'd sensed her inner turmoil this past week—their matching birthmarks kept them always connected emotionally—and she could probably sense that whatever he was doing in Pearson, it was connected to that trouble.

It was damn hard to keep secrets from a psychic, especially one he was linked to by blood. "I'd prefer not to tell you anything else just yet," was all he said.

She nodded. "Okay."

With that covered, he reached over to the backpack and took out a small, heavy plastic bag.

As an open telepath, unless someone deliberately shielded him, Angelo could pick up random thoughts and sometimes images from their minds. He had the ability to shield himself, to close the door in his mind so that the random thoughts of everyone around him didn't float through his head constantly—so only those directed straight at him could get through.

He generally kept the shield in place to protect his own sanity, as well as people's privacy, but there were times when even that didn't work. Gina and Drake, both with psychic abilities of their own, also had mental shields for the same reasons. So, right then, Caleb was the only open mind in the room, and his thoughts were starting to piss Angelo off.

"I'd never let anything happen to my sister, Caleb. She's all I have, and I love her, so lay off the threats already," he said as he pulled the folded canvas from the plastic bag and set it on the table in front of Gina.

Caleb stared at him steadily. "Stay out of my head if you don't like what you're reading."

"I'm not in your head. Your thoughts are screaming at me."

Gina leaned back and whispered something in Caleb's ear before kissing him firmly. "Trust me. Trust him," she said firmly.

Caleb nodded, and his thoughts quieted. Gina turned back

to Angelo, and their eyes met. *This is all new to him, Angel. But he loves me; give him time.*

Angelo smiled and dipped his head. Anything for her.

He shored up his mental shields, quieting his own mind, and focused on the job at hand.

"Okay," Gina said and nodded at the object on the small coffee table in front of her. "What is it?"

Knowing she wouldn't want to touch it until she had to, Angelo unfolded the cloth and showed her what they had.

"Don't," he warned when Caleb's hand reached toward it. "Not until after she's had a chance at it."

Tension filled the room as everyone looked at what he'd pulled out. It looked like a plain old chunk of metal with runes and strange symbols etched into it. And that's what it was—except, this metal was magically enhanced by a demon, and the markings were a spell. His met his sister's gaze. "Be careful. Open yourself up slowly."

Drake silently moved to sit on the sofa on Gina's other side, an encouraging smile curving his lips when he nodded to her. He'd be the first to sense if there was trouble for her, and the best bet for someone to help her if there was.

Caleb shifted in his seat. "Gina—"

She cut him off with a soft smile and firm words. "It's okay, babe." With one last glance at Angelo, she picked up the metal and closed her eyes.

There was no gentle fade of consciousness this time. Gina didn't even have to reach out for the vision—it hit her right between the eyes the second her fingers wrapped around the metal. Her heart slammed against her rib cage, and her blood chilled.

A man—tall, athletic, dark skinned—stood in front of a big white house, fists planted on his hips as he surveyed all that was around him. The sun was shining, the sky was blue, the house was beautiful. Everything looked perfect; even the man himself was good-looking.

Nothing in the vision explained the fear, the dark tendrils Gina could feel creeping into her mind. Not until his head turned slowly, a chilling smile in place, and he stared directly at her with eyes that glowed a deep, fiery red.

*Impossible! He can see me?*

Shock waves crashed through her, and she gasped, her fingers automatically letting go of the shard of metal. She clasped her hands to her head and sucked in air. Deep breaths in and then out, calming her heart rate and blocking the sounds of Caleb and Angel arguing.

When she had control of herself again, she put her hands down, one of them going straight to Caleb's thigh to give him a reassuring squeeze. She glanced from Drake to Angel, seeing the concern stamped on both their faces. "What the hell was that?"

"What did you see?"

"I saw a man standing in front of a house. I think."

"And?"

"And he looked right at me. He *saw* me. How the hell can someone in one of my visions *see* me, Angel?" A shiver whipped through her, and she shifted closer to Caleb, who was strung tighter than she was but sat silent. For the moment anyway.

Angel ignored her question, his gaze boring into hers intently. "What else did you see?"

"Nothing out of the ordinary. Trees, blue sky, warm sun. And him."

"Can you describe him?"

"I can do better than that, I can sketch you a picture. But first you need to tell me what he is because those glowing red eyes of his say he wasn't exactly human."

That got them.

Drake and Angel shared a look, and Caleb's thigh twitched under her hand. The poor guy—he'd barely accepted that people could be psychic, and now he was faced with—*they* were faced with—something not quite human.

Gina settled back against his side and waited for her brother's reply. That thing in her vision had been evil, so whatever Angelo was into, there was no way she was letting him go after it alone.

She watched him closely, and for once in her life wished she were the mind reader. He was definitely hiding something. Something she wouldn't like. "Don't do this, Angel. Don't try to tell me everything is normal and things are all hunky-dory. It never worked for Dad, and it won't work for you."

The birthmark on her wrist warmed; love and a tinge of worry settled over her, and she relaxed slightly.

"I don't want to lie to you, Gina. I'm here to do a job, and I'd rather not tell you all the details."

"Then tell me some of the details." She looked at Drake. "Like, is this something new to you guys? Do you really know what you're chasing?"

Drake nodded, his emerald eyes calm and confident. "We know."

Gina looked from one to the other and wondered if they really did. Somehow she didn't think so.

# 2

Kaz was the first of the guardians to wake up. "It was a man . . . but it wasn't," he'd croaked.

Jewel poured some of the herbal healing tea the *Shuvani* had brewed into a cup and handed it to him. "Drink."

The wise woman's tea would make Kaz feel better, faster than anything else could. And as soon as he felt better, they were going to find Jewel's sister.

Nadya was her kid sister. Fifteen years old, full of attitude, and a complete pain in the ass. And all Jewel had in the world. She wasn't going to let anyone, or any*thing*, hurt her.

The clan had been shrinking steadily for the last decade. The gypsy lifestyle couldn't compete with modern niceties anymore, and families were breaking away and settling in when they found a city or town they liked. Settling down had never appealed to Jewel. She loved the freedom she'd grown up with, and if her soul longed for a place to call home every now and then, she considered it a small price to pay for complete freedom.

Only, it wasn't really complete freedom. Not when she still had Nadya to look after. In fact, if it weren't for her sister, she would've left the pack to find her own way a long time ago. She much preferred to be on her own than to have to follow anyone's rules, even the loose ones the clan labeled as "tradition."

Jewel felt a presence behind her seconds before Leon spoke. "Nice to see you awake, Kazmen."

Kaz nodded, his gaze steady on the older man still unconscious on the other side of the fire.

Jewel put a hand on his arm. "Jimmy's going to be okay. He was awake for a minute earlier, asking about you, and he's resting now."

With only a dozen people left in the clan, there were only two guardians. Jimmy—who was in his late sixties and was not too strong physically but still in superb shape magically—and his grandson, Kazmen.

Kaz was the next generation—young and smart with a true heart and a long line of guardians in his blood. He was stronger magically than anyone else in the clan. Anyone except maybe Nadya.

A chill settled deep in Jewel's bones. Kaz was right—for something to take them both out and grab her little sister, it had to have been more than a mere man.

Leon spoke from his standing position behind Jewel. "Can you tell us what happened?"

Kaz sipped the tea for a moment and then spoke again, his dark eyes darting away from the elder and meeting Jewel's as he fingered the silver talisman that hung from the chain around his neck. "It looked like a man named Hooper who Nadya talked to at the park yesterday when she was selling her jewelry. But it wasn't him. I'd have known if the man in the park was that *thing*."

"Are you sure?"

The nineteen-year-old flushed, his fair skin turning dusky as he hung his head. "I'm young, Jewel, but I'm not stupid. This guy bought some of Nadya's jewelry and hung around talking to us for a while. I'd have sensed it. Hooper was just a businessman, a rich one Nadya was trying to make a deal with for a bulk order of her crystal necklaces. Something about unique gifts for his clients."

Jewel couldn't keep the incredulity from her voice. "And you told him where we were camped?"

"No! He was supposed to meet us at the park in two more days to pick up his order. I don't know how he found us. If it even was him." Kaz shook his head slowly, his eyes full of confusion and anger. "It looked like him, but this guy wasn't human, Jewel. And he wasn't anything I've faced before. He knocked Granddad twenty feet into a tree with one swipe of his hand, and I couldn't stop him. He was stronger than anyone I've ever met. Fast, too; he had Nadya by the throat, so she couldn't speak before any of us even knew he was there."

Their eyes met as the significance of that sunk in. "So he knew."

"He knew," Kaz confirmed. "I'm sorry, Jewel. I tried to stop him."

"I know you did. We'll be better prepared when we go get her back."

The young man nodded firmly and lay back down. "We'll get her back."

"Jewel," Leon said and walked away.

She got up and followed him away from the fire. When they were about thirty feet from the fire, Leon turned and stared at Jewel steadily. "I've spoken with the other elders, and we're moving on in the morning."

"What do you mean?" Fire leaped to life in her veins, but she took a deep breath and calmed before she spoke, hoping she'd misunderstood him. "Without even trying to rescue Nadya?"

"I have to think about everyone, and it's not safe here for us."

Nope, she hadn't misunderstood.

As a woman whose only master was her gypsy wanderlust and her love for her sister, Jewel had been around. She knew the one thing 90 percent of the people in the world had in common: they loved to talk. If you knew the right questions to ask, information was ripe for the picking.

Hooper Radisson, the owner of the big white house set on the side of the mountain just outside the city, was someone the residents loved to speculate about. He'd moved to Pearson less than a year ago and set up shop as a financial consultant. Only, he never actually opened up an office, and he had no local clients.

He was seen about town often, spending money and entertaining visiting clients, but that was it. And lucky for Jewel, it drove the locals crazy with curiosity. One mention of Hooper's name at the pub and she knew where he lived, what kind of car he drove, and, among other things, that he was a vegetarian.

Forty-eight hours after Nadya was taken, Jewel was smirking at the simple security system surrounding the big white house on the hill. Getting past the guard at the front gate had been as simple as climbing over the seven-foot cement wall surrounding the grounds.

Almost too easy, really. She knew Hooper was no ordinary man, not if he could grab Nadya so easily.

She slowly made her way through the trees and up to the house, surprised at the lack of guards patrolling the grounds. She inched her way along the side of the house and to the back, checking out each window as she went. A kid could crack the system wiring all the windows and doors, and her instincts were screaming caution.

She reached into her pocket and pulled out one of the small

pouches Kaz had given her before the clan had left town. "Let's see what we've got here," she muttered to herself and spilled some of the fine powder into the palm of her hand. With a soft blow, the powder flew off her hand and into the air . . . where it hit a shimmering wall of energy and sparkled fluorescent orange for a split second. "Ohhh, nasty."

The lovely orange color showed that the house was indeed protected by a spell. It didn't matter that the technical security sucked—the magical security was top-notch. Before Jewel could reach for her crystals, a muffled cry of pain came from nearby, and the house and surrounding grounds were flooded with light.

"Shit!" She didn't hesitate a second. Adrenaline kicked into overdrive, and she spun around on her heel and took off for the dense trees nearby. A mad dash through them wasn't the quietest way to get to the wall that separated the grounds from the winding public road where she'd parked her truck, but it was the fastest, and it offered protection from the floodlights.

Five feet from the cement security wall, a shadowy form jumped from behind a tree and tackled her. Heart in her throat, she reacted instinctively, her hands going for her attacker's throat, her knees bending and feet kicking as she tried to nail him in the balls.

The body turtled over her, heavy legs tangling with hers, pinning them, full weight on her torso as one hand covered her mouth and the other grabbed two of her fingers and yanked them back until pain made her let go of his throat. "Shut up, for Christ's sakes! They're almost here."

His whispered words registered in her mind at the same time a beam of light played over the compound wall just above them. They both froze, and Jewel finally realized that this guy wasn't hauling her to her feet or dragging her back toward the big white house.

She closed her eyes and concentrated on calming her heart rate and listening to the sounds around them. The musky scent of raw man reached her nose, and butterflies unfurled in her stomach. Sensual awareness threatened to overcome her fear as they lay there.

Neither spoke—she didn't even think they breathed—but in the distance she could hear voices raised as guards searched the grounds. A single bark split the night air, and they both tensed. Jewel's eyes popped open, and she stared at the shadowed face above hers. Eyes black as night met hers, and his hand left her lips.

"A dog!" she whispered furiously.

"Over the wall," he replied. "Now."

He sprang to his feet, and she was right behind him.

As if they'd done it a million times before, he bent his knees, and Jewel stepped smoothly into his cupped hands; he boosted her to the top of the wall with ease. The stranger was more than six feet tall, and with a small jump he was halfway up the wall. Jewel gripped the foot-wide cement between her thighs and grabbed the back of his belt as he scrabbled up the wall. As she swung her leg over and sat atop the wall, the dog came through the thicket of trees, barking madly and pulling a small man behind. A chunk of cement flew into the air as a gunshot bounced off the wall a foot to the left of Jewel, and she jumped to the other side.

She hit the ground running and was at her truck in seconds, the helpful stranger right behind her. Shoving the key in the ignition and pulling her door closed at the same time, she was surprised when the passenger door opened. She heard him say he was leaving with the girl and watched with wide eyes as he joined her.

What the hell?

"You can't—" A shot hit the windshield, and she clamped her mouth shut on the instinctive cry of surprise.

"Go, damnit!" he shouted.

And she did.

Without another thought, she slammed the truck into gear and floored it, speeding off down the twisted mountain road.

# 3

Neither of them spoke as Jewel drove into town. She concentrated on the road ahead of them, and he watched the road behind them. They must not have been followed, though, because he never urged her to speed up or take off on one of the side roads.

Jewel's thoughts whipped through her head at a mile a minute while she tried to figure things out. Every now and then she'd glance sideways at her passenger only to catch him staring straight at her.

Their gazes collided more than once, yet still neither of them spoke.

By the time they hit the Pearson city limits, it was clear that no men with guns had followed them, and reaction had started to set in. Jewel wasn't an innocent to the ways of the world; she'd dealt with a lot of scary things. Shit, she was a gypsy who made the bulk of her money hustling dart games in pubs around the country—she'd been in a tough spot or two before.

She'd seen things, natural and supernatural things that were both good and evil, but she'd never been shot at before.

Her heartbeat started to slow, and the trembling inside her

had settled down enough so she could breathe normally. She loosened her death grip on the steering wheel, and when her knuckles were no longer glaringly white, she glanced at her passenger. Her gut tightened. What now?

As if he could read her mind, he gestured to a parking stall in front of the coffee shop across from the lake. "Pull in here," he directed. "We need to talk."

The only reason Jewel did what he told her was because it was true. They did need to talk. She put the truck in park but left it running and turned to get her first really good look at her passenger.

The light from the street lamp illuminated the inside of the truck's cab enough for her to see that he was extremely good-looking. Short, dark hair, olive skin stretched over high cheekbones, and almost bottomless eyes had her pulse picking up for a very different reason than fear. His firm jawline was shadowed with a layer of stubble that only enhanced the shape of his very seductive mouth.

A quiver of excitement rippled through her. A man with a mouth like that had to know how to use it.

Jewel squashed the sensual awareness growing inside her and gave him a hard look. "Who the hell are you?"

The mouth in question twisted. "You can call me Devil."

She grabbed for the dagger tucked into the side of her right boot, but before the blade cleared leather, his hand gripped her wrist, hard. "I said you can *call* me Devil, not that I was the devil. I'm one of the good guys in this battle."

She met his gaze head-on, no fear. "I'm supposed to believe you just because you say so?"

"If I were one of them I'd have let you run right into the spotlight instead of tackling you, and I certainly wouldn't have helped you over the fence." He spoke matter-of-factly, his expression blank. "Now, why don't you tell me your name?"

When people lied, they tended to overplay their hand. If anything convinced her to believe him—and she wasn't sure she did—but if anything was going to convince her, it was his lack of emotion.

"Okay, say I believe you. What were you doing there?" She let go of the onyx-handled dagger but kept her hand by the side of her leg. His hold on her wrist loosened in response, but he didn't release her completely.

"Your name?"

Shit. "Jewel."

His head dipped in acknowledgment. "Okay, Jewel. It doesn't matter what I was doing there. What matters is it's a dangerous place, and you are not to go back there."

*Fuck that,* she thought to herself.

Tension thickened the air between them. Who did he think he was? He didn't even ask what she had been doing there, just issued orders like he was the king or something. "You think you can stop me?"

"Yes."

The one word was said with such complete arrogance that Jewel reacted instinctively.

Slapping her right hand on top of the one that held her left wrist, she pinned it there, at the same time twisting her left hand up and over his. She put her weight behind it, shifting toward him and pressing down on the wristlock. He countered by moving back and pulling her on top of him, his other hand going on top of hers and yanking two fingers back—the same two fingers he'd used to get her to release her choke hold earlier. Pain ripped up her forearm, and she let go, landing in his lap with their hands trapped between their bodies and their faces only millimeters apart.

She sucked in air and tried not to notice the hardness of the body beneath her . . . until he kissed her.

\* \* \*

He didn't think.

Her luscious lips were there, and he just went for it. He speared his tongue between them, and she opened eagerly for him. The kiss was as aggressive and fiery as she was, their tongues dueling for dominance as their hands shifted and holds released. She thrust her fingers into his hair and held him tight while he reveled in the handful of pliant womanly curves in his lap. He gripped her hips, pulling her closer, tighter against him as blood rushed to his dick and he forgot about everything but the feel of Jewel and the purr of pleasure that was filling his mind.

*More, more.*

He'd give her more. One hand left her hip and cupped a full breast, the hard nipple poking into the palm of his hand as her moans filled the truck cab. Her fingers tightened, pulling his head back and exposing his throat to her hungry lips. Teeth scraped down his neck to the connecting muscle there—she nipped, she licked, and then her lips sealed against his skin and she sucked sharply before pulling back and slamming her mouth back down on his again.

Blood rushed to his cock, and his hips bucked against her. She was wild and willing in his arms, and he was ready to give as good as he got—until the door next to him swung open and Drake stood there, not bothering to hide his smirk.

"I hate to interrupt your courtship, Devil, but Gina called. She wants us back at her place, pronto." He paused and gave Angelo a look. "And she said to bring the girl."

# 4

Jewel reared back, her cheeks flushing. "I'm not going any-where until I know what the hell is going on."

Devil took one look at the tilt of her chin and nodded to Drake. "Go ahead. We'll meet you there as soon as possible."

Drake gave him a look. *Now's not the time, dude. Make it fast.*

The mental rebuke was loud and clear in his head. Devil nodded at his partner and closed the door before turning to the only other person in the truck cab—the woman who had just short-circuited his brain until his body took over. Drake was right—now was not the time to fuck around.

Reinforcing his mental shields to quiet the erotic purr push-ing at his subconscious, he straightened up and did his best to ignore his hard-on. "Head south on Main and I'll tell you when to turn."

Jewel was firm. "I told you I'm not going anywhere until I know more."

He met her gaze. "You drive and I'll explain. If my sister wants us there fast, we need to be there *now*." Unease tickled at the back of his neck. He wasn't surprised that Gina knew about Jewel being at the house, but why did she want him to bring her back with him?

Something indefinable flickered deep in Jewel's eyes at his words, and she gave a sharp nod. She slid back behind the wheel and put the truck back into gear. "Fine. Start talking."

"It's pretty simple. That guy was my partner, Drake, and we're after the bad guy that lives in that big house you were trespassing on, so you need to stay away from there."

She snorted. "Are you guys cops?"

"Not exactly."

"Then what exactly are you? And why were *you* skulking around the house on the hill?"

"I work for a private security firm hired to get something Hooper stole."

"So you're going to steal it back?" She glanced at him, her mouth twisted in disbelief. "That doesn't sound like something a security firm would do. Why not call the cops?"

Fuck, she was stubborn. The brief glimpse of her thoughts he'd gotten when they were wrestling back at the house had told him she was scared but determined.

He was pretty sure she was one of the good guys, but that didn't matter. She was in his way.

The more people involved in an operation, the more chances there were for someone to get hurt—or worse, dead. Dragging his sister into this mess had been necessary, but that was it. "All you need to know is that he's a bad guy and not in a way the cops can handle. Turn left at the light."

She glanced at him, brows pulled down in a frown. "But you can?"

"Yes."

"Whatever," she spit out.

Frustration hit him, and his hands tightened into fists pressed into his thighs. He was not going to let her know she was getting to him; he just needed to figure out how to keep her out of his way.

"Park in front of that pinkish apartment building," he said with a wave of his hand.

The truck pulled to a stop, and he dropped his mental shields and reached out to her. When he found what he was looking for, sympathy whispered through him, but he shoved it aside and faced her. "Listen, Jewel, your getting caught by Hooper won't help Nadya any, but Drake and I can get her out for you when we go after what we want. But we can't do our jobs if you get in the way."

Her head snapped around, eyes wide, and she snarled at him. "Stay out of my head and *don't* try to tell me what to do."

Shock rippled through him. She hadn't been surprised when he'd mentioned Nadya's name, and she knew how he'd gotten it. Why?

They glared at one another for a full minute, the air in the cab of the truck getting thicker as they sized one another up. Devil noted the long tumble of curls, the dark eyes, the silver rings, and the crystal pendant at her throat. He pushed aside the heat of attraction that was building inside him and focused on her other energy that made the tension so thick.

It felt different than regular persons—stronger, more primal . . . earthy. A wtich? If demons were real, why not witches? And he'd had to fucking run into one while hunting a demon!

Devil fought the urge to bang his head against the dashboard. What the hell could happen next?

Swallowing a sigh, he jerked the door open. "C'mon. Let's go see what's going on."

Questions swirled around inside her head as Gina paced back and forth inside the small apartment from the kitchen to the living room, where Drake sat on the sofa. *Where are they? What are they doing? What were they doing at that house? Do they even know what's really inside it?*

It was three in the morning, and most of the city was asleep, including her new fiancé, but not for much longer. As a construction guy, he was naturally an early riser, and she needed to find out what was going on before he woke up and freaked out.

Normally the one to sleep late, she'd gotten up to do some sketches because the muse kept jumping up and down in her head, making her toss and turn. Then, shock of shocks, she'd gotten a vision—unlike any she'd ever experienced—and if Angel didn't get back soon, *she* was going to flip out.

"Will you please stop stressing, Gina? I told you they'll be here in a minute," Drake said from his seat on the sofa as he rubbed the bridge of his nose.

Gina stopped, forcing a small smile. "Sorry. Am I giving you a headache?"

"This whole case is giving me a headache." He met her gaze. "We're missing something important. I can feel it."

"I, um, might be able to help you with that." She went and sat beside him. She'd known Drake close to ten years, and she trusted him with her life. As if he were another brother to her. "You need to tell me everything about this case, Drake. I know Angel is trying to protect me, but keeping me in the dark isn't working. You and I both know it."

Acceptance spread in his emerald eyes, and she blew out a slow breath. But before Drake could tell her anything, the front door opened, and Angelo strode in, a brunette with a tight body and an angry frown right behind him.

"Took you long enough," Gina snapped.

"Gina Devlin, meet Jewel." He waved at the woman behind him while he scanned the room quickly, meeting Drake's gaze for a second and then focusing on Gina with concern. "What did you see?"

"Everything." She shifted to the chair and waved the two of them to the sofa next to Drake.

Gina eyed Jewel, quickly summing her up. She wasn't super-pretty, but there was certainly something about her that made her stand out. Energy, charisma, even a touch of machismo. The perfect match for her big brother.

"Gina," Angelo growled, impatient.

She took a deep breath and spit it out. "I was there when you tripped the alarm."

"You saw what we were doing?"

Gina's heart pounded, her blood racing. She knew what she was about to say was freaky, even for them, but he had to believe her. "Not you. I was with him, the red-eyed thing from my vision two days ago. And I more than saw him, I was with him. I was actually inside the vision. I could feel the heat in the room and smell the sweat of the men he had building whatever it is they're building under his house. It was more than a vision." She glanced at Drake and then Jewel, thankful to see that both were taking her seriously.

Her brother's face was a complete blank, and she knew what that meant. He was fighting very hard for control of his own emotions.

"It's okay. As much as I could feel what was going on, he didn't see me this time. He was too distracted by the other girl that was there."

Jewel sat forward, her brow furrowed with concern. "You saw Nadya, didn't you?"

Gina nodded. "Your sister, right? You two could almost be twins. When the alarm went off, and Hooper went to the window, he saw you running for the trees."

"Did he see me?" Angel's voice was tight.

"No, only her. I don't think he knew you were there. I only knew because when I came out of the vision and I reached for you, there was that particular brand of nothing I get when you're blocking me. I figured you guys had to be going after him tonight."

"Damnit, Gina. You promised you'd stay out of this. You pointed us in the right direction—that was it. Your part was done!"

Anger stirred inside her, but she spoke softly and clearly. She wanted no misunderstandings here. "I kept my promise. Even though I knew you were hiding something, I didn't go looking for this. I trusted you and went about my work."

Angel stood, running his hands through his hair as he paced the small room. "Then why did you pick up the metal again?"

"I didn't! How could I when you took it with you? I was sketching, Angelo." Gina stood up and, stepping in front of her brother, stabbed him in the chest with a stiff finger. "I was working, when all of a sudden I wasn't in my apartment anymore but in a basement full of noise and sweat and heat while some *thing* was interrogating a teenage girl about a gateway to hell. I didn't go looking for this, but I got it, and you need to tell me what is going on."

Jewel stood next to Gina. "I think you need to tell us both what's going on, stud."

"Make that all of us," Caleb said from the bedroom doorway.

# 5

Angelo looked at Drake helplessly. There was no way to avoid telling them everything now. Frustration—and a touch of panic—fought to find a hold inside him.

He didn't want Gina to know about all the bad things in the world. She'd been so young when their mother had died, just a toddler, and their father had raised them both as fighters. They'd always moved around, always struggled to fit in. If she learned too much, she'd never truly fit into the world around her again. He didn't want her life to end up like his.

She was the reason he did what he did, why he was so tough, why he'd killed so many. To keep the world safe for people like her.

He looked at her, begging her to let it go. "Gina, can't you just leave it alone? Trust us to keep you and your man safe?"

"No, Angel, I can't." She reached out, her hand grabbing his and holding it tight. "I do trust you to keep me and Caleb safe. But who's going to keep you and Drake safe?"

"We've got each other's backs."

"Don't be stubborn, big brother. I'm not letting it go any

longer. I know in my gut that you need me to get through this. And you know my gut is always right."

The shit thing was, he did know that. Gina's instincts and premonitions had saved his life more than once, without her even knowing exactly how. With a step back, he glanced at Drake and nodded. "Go ahead."

"You already know that the man in your visions isn't just any man, right, Gina?" Drake said. "He's a demon who's been searching out psychic hotspots around the world and building gateways to alternate dimensions." Calm and confident as ever, Drake stood, speaking quietly as he walked to the center of the room. "HPG has been tracking his activities for almost a year, and we've always managed to destroy the gateway before he could find a *key* to unlock it, but we've never been able to get close enough to him to put him out of commission permanently. Two weeks ago we tracked him to South America, but when we got there, he was gone. Our intel is that he heard about a key here in Pearson and came to get it. We destroyed the gateway he'd built there—that was a piece of it we gave you to try to find him with, by the way—and followed him. Now, thanks to your vision, we're closer than we've ever been to getting him. We have a name and a face to go with the location. And from what you saw tonight, it's clear he's building another gateway, this time under his house."

The room was silent, everyone staring at Drake.

Angelo had been gauging their reactions as his partner spoke and was a bit thrown by the lack of surprise on the two women's faces. They seemed to be taking the whole "demons do exist" thing completely in stride.

Caleb, however, was visibly struggling with the information.

Slumped against the chair Gina had previously been sitting in, he looked at Devil's sister with wide eyes. "I thought you said there were no such things as witches and demons and vampires?"

"What do you mean, a name and a face?" Jewel said. "You've been following him around the world for a year but you never knew his name or what he looked like?"

Angelo answered Jewel first, noting how Gina had settled back into the chair, her hand on Caleb's thigh, their heads bent together. "He is Vetis, the demon of corruption, but his human identity has been more . . . difficult to discover than we'd expected. Our information on him is all about the mystical aspect of things and is mostly based on legend. Rumors of demons have always been around, and like most people, HPG didn't think they existed on earth. Not until one of our teams ran into him, completely by accident, when in Rio last year."

Jewel's eyes narrowed. "If you didn't know they existed, how did they know what he was when they ran into him?"

"All the hunters at HPG are psychic in some way. One of the men who first found Vetis was a die-hard Christian who fully believed in demons as well as angels. He's the one who told us it was Vetis. We believe him."

Jewel quirked an eyebrow and looked down her nose at him. "And in a year, all he's been able to tell you is a name? A *demon* name?"

Angelo clenched his jaw. "Tracking his human side has been a lot harder, since he killed the only team that's actually seen him. All we've had to go on was a garbled radio transmission of their murders."

Pink colored Jewel's cheeks, and she backed up a step. "Okay. So what *do* you know about him?"

Drake stepped up, putting a hand on Angelo's shoulder, taking away some of the anger swelling inside him. "We know he's become bored with corrupting individuals on earth and has decided to corrupt the entire planet as a whole by opening up the portal to a hell dimension and inviting some friends to join him here. And now we know he's Hooper Radisson."

"Hooper Radisson?" Caleb's head came up. "I know him. He's not a demon. Demons aren't real."

"How well do you know him?" Drake asked.

Angelo had watched the interaction between his sister and her lover out of the corner of his eye as he told his story. He'd heard her whispered assurances to Caleb, and Caleb's half-hearted arguments, and seen the small touches they shared. They were there for each other—all the way.

"Not real well. My company built his house when he moved here about a year ago." Caleb shifted his gaze to Angelo. "Really? He's a demon?"

"Yes, he's a demon," Jewel snapped before facing Angelo head-on. "And he's got my sister, so no matter what you say, I'm not staying away from that house. I am going to get her back."

Any calm that had started to settle over Angelo at seeing his sister taking the whole thing so well went up in flames at Jewel's words. "Witch or not, you'll only get in our way. You need to back off and give us a couple days. I'll get Nadya back for you, I promise."

"I'm a gypsy, not a witch!" She was mad. Her eyes shot sparks, and her body was strung so tight she was vibrating as she faced off with him. "And you can't tell me what to do."

"A gypsy?"

Angelo ignored Caleb's query as heat that had nothing to do with Jewel's words, and everything to do with the way her skin flushed and her breasts jiggled, shot through him. "I can, and I am."

"Keep on dreaming, stud." She stepped closer and shoved a stiff finger against his chest. "You're the klutz that set off the alarm tonight, not me. You need me to get you into that house."

"I didn't set off the—"

"Guys, stop for a minute, would you?" Gina snapped. "There's more."

"Are vampires real, too?" Caleb's voice was soft, as though he might be talking to himself.

"I don't know, babe," Gina said, patting him on the thigh, her eyes on Angelo. "But I do know that Jewel's sister is more than just a hostage to Hooper."

"Oh, shit."

Drake's soft curse echoed through the room at the same time that Angelo became aware of the tingle in his bicep, right where the birthmark that matched the one on Gina's wrist was; a shiver of anxiety ripped down his spine.

"What is it? Why her?"

Gina's gaze met his. "While I was with them in the basement, he told her that on the next full moon she becomes the key that can open any gateway."

# 6

The heavy curtains in the cheap hotel room kept the sun from blazing in, which was nice since Jewel didn't crawl into bed until almost nine in the morning. The motel was a small, cheap place on the highway, but it was quiet and clean, and they welcomed her paying ahead of time so she could leave at any moment. Everything she could ask for.

And wasn't it fortuitous that the two hunters were staying in the same hotel?

*Devil and Drake.* She snorted softly and punched her pillow, searching for comfort. As hot as they were, they didn't have a clue what they were up against. If Devil hadn't set off the alarm earlier that night, she and Nadya would've been on the highway out of town already. A spurt of frustration had her flipping over in bed and punching the pillow again.

She'd be keeping an eye on them. It didn't matter that they'd agreed to include her in the planning of their next attack on Hooper's house; she didn't trust them—not to let her in on what they were doing, and not to make getting Nadya out a priority. Why should she? She'd trusted the clan to treat her and Nadya like family after their mother had died, but it hadn't happened.

At the first hint of trouble, Leon had packed up the caravan and hit the highway, taking everyone with him.

Kaz had fought to stay behind, partly because of his sense of responsibility, but also because he was just a little bit in love with Jewel. Some might think a nineteen-year-old was too young for her, but that wasn't why she'd never hooked up with Kaz.

In the gypsy lifestyle, sex was natural, and Kaz was very mature for his age. But Jewel wasn't interested in tying herself to the clan any more than she already had, so she kept her pants zipped when it came to the gypsy men and found her entertainment in the towns they visited. With men who only wanted a good time, for a short time.

It seemed it had been a good thing to protect herself that way, since, good gypsy guardian that he was, Kaz had stayed with the clan when they'd moved on. None of the other gypsies had offered to stay behind and help her get Nadya back either. Sure, they'd welcomed Nadya's power when they wanted something, help with a spell or a healing, but when she was in trouble . . . they ran.

At least Kaz had done what he could, arming her with a couple potions that could help her against a malevolent spirit or supernatural being.

She still hadn't decided how much to share with Devil and his partner or if she was even going to work with them. She might have a better chance at getting Nadya out if she went in on her own and left Devil behind.

Devil.

His sister had called him Angel, but Devil certainly suited him better. Tall, dark, and handsome . . . and arrogant as hell. He fired up her blood in more ways than one.

The memory of their brief insanity flooded her system. The

way his mouth had felt on hers, his big body beneath her. God, how good it had felt. His hardness rocking against her core, his hand cupping her breast, the taste of him on her tongue. . . . She rolled over and groaned into her pillow. Why did he have to kiss her? She really didn't need the distraction of horniness right then.

As though her thoughts had called trouble to her, there was a hard knock on her door.

She opened it without looking out the peephole. The bolt of desire that had whipped through her at the knock told her who stood on the other side. "What?" she asked, hand planted on her hip to still the urge to grab him by his shirt and throw him down on the bed. A long bout of hard and fast fucking would be the perfect thing to tire out her brain enough so sleep would come.

"Is that how you always answer the door?" Devil asked, tight lines forming around his full lips as his gaze swept over her.

She didn't bother to glance down at the white undershirt and panties she had on. She knew her nipples were poking out and the shadow of her pubes were visible through the thin cloth. And she didn't care. "It is when I'm pulled out of bed."

He nodded, as if coming to a decision of some sort.

"I just came to tell you to get some rest. Drake and I are meeting with Caleb at five to put together a plan. Since Caleb built the house Hooper lives in, we should be able to find a way in easily enough." He paused, his eyes shuttering. "I still think you should stay away, so if you want in on this, you better be there, 'cause I'm not coming after you."

"Fine. I'll meet you at the truck at quarter to the hour." She smiled sweetly and closed the door on his face.

Arrogant bastard. It was really too bad she didn't like him.

\* \* \*

Devil closed the hotel room door behind him and started stripping. When he was down to his shorts he crawled into bed and closed his eyes. He was tired, so very tired.

"That was quick," Drake said from the table near the window. He had his laptop set up and was doing his thing.

"I decided we could wait for answers from her. I wasn't in the mood to argue anymore."

Drake laughed. "You mean you weren't sure where an argument would lead with you two alone and near a bed."

He rolled over, pulling a pillow over his head. "That, too."

# 7

Turning into the parking lot of Mann's Construction, Gina tamped down the trepidation that had been rising ever since Caleb had left the apartment muttering about work and "the real world." He'd managed to stick around her living room that morning long enough to hear that demons and witches and other supernatural beings of legend were real but not to talk to her. He'd agreed to give Drake and Angelo the blueprints for Hooper's house and then left, shaking his head and avoiding her gaze.

She parked her bike next to Caleb's truck and waved at a few of the workmen sitting on some scaffolding eating lunch. The offices for Mann's Construction were in a simple trailer that moved from job site to job site. A month ago, when she'd dropped in on him for the first time, it was just outside of town, and now Caleb's "office" was a five-minute drive from her apartment, making it easy for him to come to her place for lunch. Only, he didn't do that today, and that was why Gina was there.

On the other side of Caleb's truck was Gabe's car, and as

soon as she turned off her bike, sounds of the brothers arguing could be heard clearly from where she was. She glanced at the workmen on the scaffolding, but they didn't seem to hear it from where they were, which was probably a good thing. She set her helmet on the seat of the bike and started for the trailer, only to stop next to Gabe's car.

Should she go in just yet? Right after she and Caleb had started dating, she'd met Gabe for the first and only time. They'd gotten along fine, but Gina knew Gabe wasn't 100 percent behind the idea of them getting married. And that was okay.

It warmed her heart to know that Gabe was protective of his older brother; after all, Caleb had given up a lot to raise him when their parents had died, and they were very close. Gina understood that—she was close to her brother, too.

Although, not as close as she'd thought.

A fist tightened around her heart. He'd hidden a lot from her.

His heart had been in the right place; Angelo only ever wanted good things for her. She knew that. She trusted that. But if she lost Caleb because of this new demon/witch stuff, she wasn't sure she'd be able to forgive him.

The door of the Mann's Construction trailer slammed open, and Caleb's younger brother stalked out. The sun glinted off Gabe's blond hair as he slid dark sunglasses on his nose and stormed down the steps. There was a slight hitch in his stride when he spotted Gina standing next to her bike—next to his car—but he didn't stop. He gave her a small smile and a nod. "Gina."

"Hi, Gabriel. How are you today?"

He chuckled. "Aside from having to deal with brother bear in there? Very well. Maybe you can cheer him up—he won't talk to me about whatever's wrong."

"I'll give it my best shot." She smiled at Gabe, straightened her spine, and headed toward the trailer and her fiancé. *There is no way I'm letting a demon mess up my love life.*

Confident strides took her up the steps and into the trailer. Flipping over the GONE TO LUNCH sign on the door and giving the watching workmen a flirty wave, she shut the door on their laughter. She moved past the small, empty reception area and leaned against the door frame to Caleb's office.

He sat at his cluttered desk, chin propped up on one tight fist while his other hand rapidly tapped a pencil against the file in front of him as he stared into space. Shadows had formed under his eyes, and his lips were pressed tight together.

"Caleb?" she called out softly.

His head snapped around, his eyes meeting hers. "Gina! What are you doing here?"

"You rushed out this morning without us having a chance to talk, so I came down to see how you are."

Caleb leaned back in his chair, waving her into the room. "I'm okay. The real question is how are you?"

Licking dry lips, she stepped forward, all the way into the room, and over to him. With three more steps, she was sitting on his desk in front of him, close enough to see the dark worry in his true-blue eyes but far enough away to show him she really was there to talk. "I'm . . . surprised but not shocked, really. Some part of me always knew there was more to what my brother did than basic security work. There were times I thought he was an assassin or something."

That got Caleb's attention. "An assassin?"

"There's been a darkness growing in him for the last few years. As if . . . as if he'd shut off part of himself from the world or given up hope. I've been worried."

"And now?"

"I'm still worried but more for his life than his soul." She chewed on her bottom lip, remembering.

Caleb inched his chair closer, lips tight. "What?"

"I'm just wondering about my dad and how he died. This sheds a whole new light on the nightmares I had."

Caleb knew all about how her mother, a soft-spoken empath, had died from a brain aneurysm when Gina was just a toddler, and then how her military father had died when she was a teenager. They'd told her he was killed when taking down a stalker, but . . . she'd had a dream about him being killed by a giant dog or wolf.

Angel had convinced her it was just that—a nightmare.

Caleb leaned forward, resting his arms on her denim-clad thighs and his hands on her hips. Not grabbing or groping, just touching her, holding her. Comforting her.

"Do you think Angelo has always known?"

"About the demons and things?" She bit her lip and shook her head. She'd come here to comfort him, to see how he was handling the shock of things, and instead he was there for her. "I don't think so. But that doesn't make it right for him to hide it from me when he did find out."

Caleb pushed back his chair and started pacing, restless and angry energy coming off him in waves. "Oh, I don't think hiding it from you was his mistake. I think getting you involved was his mistake."

"No, Caleb."

"What was he thinking? Bringing a demon chase—a *demon* for Christ's sake—right into your home? He's crazy!"

"Caleb."

"What?" He stopped pacing and stared at her.

His forehead was wrinkled in a frown, his lips pressed together, hands planted on slim hips . . . and love shone from his eyes. Gina's heart thumped in her chest, and she held out her hands. "Come here," she whispered.

When his fingers wrapped around hers, she spread her legs and pulled him close, hooking her feet together behind his knees. "I'm not so worried about the demon as I am about how you're handling the idea of him."

Color crept up his cheeks. "You mean, am I still stuttering like an idiot at the thought of it all? No, it's sunk in a bit."

"And? You're, um . . ." How did she say this? Straight out always seemed to work. "You're not running for the hills or calling the men in the white coats?"

"I love you. You can't get rid of me that easily." He leaned in and kissed her hard. His lips covered hers, and his tongue delved into her mouth, claiming her. When he finally pulled back, she was panting heavily and clutching his ass firmly.

"Prove it."

He stepped back with a grin. "Gladly."

With sure hands he pulled her off the desk, spun her around, and reached for the snap on her jeans. His breath tickled her ear as his knuckles brushed against her bare skin. Lust mingled with love and rushed through her veins. Eagerness whipped through her at his confident handling as he shoved her pants down and pinned her to the desk with his hips.

The rasp of his zipper coming undone was closely followed by the heavenly feel of his hot hardness sliding between her legs. Gina groaned as the connection between their bodies was made and braced herself against the desk. He gripped her hips as he took her slowly, withdrawing and then thrusting deeper.

"Yes," she hissed, pushing back against him. "Mine. Fill me more."

Her insides tightened as he picked up the pace, the feel of him coming home again and again bringing her a pleasure that was more than just physical. She felt his cock swell and twitch and knew he was holding back for her sake. But she didn't need him to. She didn't want him to. All she wanted was to give him pleasure, to be there, a part of him.

"Come inside me, Caleb. Give me part of you. Please."

His grip dug into her hips, and he slammed into her one last time, seating his cock deep and letting go. Warmth flooded her insides, reaching all the way to her heart and soul as his grunt of satisfaction echoed through the room.

A few seconds later Caleb's hands left her hips and covered hers on the desk. He leaned forward, his breath tickling her ear as he spoke, resting against the length of her. "You have all of me. Without you, I'd be more than dull, I'd be dead inside."

She looked at his hand covering hers, felt the beat of his heart against her back, and didn't need a premonition to know that nothing could tear them apart.

# 8

---

Angelo scrubbed his hands over his face and swallowed a groan. They'd been at Caleb's house for almost six hours, staring at blueprints, going over various plans, options . . . arguments. They were getting nowhere, and it was all *her* fault. "Can't you do a spell to put everyone in the room asleep or something?"

Jewel's eye flashed at him. Again. "I told you—I'm not a witch, I'm a gypsy."

"But you can do magic—"

"Contrary to popular culture, gypsies are not the same as witches. I'd think a big-time demon hunter like you would know that."

The image of what he knew about her, of her tight little body in a see-through wife beater and skimpy panties, flashed through his mind, and he smirked. "I'm more than a demon hunter, baby."

"Would you two stop already?" Gina snapped. "The next full moon is tomorrow, and the rest of us would like to come up with a plan tonight. You're not helping."

Angelo glared at his sister. "I think the best plan is for you three to stay here while Drake and I go in, blow up the gateway, kill Vetis, and rescue the girl."

A chuckle echoed through Angelo's mind. *Smooth.*

He ignored Drake's ribbing, along with the evil looks the two women threw him. "What? Caleb agrees with me, don't you?"

Caleb shook his head. "I think you're right about Gina staying here, but I think you're an idiot if you don't take Jewel with you."

"Oh, really? And why is that?"

"Because he's expecting her to try for her sister again. And we can use that to distract him."

"But that would require her trusting us to get Nadya out," Angelo said, his gaze meeting Jewel's directly. "And if she trusted us to do that, we wouldn't need her there at all."

No one spoke while they looked at each other. There were two ways they could do this job—a quick and messy smash-and-grab, or super stealth. And it was make-or-break time. One of them needed to trust the other.

A sharp gasp broke the silence, and all eyes turned to Gina.

Angelo's chest tightened, and his gut churned when he looked at his baby sister. She stood rigid, glued to the spot, her head up and eyes staring out unseeingly. Slowly her eyes started to glow, the whites turning pink and then red as her mouth opened and closed but no words formed.

"Gina?" Caleb reached for her, but Drake stepped between them quickly.

"Don't touch her right now."

"Get out of my way." Caleb's words were quiet but full of deadly promise.

Angelo saw Drake hesitate; then his fist snapped out, and Caleb went down. "Sorry, man, but you'll only hurt her right now."

*Angel! It's him! Here. Now!*

Her voice faded from his mind, and numbness began to spread from his birthmark down his arm, their connection fading. Angelo's heart pounded, and he leaped forward, only to be blocked by his partner as Drake stepped in front of her and grasped her shoulders.

Jewel's fingers clawed into his arm as they watched Drake put his face close to Gina's and speak fiercely.

"Leave her be, you bastard. She's not the one you want. You think I can't feel you? You think we won't get you this time? Your arrogance is what will ensure we do. Now leave her alone!"

Pain lanced through Angelo's arm, his connection to his sister snapping back into place. Anger and fear washed through him, blending with his own until he was reaching for Gina himself. *I'm here, Gina. Focus on me. Let Drake do his thing.*

*It's not working! He's hurting Drake. Angel!*

"Fuck! It's not working." He shook Jewel off and stepped around his partner. He put his hands on Gina's head and focused, trying to get as far into her head as possible. But nothing happened.

*Angel. Help.* Helpless anger whipped through him as he felt their connection start to fade again, her call a mere whisper in his mind. "No! Damnit, I'm not losing you, Gina!"

Then, suddenly, Jewel stepped forward, palm up and lips pursed as she blew dust of some kind in Gina's face. Drake pulled back sharply and sneezed while Gina collapsed back into Angelo's arms.

"What the fuck just happened?"

Angelo raked a hand through his hair and stared over his partner's shoulder into Caleb's living room. Caleb was leaning against the far wall, glaring at him and Drake while Gina tried to calm him down.

"He was right, baby. You couldn't have helped with something like that, and if you'd tried and somehow gotten hurt, I'd never be able to forgive myself," Gina said.

Angelo didn't blame Caleb. No man wanted to be out like a light on the floor when the woman he loved was in trouble.

Not that he himself had been much help. He turned to Drake. "Talk to me, partner. What just happened to my sister?"

"It's hard to say—we know so little about how much actual power this thing has—but it was definitely Vetis. Somehow he's formed a connection with Gina, or knows about her anyway, and was trying to see through her eyes." Drake looked at him, his smile grim. "He wasn't hurting her—her own panic did that. Although, there's no telling what he would've or could've done if he hadn't been stopped."

"I'd panic, too, if a demon was suddenly inside my head," Jewel threw in.

"No shit." Angelo turned on her. "And what was it that you did? What was that dust?"

She smiled, baring her teeth. "I may not be a witch, but I do know one. One who's already had a run-in with your demon and who wants very much for me to get my sister back. He gave me a couple of potions to help me out."

"Potions?"

"Yes, potions."

Anger started to boil deep inside. "You've had these potions the whole time and never mentioned them?"

"I, uh, I'm going to check on Gina and Caleb now," Drake said. *Take it easy on her, Devil. Her potion just might've saved Gina's sanity.*

Jewel planted her hands on her hips and faced Angelo. "Yes."

"When were you going to tell us about them?"

"I hadn't decided yet."

He stepped closer, invading her personal space, and lowered

his voice to a deathly quiet threat level. "So you let us waste precious time trying to come up with a plan when we didn't even have all the facts, and that allowed Vetis to find a way to get to my sister."

"I think your giving her a piece of his last gateway was what gave him a way to your sister. Don't try to put that on me."

Guilt started to settle on his shoulders, but he shoved it away. "Uh-uh. If everything had gone according to plan, Vetis would be dispatched by now and this would all be over. It's only since I ran into you that things have gotten messed up."

Her chin lifted eyes flashing fire. "It wasn't me who set off the alarm last night."

"You keep saying that, but I didn't set off the alarm. I hadn't even touched the house yet. You set it off."

She threw up her hands. "You didn't need to touch the house! The alarm was a mystical one, a spell put around the house, not the normal windows-are-wired kind of thing. *You* did set it off, because I knew it was there and was about to get rid of it when all hell broke loose!"

Angelo's blood heated as they glared at one another. It pissed him off to no end that she'd had a secret weapon she hadn't shared with them, and he still couldn't help but admire the way she stood firm and never backed down. Even from him.

Her cheeks were flushed, her chest was rising and falling rapidly, and his cock was throbbing to the same rhythm. She stared at his mouth and licked her lips . . . and he reacted. His hands cupped her head, fingers tangling in her hair as he held her still and slammed his mouth down over hers. A quick swipe of his tongue and he was in, tasting her, taking her.

Her body surged against him, her hands reaching out, nails digging into his shoulders, before he pulled back abruptly. "You and I need to get some things straight. Now." He grabbed her hand and pulled her toward the front door of the house. "We'll be back in a few minutes!" he called out over his shoulder.

"A few minutes? That's disappointing."

Jewel eyed the way Devil's jeans hugged his ass as he pulled her along behind him, giddy lust overtaking any rational thought process. "A few hours would be much better."

"This isn't a joke," he said as he stopped at the side of the house. He pulled her close and pinned her against the wall of the garage, hands above her head, his forehead pressed against hers.

The sun had set hours earlier, but the air was still humid and sultry. Especially in the small space between them. When Devil spoke again, the damp heat of his words caressed her lips. "You and I need to come to an understanding."

"I think we understand each other perfectly fine," she said, rubbing against him as best she could. Lord! He felt good. So hard and muscled . . . and hard. "This is all about chemistry; we don't need to like each other."

"Not this," he panted and swiveled his hips, getting right between her thighs so his denim-clad hard-on was rubbing against her sex.

She whimpered, wrapping a leg around his, hitching closer, wanting less talk, more action. She lifted her chin, nipping at his bottom lip before he turned his head slightly.

"I'm talking about the trust thing." His lips brushed her cheek as he spoke. Kissing her but not really kissing her. "We need to come to an agreement—we have to trust each other—or one of us is going to lose a sister."

They both stilled, the words hanging between them. Their rapid breathing slowed, her leg slid to the ground, and he let go of her hands.

She felt the soft brush of his lips across her forehead before he stepped back. "We need to work together, Jewel."

"I know," she whispered.

What a freakin' idiot! She'd been so focused on the sensations flooding her body she'd forgotten all about Nadya. Idiot, idiot, idiot. She banged her head back against the wall a couple times before Devil's hand cupped her chin, stilling her. She opened her eyes, surprised at his gentle touch.

"Don't beat yourself up." His smile was a wry twist of his lips. "As soon as we get Nadya and destroy Vetis, you and I will finish this. And it's going to take a lot longer than a few minutes."

Her breath caught in her throat at the promise in his gaze. *Oh, baby. When I get my hands on your body, you are not going to get any rest!*

He grinned, and she suddenly remembered that he could read thoughts. Heat flooded her cheeks, and they both chuckled.

"Don't worry," he said. "My thoughts are running along that very same line."

# 9

---

Jewel opened the front door to Caleb's house and strode back in as if nothing had happened. Except, the heat of Angelo's gaze on her butt had her putting a little extra swing in her hip. No reason why she shouldn't show him what he was going to be getting his hands on in the future.

Drake, Caleb, and Gina were all gathered around the dining-room table with the blueprints still spread out. Drake straightened when they came in. "We have a plan we think will work."

The cell phone in Jewel's back pocket trilled the first few bars of ZZ Top's "La Grange," and she reached for it. Watching as Devil hugged his sister, she flipped the phone open and held up two fingers to signal she needed a minute. "Kaz, what have you got for me?"

"I've got it all." His voice was confident. "Granddad came through. You got a pencil handy?"

Jewel snatched the pen out of Caleb's hand, ignored his vexed look, and pulled the legal pad from in front of him, too. "Go for it."

He rattled off a list of simple ingredients any kitchen would have, and she wrote them down. "Once you've got them all together, throw them in a blender and whip them until they are a fine dust. Now, listen carefully, this next step is very important."

"I'm listening."

"The crystal you wear around your neck—it's quartz, right?"

"Quartz, and I carry a piece of Obsidian in my pocket." There were whispers behind her, but she ignored them.

"The quartz will do," Kaz said. "But if you can get your hands on some turquoise, it'd be better."

"Okay. What do I do with them?"

He described the rest of the ritual. How to blend the new powder with one of the potions he'd already given her and how to bury the gemstone in the potion. "You need to let the stone, buried in the potion, sit in the moonlight. Then, as the sun rises, unbury it and say the spell. It will draw in the sun's power."

Jewel scribbled down the four-line spell before straightening up, confidence soaring. They were gonna kick demon ass. "And how do I use it?"

"You can't." Kaz's voice dropped, taking her confidence with her. "I'm sorry, Jewel, but the magic won't come for you. You can load the stone, but only someone with magic in their blood can release it. The only way to actually use it is to get it in Nadya's hands. She'll know how to release it."

"Shit." She tossed the pen on the table and walked away, keeping her back to the others.

"Yeah, it sucks. I wish I was there, Jewel, but Granddad . . ."

"I know you do." A fist tightened around her heart. While the rest of the clan had been quick to leave them behind, having a healthy fear of Nadya's growing power and her tendency to blur the line between right and wrong, Kaz had not wanted to leave them. He wouldn't have, either, if his grandfather hadn't been so near death. "How's he doing?"

"As good as can be expected. I don't know if he'll ever fully recover from that attack, but he's awake, lucid, and starting to get cranky, so those are good signs." There was a pause, and Kaz cleared his throat. "You get that demon, Jewel, and send it straight back to hell."

"I will, Kaz." Jewel turned back to look at the people surrounding the table ten feet away. Devil and Drake were pretty intimidating, and the determination and anger radiating off Caleb and Gina made the whole group pretty formidable. "I promise."

They chatted for a few more minutes before Jewel thought of something else that might help them. A minute later she hung up and went back to the table.

"What's this? A spell?" Caleb held up the legal pad.

She snatched it out of his hand and scribbled a few quick instructions and some well-chosen words. She tore the page off and held it out to Gina. "I told my friend about that little hijacking stunt Vetis pulled on you tonight. He said if you do this, it'll muffle your connection and keep him from doing it again."

"Thank you." Gina reached for the paper.

"There's only one catch." Jewel met her dark gaze. "It'll muffle *all* your psychic connections for a few days."

"All of them?"

Jewel nodded, watching the interplay between Gina and the two hunters. Caleb, who was also watching the silent exchanges, put his arm around Gina and smiled grimly. "She'll do it. Thank you."

Jewel met Devil's gaze. *One sister safe; now let's rescue the other.*

# 10

---

While the others were in the dining room, creating a plan of attack, Jewel went to check out the kitchen. Caleb had most of the stuff she needed, but a quick run to the market was in order, so she told the others she'd be back in a few and dashed out before anyone could say another word.

So much had happened in the last few days she just really needed a few quiet moments. Her emotions were all tangled, just simmering below the surface, and if she wasn't careful, she was going to lose it.

Jewel parked her truck in front of the market but didn't get out. She closed her eyes and tried to center herself. She had a ritual to do, and she needed to get a grip or it wouldn't work.

Deep breaths in; blow them out slowly . . . search for the calm within. Only, she didn't find calm. She found anger, and fear, and . . . desire.

The simmering anger at Leon and the clan for leaving her behind was underscored by an understanding that it *was* Leon's responsibility to do what was best for the whole clan. Intellectually she knew this, but that didn't stop her from feeling betrayed by those who were supposed to be her family. No, being in Pearson right now was not safe for them, but then again, with Nadya taken, they *were* safe. Nadya was always the one who attracted supernatural trouble.

But she was also usually the one who got them out of it.

Now it was up to Jewel to get Nadya out of trouble. But she couldn't do it alone, and she hated to depend on anyone else. Especially a man. She had her mother's bad taste in men, which was why she'd always gone for the quick fling and never let her emotions get involved. Only, now she could already feel her heart opening up to the warrior.

And Devil was a warrior; no matter that his sister called him Angel. Jewel knew the look of a man who'd killed before and was willing to do it again. Yet she also sensed gentleness in him. It was there in the way he looked at his sister and even in the way he'd kissed Jewel's temple when they were outside earlier. The man was dangerous, in more ways than one.

It was a good thing she knew how to protect herself—in more ways than one.

She sucked in a deep breath and let it out slowly and then climbed out of the truck. It was time to get to work.

As soon as Jewel stepped inside the house again she knew she'd been the topic of discussion while she was gone. She focused on reciting her grocery list as she met each person's gaze; she didn't want Devil getting into her head when she wasn't prepared.

"What's up?" she asked, setting on the table the small bag she'd brought in.

"We have the outline of a plan," Devil said, shifting closer to her. "But we need some answers from you before we can solidify it."

"Okay." She ignored the shiver of awareness that danced down her spine at his closeness. "What do you need to know?"

Drake smiled at her softly. "Why don't you start with telling us what those potions you have do?"

That was easy. "I have three basic ones. A sensing powder—when dusted over or around an object, or in the air, it shows if there's a spell or anything mystical there. The second powder, the one I used when Vetis was trying to get into Gina, is a general kill-all type of dust. It kills almost any spell when the be-spelled person inhales it. The third is a liquid healing potion, like a really strong herbal tea."

"Perfect; we can use the sensor one for sure, and hopefully the other two won't be needed." Devil smiled at her, and her heart skipped a beat. "But you're hiding something, Jewel. Something I think we need to know."

Damnit.

She tore her gaze away from Devil and started talking. "Gypsy lore doesn't have a lot of demons in it, but fifteen years ago one of the men in the clan had a run-in with what he thought was a demon, so he's sort of taken it on as a hobby."

"Nice hobby," Caleb muttered.

Jewel shot him a look. "It is, since his hobby has just given us a way to send Vetis back to whatever hell he came from."

"Our orders aren't to send him back to hell, we're to kill him—destroy him so can't ever find a way back again." Devil was firm in his conviction.

She recognized stubbornness when she saw it and didn't bother to argue the point. Right then, she didn't care about much beyond getting her sister back anyway.

"Jimmy's given me a ritual that will . . . well, load a magical gun. Except, the only person who can pull the trigger is Nadya. I'm not the magical one in the family," she said with a small twist of her lips. "But I've seen enough to know that not all spells require magic; most require only faith."

"Exactly what is it that makes your sister so special? Why is she the key?"

When Jewel met Gina's gaze she saw that Gina wasn't being anything but sincere. Her questions weren't meant to put Jewel on the spot or to be derisive. She honestly wanted to know.

Dread settled in her gut. They'd guarded Nadya's secret since before she was born, but Jewel knew now she needed these people to get her sister back.

Devil had said they needed to trust each other, and it looked like she was going to be the one to start the ball rolling. She straightened her spine and braced herself mentally.

"Nadya's father was a shape-shifter."

Caleb folded his arms across his broad chest and shook his head. Drake's expression remained carefully blank, while Gina's cheeks flushed bright pink. Devil put a hand on his sister's arm and spoke. "A werewolf?"

"No," Jewel shook her head. "A true-blood shape-shifter. A man who could shift to any animal he had a piece of. With an eagle feather in his hand, he could become an eagle; with a bear claw in his pocket, he could become a bear."

"Was?"

"He died before Nadya was born," she said quietly.

"But he wasn't your father, too?"

She shook her head slowly. "I was six years old when we moved to Canada, and back then the gypsy clan stuck together, no matter what. Until about ten years ago, the caravan was a traveling carnival, with everyone having a part to play. My mother was a dancer with the carnival—as in *exotic dancer*. Whenever we hit a new town, her beauty became legendary, and her moves . . . well, they say she was hypnotic. She made lots of money, and unfortunately she fell in and out of love almost as often as we changed cities."

Sweat trickled down the back of Jewel's neck. What were they thinking?

"How did the shape-shifter die? How did your mother die?"

She shrugged. "When the elders in the clan found out what he was, they sent the guardians—who are basically magical security guys or bodyguards for the clan—after him."

"And your mother?"

"She died while giving birth to Nadya."

Gina leaned her hands on the table and glared at Jewel. "Correct me if I'm wrong, but aren't shape-shifters evil?"

"Good, evil . . . I still can't believe they're real," Caleb muttered under his breath only to hold up his hands in surrender when Gina turned her glare on him. "Sorry."

"It's hard to say if they're all evil or not. There aren't many shape-shifters left in the world today. Werewolves are a bastardized branch of them, but true shape-shifters . . . There hasn't been a sighting of one in more than a decade. Basically, they're like any other race—some good, some evil."

"And Nadya is half pure-blood shape-shifter, which makes her stronger than even werewolves. And the full moon does what?" Drake asked.

Oh, boy!

"First of all, you need to know that Nadya's already stronger than even our strongest guardian. She can make any command into a spell, just by saying it with the right—or wrong—intent. It's made her a bit . . . unruly to handle at times. But obviously Vetis knows more than the clan could find out about Nadya's magic because this full moon is the first one since she turned sixteen a week ago." She looked at the group. "According to legend it's when her blood heritage should come to her, and none of us are sure how it will manifest."

Drake must've sensed Jewel's sincerity, and her fear for her sister, because he stepped up and put a big, warm hand on her shoulder. "Then we'll have to get her back before the moon rises tomorrow. Which fits in perfectly with our plan."

## 11

---

Angelo scrubbed a hand down his face and glanced at his watch. "The sun will be up in about half an hour, and we've planned everything we can plan for, so let's get some rest. We'll head out at oh–nine hundred—that gives us four hours." He glanced at the door to the kitchen. It had been silent in there for a while now, and he wondered what Jewel was up to.

"There's the couch and the spare room," Caleb said with a yawn and a stretch. "You guys can fight over who gets what."

Caleb started from the room with Gina behind him, but she stopped in front of Angelo. She placed a small hand on his shoulder and looked up at him with her big brown eyes. "Now's not the time to deal with this, but just so you know, I am pissed at you for not telling me the complete truth about what you do. We *are* going to have a talk about it."

He nodded. "I expected nothing less, baby sis."

"Try to get a bit of sleep; we'll wake you up in a few hours so you can go kill this thing." She stood on tiptoe and kissed his cheek and then did the same to Drake.

The men looked at each other after she left, neither saying a word. Then Drake spoke. "Jewel can have the spare room, I'll take the sofa, and you're stuck with the floor."

"I'll wrestle you for it."

Drake smirked. "No way, I called it first. It's mine."

Angelo watched him walk away and debated tackling him just for the hell of it. Instead he went in search of Jewel.

She'd been cloistered in the kitchen for hours working on whatever ritual her friend had given her, everyone leaving her alone. He pushed open the door to the kitchen and saw that it was empty and sparkling clean. Turning off the kitchen light, he walked over to the window and saw Jewel in the backyard.

His eyes landed on her and stayed there as the sky began to lighten from a deep gray to purple. She'd removed her boots and knelt on the ground, sitting back on her bare feet, in her jeans and a skimpy black tank top. Through the open window he could hear her soft muttering as she dug into the earth with her bare hands. Her voice blended with the sounds of nature waking up—birds chirping and leaves rustling in a soft breeze. Natural, primitive.

Jewel herself was natural and primitive.

She raised a need inside him that went beyond the simple desire to fuck. She was willful and strong, a true fighter. Her determination was matched only by the seductive lure of her fiery eyes and lush lips. His chest got tight, and his dick hardened as he watched her get to her feet. She straightened up and raised her hands to the sky as the sun peeked out over the horizon.

Her posture was erect, her breasts thrust forward and head tilted back, as if drinking in the sun's first rays. She raised cupped hands to the sky and, transfixed, Angelo drank in the long lines of her body—the arch of her back, the curve of her ass . . . Even her bare feet digging into the earth was sexy.

She lowered her hands and turned to the house, her eyes meeting his through the window. Angelo didn't smile, didn't move. He ignored the pounding heat rushing through his veins and focused on the light in her eyes as she walked back to the house.

The back door opened, and she stepped into the kitchen and padded over to him. Every muscle in his body tensed with the urge to grab her, lift her onto the counter, and step between her thighs. But the house was full, and he wanted nothing less than to make her scream her satisfaction—over and over again.

He leaned down, skimming his nose over her neck, ruffling the whisp of hair near her ear as he inhaled her scent, the earthy smell of dirt, sweat, and aroused female filling his head. He pulled back a bit, but, hovering over her mouth, their breaths mingled. He could almost taste her.

A groan rose in his throat at the sight of her little white teeth sinking into her full bottom lip. "We leave in just over two hours," he whispered.

"Okay," she murmured.

Neither of them moved.

"More than a few minutes," he reminded her.

"Much more," she agreed.

Finally, after another minute of torturing himself with her nearness, Angelo stepped back. "There's a spare bedroom across from the bathroom. The bed's yours; Drake and I are in the front room. Try to get some rest."

"Yes." She cleared her throat and stepped back a bit farther. "I'll do that and see you in a little while."

Steeling himself, Angelo spun on his heel and left the kitchen while he still could. That woman was potent, and that made her dangerous.

# 12

The plan was simple, and because of its simplicity, Devil hoped it would go off without a hitch. Once it was all laid out, it looked perfect. They all knew perfect never happened, but hopes were high that success was just around the corner.

Since they didn't know exactly how much Vetis had learned from his little excursion into Gina's head, they'd decided to scrap everything they'd even considered and go in during daylight hours.

The full moon was that night, so they didn't have any time to waste. A daylight siege was the last thing the demon would expect. Not that they wanted a siege. The plan was to get in, get Nadya out, and then blow the place up.

Devil had killed men, he'd killed beasts, he'd even killed a werewolf or two, but he'd never run into a demon before. HPG's objective had always been to destroy the gateway and kill Vetis, but the more he learned, the more he wondered if killing Vetis would be as easy as they'd expected. All wondering aside, it was time to get to work.

Gina and Caleb were picnicking in the cemetery just north

of Pearson—safe—while Devil, Drake, and Jewel made their move on Hooper's big white house. He knew Gina was pissed at not being more involved, but her anger was mostly from fear. Fear for him and of being completely unable to connect with him, or anyone, psychically. But between the spell Jewel had given her, and being on hallowed ground, she was safe, and *that* would allow him to concentrate.

"The guard is practically comatose, he's so bored. You two ready?" Drake asked as they walked past the guardhouse at the end of Hooper's driveway.

"Ready," Jewel replied.

Devil nodded. And the three of them veered off the road and into the thicket of nearby trees.

"Wait!" Jewel stopped them before they reached the cement fence bordering the property. "Let me check it for a spell."

The two men stopped and watched as Jewel stepped forward, pulling a green pouch from the small satchel strapped across her body. She poured some of the powder in the palm of her hand, closed her eyes, muttered a few words, and then pursed her lips and blew. The dust flew from her hand and sparkled in the sunshine leaking in through the tree branches.

"Well?" He asked impatiently.

"Give me a second."

*Pretty nice trick.* Angelo met Drake's gaze as they waited for Jewel to do her thing. *We should try to make that powder part of our standard assault kit.*

*Yeah, right,* Angelo thought. He was sure old-man Hunter would love to add a witch to the HPG staff roster.

"Okay, boost me up."

Angelo boosted Jewel and then Drake; then he reached for Drake's hand and got pulled up. The three of them were off the wall and into the trees in less than a minute, with no alarms going off.

A chill of unease slithered down his spine, and he looked at Drake. Something was wrong. They made it to the house without incident, and Jewel repeated her mystical lock picking. When she nodded and stepped back, Drake stepped forward and slid a card into the electronic security pad at the garage door.

It beeped its welcome, and the door unlocked.

No one spoke as they moved smoothly through the garage to the house entrance. Gina had said when she was "in" the vision with Hooper that they were in the basement, and the blueprints had shown that the stairway to the basement was just inside the garage door.

It would be easy enough, as long as no one was in the kitchen when they opened the back door. Drake put his hand against the door and closed his eyes. A few seconds later he turned to Devil. *I can't feel anything, can you hear anyone?*

Angelo reached out, listening for random thoughts. He pushed past Jewel's impatient mutterings and reached further. There was something, a whisper, but it was far away. Farther than on the other side of the door. He put his hand on the knob and turned it, easing the door open.

He took four steps in and peeked around the corner. About thirty feet in were three guys in suits, playing poker at a small card table in the front entrance way.

A couple of sharp hand signals had Drake pushing ahead of Jewel to take point on the stairs, while Devil took the rear.

Tension had every muscle in his body tight, but his mind was relaxed, his eyes scanning, his mental shield down as he listened for anything, anyone.

There was nothing.

And that made all the little hairs on the back of his neck stand on end.

Drake reached the bottom of the stairs and stalled. *Devil?*

He looked up from the last stair. *I can't sense anyone. Not even Nadya.*

Shit!

Angelo nodded. Drake was uneasy, too, and that could mean nothing good, but there was no turning back now. They had a job to do, never mind a mission to save a girl.

He shared a look with Drake, steeled himself, and then gave a sharp nod. Ready.

Sure enough, the minute Drake set his foot on the concrete floor of the basement, all hell broke loose.

Noise, alarms, drilling, shouting, and—for Devil—mental chaos. He slammed his shields shut and dashed back up the stairs. He reached the top just in time to grab the first poker-playing gorilla around the neck and toss him down the stairs. He dropped low, punched the second guy in the balls, and came up with a hard knee to his face, snapping the guy's head back so that he fell into gorilla number three.

Angelo stepped out of the stairwell and booted gorilla three in the head, knocking him out, too. A couple of zip ties had them secured within a minute, and Angelo did a quick sweep of the first floor. No more guards, or anyone else, there. All the action was happening in the basement. He lowered his mental shields and reached out for Drake and Jewel. Drake's mind was that calm quiet of a fighter reacting on instinct, and Jewel's mind was full of angry curses.

Both were alive and fighting as he started down the stairs.

Gina tried desperately not to think about what was happening on the other side of the city as she lay on a blanket in the sun with her lover.

"They're going to be fine. The plan was a good one," Caleb said as he smoothed a hand over her back.

"Oh. Are you the psychic now?"

"No, but we both know your brother and his friend have to be damn good at what they do or they wouldn't still be alive."

Shame tickled her belly. Caleb was doing his best to distract her and keep her mind off the fact that for the first time in her life, she had no connection to her brother. "I'm sorry," she whispered.

The first thing she'd noticed after doing the ritual Jewel had given her was the absence of heat in her wrist. She'd always thought the birthmark heated only when Angelo was near or was thinking of her . . . but once the ritual was done, there was nothing there at all. Her birthmark had stopped being a link and was nothing but a purple spot on her wrist.

"It's only temporary," Caleb muttered as he pressed a kiss to her temple and cuddled her against his side.

"I know. And I know you were right to insist I do it. If somehow Vetis got through to me again, it would put Angelo and Drake in a lot of danger."

"Not to mention you."

Gina tilted her head back and smiled at her dream man. If he really wanted to help take her mind off things, there was a better way than talk. "Sex in a cemetery would take you off the boring-and-stodgy list forever, ya know."

"Is that a promise?"

"Oh, yeah," she murmured, pulling his head down for a kiss. "Especially if we get caught."

# 13

Angelo swung around the corner at the bottom of the stairs and immediately dashed into the fray. Just in time to stop a muscle-bound monkey from cracking Jewel over the head from behind while she fought with the goon in front of her. Instinct had him reaching for the eight-inch Tanto knife from his thigh holster instead of the gun at his hip. He stuck the blade between the guy's ribs and moved on.

These guys weren't playing around, and he'd run out of mercy. Grabbing Jewel by the shoulder, he swung her away and faced the guy she'd been fighting. She'd been winning, but he'd do it faster.

"Find Nadya!" he instructed.

Without a second look, Jewel took off, dodging Drake and the two guys he was fighting. Where was Hooper? A swift crack to his jaw reminded him to keep his mind on the man in front of him.

Three moves later he was wiping the blood off his knife and sheathing it as he watched Drake put down the last of his opponents. When the last guy hit the floor, they shared a look.

The house was silent again.

"This can't be good, man."

"You wire up the gateway; I'll find the women," Angelo said, waving at the structure on the far side of the room. It was a large metal rectangle built up against the cement wall, like the frame for a new doorway. Only, this frame was six-inch-thick metal with weird symbols carved into it. Almost identical to the gateway they'd found deep in a cave in the side of an Ecuadorian mountain.

Leaving the gateway to Drake, he spun around and followed the panicked thoughts running through his mind. He found Jewel in a small room off the main one, on her knees next to the limp body of a young woman.

Jewel's head snapped up at his entrance. "She's alive but feverish and completely out of it."

He moved past the hot-water tank and looked out the small window, which was at ground level. He expected to see guards running up to the house or *something*, but there was nothing. "Let's get her out of here then," he said.

When he saw Jewel struggling to lift her sister, he pulled out his knife and held it out to her. "You take point; I'll carry her."

Jewel glanced at his knife, smiled grimly, and tugged a wickedly long dagger from her boot. "I've got my own, thanks."

Shit, he was glad that dagger had never cleared her boot the day they met.

Once Nadya was firmly over his shoulder in a fireman's carry, they exited the small room. Drake was waiting by the bottom of the steps with a grim expression. "Nothing."

Devil glanced at the gateway, saw that it was wired up, and nodded. Drake pushed the detonator, and the wires blew, the metal frame shattering at the joints. They waited for the smoke to clear before Drake snatched up a chunk of the metal and stuffed it in his pocket. "Let's get out of here."

Drake took point, heading up the stairs with Devil and Nadya in the middle and Jewel taking up the rear. Things had gone smoothly so far, but it wasn't over yet.

Yet they made it all the way to the wall, and over it, without running into anyone or anything. Not even the dog from the other night.

"This is creepy," Devil muttered as he crouched in the shrubs with Jewel and Nadya while Drake jogged up the road a bit for the truck.

Jewel looked up from her examination of her sister and arched an eyebrow at him. "Hiding in the bush?"

"The whole thing. Where the hell is Hooper, and if he's not around, why didn't he have more security?"

"Isn't that why we did it during the day? Because he wouldn't be expecting it?"

"Yeah." But something just wasn't right.

Everything was too still, too quiet. Where could Hooper be? What could possibly be more important to the demon than guarding the gatehouse?

Dizziness swept over him. "Gina."

Gina was thoroughly enjoying her lover's kiss when a sudden chill seeped into her blood. She pulled back and lifted her head to look around while Caleb dipped in under her chin and nibbled on her neck, whispering naughty instructions to her until she pushed back.

"Caleb, someone's here."

He straightened, cheeks flushing. "Oops."

He followed her gaze, and when he saw the man on the road, he stiffened. Gina clutched him tight. "It's him, isn't it? That's Hooper."

Caleb jumped to his feet and stalked over the grass toward

the road where Hooper leaned against his shiny car. Gina ran behind him, heart pounding.

"What are you doing? You can't just attack him. Caleb, stop!" She grabbed his arm and spun him around. "*What* are you doing?"

Caleb placed both his hands on her shoulders, their heat seeping through and chasing away the chill that had settled over her moments earlier. "I'm going to talk to him."

"You can't reason with him, Caleb. He's a demon."

"He was just a man when I met him before."

Gina looked into Caleb's eyes, and her heart fell. "You still don't believe it, do you? You think there's no such things as demons."

He shrugged, looking away from her steady gaze. "I don't know what to believe. But I do know he's standing right there, and he's not hurting either one of us. He could've easily snuck up on us if we'd kept making love."

"We're in a cemetery, Caleb, consecrated land. He probably can't come in here. That's why he's on the road." She saw the determination in the set of his jaw and the way his fists clenched by his side. He was determined to confront Hooper. "Okay, but I'm coming with you. Just do *not* step off this land!"

They walked toward where Hooper still stood, a good-looking, clean-cut man in neatly pressed slacks and a white button-up shirt. The glowing eyes were gone, and he actually smiled. He certainly didn't look like a demon. Except for the pressed slacks, maybe. Gina hated buttoned-up-and-pressed men.

She threw a glance at Caleb, remembering the first day they'd met, and how his denim jeans had been pressed so neatly. Okay, so she couldn't judge a man by his clothes. Hooper was still a demon.

Caleb stopped five feet from the edge of the road. "Hooper Radisson, what are you doing here?"

"Caleb Mann, I could say the same thing to you. You never struck me as the type of man to hang out in cemeteries." The man's lips lifted charmingly, and he eyed Gina. "Or to get involved with the mystical."

Caleb jerked, as though to step forward, and she grabbed his belt with a sweaty palm. Caleb's disbelief could be a dangerous thing for them both. "What do you want?"

Hooper settled his gaze on her. "If I tell you, will you give it to me?"

She snorted. "Not likely."

"Hooper." Caleb stepped forward, only to have Gina pull him back. "What!"

"Don't get any closer," she muttered.

"Yes, Caleb. I'm evil, don't you know?" He stared at Gina, the whites of his eyes starting to turn pink and then red. "You turned yourself off. I'm disappointed."

Turned herself off? Oh! "You mean because you can't get into my head anymore? Seemed like the smart thing to do after your last little visit."

"Not so smart, after all; now you're no good to me." He raised his hands, his eyes glowed fully red, and a vice started to slowly squeeze around her neck. Her eyes bugged out, and she gasped, clawing at her throat, feeling nothing there yet still unable to breathe. The color drained from Caleb's face, and he charged at Hooper, only to go flying backward through the air to land against a tall headstone.

Gina's heart screamed when he didn't get up, and she dropped to her knees, trying to crawl toward him. The vague sound of screeching echoed in Gina's ears, louder than her own heartbeat. She reached out for Caleb's foot and felt the hand around her throat loosen. Sucking in a deep breath, she pulled her way up his body and, holding him close, rolled around to see what was happening.

"No!" she screamed as she saw Angelo, gun in hand, fly through the air and land on the hood of his own truck. Drake rushed Hooper, but the demon opened his mouth, and a horrible garbled shrieking noise came out, sending Drake to his knees, hands clutching at his head.

Gina struggled to stand, unsure of what she could do, but instinct had taken over. She reached her feet and took a step, only to fall forward and see a knife slice through the air and embed in Hooper's throat. Hooper turned to Angel, pulled the knife out of his throat, and dropped it to the pavement while blood gushed from his neck.

With a final glare, he spun around and climbed back into his fancy car. Within seconds he was gone, leaving Gina next to a dazed Caleb, and Angel rolling off the hood of the truck to help Drake to his feet.

All four of them stared at the taillights of the silver Mercedes.

# 14

By the time Jewel got out from the backseat of the truck, the Mercedes taillights were long gone. The whole incident had taken about thirty seconds to go down, and she'd been busy trying to get out from under the unconscious Nadya in her lap, after force-feeding her some of the *Shuvani's* healing potion.

She reached Devil just as he was holstering the pistol that had flown from his hand when he'd landed on the truck. "You okay?" he asked.

She nodded, breathless, as she watched him jog over to Gina and Caleb. Once it was determined everyone was alive and unhurt, a quick plan was made to head out and meet back at Caleb's.

The fight wasn't over, and Caleb's house was now command central.

Drake stopped the truck at the motel so Jewel could grab her bags. She didn't want to leave the still-drowsy Nadya in the back of Drake's truck alone, so Jewel stayed with her sister, and Devil followed them back to Caleb's in her truck.

When they arrived back at the house, Drake carried Nadya

in and laid her down on the sofa. Fear sent a chill down Jewel's spine as she looked at her sister, laying on the sofa and muttering, "Don't kill him," over and over again.

"Who's she talking about?"

"I don't know." Jewel continued talking as she monitored her sister's temperature. The fever had broken, and she was cooling down fast. Too fast for it to have been the potion that had helped her. "Maybe Jimmy or Kaz, the guardians that were with her when she was taken? The fever seems to have broken, but she's still not making sense."

She stood and looked at Drake. "How are you?"

"Fine." He nodded his thanks and faced the others. "But we have a complication."

"No shit," Gina grouched as she held a bag of ice against the shoulder Caleb had injured in his fall.

"More than one," Devil added.

Emotions swirled around in Jewel's belly as reality set in. She had Nadya, and the gateway was destroyed, but Vetis was still on the loose. Would he come after Nadya again? Now or after he built another gateway? Could she fight him off on her own?

Swallowing her panic, she peeked at Devil from under her lashes. He looked so tense, yet his expression was carefully blank. She had to fight the urge to go to him—whether to cuddle up against his side or smack him in the face for a reaction, she wasn't sure.

*Get a grip,* she told herself. "Okay." She lifted her chin and stared at Devil. "What's the first complication?"

"How was he able to attack us while we were on consecrated ground?" Gina asked.

They all looked at each other. It was a good question—one no one had an answer for.

Devil turned to Drake. "What did he do to you, Drake? He opened his mouth, and you dropped like a stone."

"Sorry, man, I've never been hit with something like that."

"Like what?"

"That's the complication I was going to mention." He shook his head slowly. "Hooper isn't Vetis, he's just possessed by him. When he opened up like that, Vetis sent me all the pain, anger, humiliation, and fear Hooper was feeling. It's like Vetis took over Hooper Radisson's body and swallowed his soul whole."

"How the fuck did he even know you're an empath? How did he know to do that to you?" Devil didn't move, but Jewel could see every muscle tensed and twitching just beneath the surface. He was ready to kill.

"He got it from Gina's head."

"Nadya!" Jewel spun around and dropped to her knees and hugged her sister. "You're awake! You're okay! You are okay? Are you okay?"

Jewel's heart swelled when her brat of a little sister met her gaze head-on. Nadya had never truly been an innocent either—the way they'd grown up had taken care of that—but the petulant teenager was gone. In her place was an adult. "I'm okay. Vetis kept me drugged with some mystical gag, but it never lasts long, and it's pretty much out of my system now." She stood, looking a little wobbly but determined.

"Don't push it," Jewel ordered. "We're not going anywhere, so sit back down."

"You guys need to know what you're up against." She spoke firmly but weakly lowered herself back down to the sofa. "And I can help with that. Whatever he was giving to me kept me from being able to talk, but I wasn't completely out of it all the time. I heard a lot of what was going on, and let me tell you, Vetis knows all about each of you. He knows everything Hooper knows, which means he probably knows where we are. We should get moving."

"Hooper never knew where I lived. Even if he did, I didn't live here when I was working for him, I was living with—Gabe!"

Gina handed Caleb a phone, and the others watched as he dialed. There was no answer, so he tried again. When Jewel caught Devil's eye, he mouthed the word "brother," so she waited with the rest. When Gabe answered his cell phone, Caleb asked him where he was and visibly relaxed when he heard the answer. "I forgot, sorry. No, everything's fine. I'll see you in a few days."

"Vancouver for a week," he explained when he hung up.

Devil stepped forward. "So the sit-rep is we're all here, we're all alive, the gateway's destroyed, Hooper's a man, not a demon, and Vetis, who's possessing Hooper, knows all about us."

*Great.*

"What's a sit-rep?"

Devil smiled at Nadya. "Sorry, military talk. It means situation report."

"Oh. Cool, so you're a soldier?"

Jewel watched in amazement as Nadya talked to Devil. The teenager of a week ago—the one who had sneered at any form of authority—was gone.

"Do *you* know why Vetis could still attack my sister when they were in the cemetery?"

"Sure." Nadya almost preened under Devil's attention. "He's a superdemon or something. A really old one; he said he basically punched his way through the veil between Hell and earth—took him centuries. A lot of the normal stuff won't work on him, including holy water and crap. While he can't actually walk into a church or stand on consecrated ground, he can still use his mind on you, even if you're on it. He's not as strong over it, and he can't reach far, so they must've gotten too close to him."

Drake sat next to the girl and smiled at her encouragingly. "What else can you tell us?"

# 15

The sun was high in the backyard as Devil paced through Caleb's almost silent house. The house had begun to resemble one of HPG's shared units. The furniture wasn't as nice—old man Hunter was wealthy, and he treated his operatives well—but the weapons, of the traditional and mystical variety, were spread out around the living room and dining area.

It was late afternoon, and everyone had settled in somewhere with their own thoughts after the question-and-answer period with Nadya had finished.

Caleb and Gina were in Caleb's bedroom; Jewel was sitting quietly on the sofa in the living room with her sister. Drake was sleeping in an armchair next to them, and Angelo was prowling.

Nadya had put some sort of protective spell around the house and assured them they were safe for a while, but Devil still couldn't relax.

The timer on the oven went off, and he headed for the kitchen to pull out another batch of peanut-butter cookies. The added heat from the oven made the kitchen a bit uncomfortable, but he didn't care. Baking helped him think. Something about keeping his hands busy gave his brain time to sort through all the data he'd stored up in the last few days.

He used the spatula to place the hot cookies on the newspaper he'd spread out on the countertop and started to roll more for the sheet.

HPG had been way off base in their knowledge of the demon. It fucked things up big-time when men were sent on a job without good intel, and he was struggling not to call his boss and ream him a new asshole.

Of course he couldn't do that. As frustrated as he was at the whole Vetis situation, Ethan Hunter was a good man, and he'd given them what he had. When it came to demons, all they really had to work with was lore and legend. HPG itself had originally started as just what it was labeled as, a private security company. But then Old Man Hunter had had a run-in with a malevolent ghost, and he'd gotten sucked into the world of paranormal protection. That was when he'd started recruiting psychics to work for him.

A fight-fire-with-fire sort of thing.

It would be better if they had a few ghosts, werewolves, or witches on staff to help shift fact from fiction in the legends, but life wasn't that easy.

He put the last batch of cookie dough in the oven and set the timer. Filling the sink with soapy water, he started on the dishes.

Maybe when they were done with Vetis, he could convince Hunter to hire Jewel. Her mystical lock picking would be only one of the pluses of having her around.

"Why is a man doing dishes so sexy?"

Devil looked over his shoulder and saw Jewel standing in the doorway, a little smile lifting her lips.

"Because the man is me," he answered with a wink.

She chuckled and walked away. "Don't use the water for a while—I'm going to take a shower."

The image of her naked and all slick and soapy filled his head, and he was instantly hard. Pulling the plug on the sink, he left the dishes to dry, pulled the last batch of cookies from the oven, and tried desperately to concentrate on how the hell they were going to get out of the situation they were in.

If what Nadya had told them was true, they could destroy Vetis forever by killing Hooper while he was still possessed. But killing him obviously wasn't going to be easy, since he'd already taken a knife to the throat and walked away. Plus, Hooper was an innocent, really.

A man possessed didn't have control over anything he did.

Devil let out a big sigh; he was tired. He filled a plate with cookies and headed out to the living room. After setting them on the coffee table in front of Drake, he stood at the window, staring out.

The muffled sound of the running shower could be heard, and that was all it took. His blood started to heat again, and his body reacted. Unable to stop himself, he dropped his mental shields and searched for Jewel.

She was wide open and thinking of him. His pulse picked up, and he felt a growl build from deep within.

*Go to her, already; you two are driving me nuts!*

Devil swung around to see Drake still slouched in the armchair, his eyes slitted open and glaring at him.

*Hello! Empath over here not getting any peace until you two stop drooling over each other and go at it.*

Angelo could be the chivalrous type and stay away—stand guard while the house rested. But, truly, he wasn't that virtuous. Besides, the house had a protection spell around it, right?

Without another thought, Devil spun on his heel and headed down the short hallway.

\* \* \*

Jewel heard the bathroom door open, and her gut clenched. She didn't need to look to know who it was. Devil.

There were soft rustling sounds, and she pushed back the curtain a bit. Their eyes met as he stood there, barefooted and bare-chested as he unzipped his pants.

"Oh, yes," she whispered. "It's about time."

She didn't bother to hide how much she wanted him. She watched as he shucked his pants; she was eager to see him naked. When he stood tall and moved to step into the shower, her breath caught at the sight of him. He wasn't massive, but his lean body and defined muscles were the perfect frame for the long, thick cock jutting out from a tidy nest of tight little curls.

She shifted under the spray while he silently stepped into the shower and pulled the curtain closed behind him. Without hesitation, his hot hands circled her waist, and he pulled her tight against his nakedness, his head dipping under the spray, and his mouth covering hers.

Skin slid against skin; his hardness cushioned her softness as they ate at each other. Fire roared through her veins as she nipped at his lips and chased his tongue with hers. His hands were sure and strong as they roamed her curves. Cupping a breast, squeezing a nipple, squeezing her ass as he bent his knees and thrust a leg between her thighs.

The hard muscle rubbed against her eager sex, and she moaned into his mouth. He ducked his head and scraped his teeth down her neck to her shoulder. Her insides tightened, and she rode his thigh and clutched at his shoulders. Digging her nails in, she threw back her head and welcomed the orgasm that washed over her with a low purr.

The second her writhing against his leg stopped, Devil gripped her ass with both hands and lifted. "Wrap your legs around me," he ordered. Her back hit the shower wall, and he thrust deep into her slick sex.

She bit her lip against a squeal of pleasure and locked her ankles at the small of his back. He pulled back and met her gaze.

A slow, sexy smile spread across his face as he began to thrust in and out. "God, you're tight," he panted. "So hot and tight, and I never want to stop."

"Then don't," she whispered, burying her hands in his hair and pulling him in for another kiss.

She was panting by the time Devil tore his mouth away from hers. His hips never stopped thrusting as he dipped low and sucked a hard nipple into his mouth. Jolts of pleasure shot from nipple to pussy, and her insides began to tighten again. "Oh, yes," she begged shamelessly. "Again."

He switched to the other breast, his teeth lightly scoring the skin before clamping onto the nipple, setting off her second orgasm. Just as she was coming back down to earth, Devil slid a hand between them, thumbed her clit, and pumped his hips faster, harder, and she shattered in his arms. She was vaguely aware of an unexpected emptiness as her sex clenched, but then hard cock rubbed up and down her slit, rubbing her clit and keeping her body quivering as his own guttural groan of satisfaction echoed through the small space and a sudden hotness splashed over her lower belly.

They stayed like that, with Devil pinning her to the shower wall, his arms around her and hers around him, for a few minutes. Finally he pulled back and met her gaze. He gave her a lazy smile and winked. "How are you doing?"

Lightness filled her soul, and she grinned back at him. "I feel like more. How about you?"

# 16

Devil didn't hesitate.

With a few quick swipes of the washcloth, he had them both cleaned up and the shower turned off. "A little eager?" Jewel laughed at him as he wrapped a towel around her shoulders.

He quirked an eyebrow at her. "You're not?"

She dropped the towel and bent over the bathroom sink, her pert ass taunting him. With a toss of her hair she grinned at him over her shoulder. "I'm ready when you are."

*Oh, what a woman!*

Angelo dropped to his knees and palmed her ass. Firm, resilient flesh yielded to his grip, and he leaned forward, flicking his tongue against her pouting pussy lips. He breathed deeply, inhaled her scent, and bit back a groan. He could get high off that scent.

Taking his time, he savored every texture, every flavor she had. Her mind was blank, everything she was thinking coming right out of her mouth. Sighs of pleasure, gasps, and the occasional "Oh, yes, *there*" guided him well. He slid two fingers into her sex and pumped them while nipping and biting at the pillowy flesh surrounding her entrance. Her insides clenched around his fingers, and a small cry of pleasure was cut off. When her cunt stopped spasming around his fingers, he withdrew and reached for the drawer beside her.

Pulling a condom from Caleb's stash, he sat back on the floor, leaned against the side of the tub, and rolled the condom on. When he was ready, he reached up and grabbed Jewel by the hips, aware that she'd been watching him with sleepy eyes. She started to turn, to straddle him while facing him, but he stopped her. "Oh, no," he said. "I like the view from here."

He pulled her backward, with her feet on either side of his legs. "Come on, baby, sit down and ride me this way. Please?"

Her eyes glowed, and she smiled softly before facing away from him. She lowered herself right onto his rigid cock, and he sighed. So warm, so tight, and oh, so good.

"That's it," he praised as she raised and lowered herself. He leaned back a bit and watched as his cock slid in and out of her, pleasure filling him and tightening his balls. He wasn't going to last long like this. He started to pant, his hips clenching as he moved with her. Giving up the view, he leaned forward, reaching around to cup Jewel's breasts. Her nipples poked against the middle of his hands, and she lowered her head, her hot breath drifting over his hands as they picked up speed.

"C'mon, Devil," she urged. "Fuck me harder."

Her crude words spurred him on, and he pumped harder, lifting them both higher. He licked his lips and tasted her, and his balls exploded, heat exploding from him as pleasure ripped up his spine.

He settled back against the cold tub and gathered Jewel in his arms. He'd needed that.

They sat cuddled up like that for a few minutes until there was a light knock at the door, and Drake's quiet voice drifted through it. "House is waking up, Devil."

Jewel pulled away from him, and he was actually sorry to let her go. They stood and dressed silently. When Jewel was about to reach for the door without speaking, Angelo covered her hand with his.

She looked up at him, a pleasant glow in her cheeks, and her lips lifted at the corners. His chest tightened, and he realized he didn't know what to say.

So he leaned down and placed a gentle kiss at each corner of her mouth and then stepped back. It was time to go back to work.

Gina smothered a grin as she watched Angel and Jewel enter the living room. Despite the shadows under their eyes, each of them had such a strong sense of satisfaction a blind person would be able to see it.

"Feeling a little rejuvenated, I hope?" she teased.

Angel glared at her, but Jewel just grinned. "Very much so, you?"

Angel growled and barked out an "I don't want to know" before Gina could answer. The women laughed, and he shook his head.

"Where's Nadya?"

"In the kitchen, chowing down on cookies while Caleb makes dinner."

"He shouldn't be cooking for us," Jewel exclaimed.

Pride made Gina boast. "He's a good cook. Don't worry."

"Plus, it makes him feel useful," Drake said when he stepped up to the small group.

Worry rose within Gina. "He's okay, though, right, Drake?"

She'd been so glad she had a man who'd rather stay with her than go off and slay the demon—not that he wouldn't slay the demon if he had the chance, but she was his main concern, and that warmed her heart. It never occurred to her that he'd feel less of a man or left out by not actively going after Vetis.

Drake's arm landed heavily on her shoulders, and he hugged her. "Don't worry, he's good. In fact, he's completely gotten past his disbelief in the paranormal and supernatural."

"Ha-ha." She punched him in the ribs and headed for the kitchen.

The others followed, and when they entered the room, they were greeted by a strong garlic aroma. "Chicken fettuccine, anyone?"

"It's to die for," Nadya said from the table.

"I hope not literally," Angel joked.

Caleb gestured with a wooden spoon at the pot on the stove. "I figured I'd cook something heavy on the garlic. You know . . . to keep the vampires away."

Everyone laughed, and Gina went over to kiss her man. It was so good to see him joking about everything. It did her heart good to see them all joking, especially since they all knew the fight wasn't over yet.

Caleb's arm slipped behind her, and he patted her on the butt as he whispered in her ear, "Vampires are real then, right?"

Gina chuckled and patted him on the chest. "I told you, babe. I don't know."

They joined the others around the table and began to eat. Drake's phone rang, and he got up from the table to answer it. When he came back, the first words out of his mouth were, "Does anyone have a Bible?"

"Huh?"

"No."

Nadya's fork clinked against her now empty plate. "You mean you guys came to exorcise a demon and didn't bring a Bible?"

"We didn't plan on *exorcising* the demon," Angel said.

"Oh." Comprehension dawned on the teenager's face, and Gina felt a small twinge of sympathy.

Angel and Drake put their heads together, talking in low tones . . . planning.

Gina wasn't sure what to make of the girl. Young, attractive, seemingly pretty smart, too. But she was a shape-shifter. Gina was now pretty certain her father had been killed by a were-wolf, and she wasn't sure how she felt about a shape-shifter being so close to her loved ones.

"But you're not going to just kill him now, right?" Nadya interrupted the men. Her forehead puckered in a frown. "If you, like, blow him up, then Hooper dies, too."

Angel met the girl's gaze. "We don't know how else to kill it, Nadya."

"I can exorcise it! I don't need a Bible. Just the gem Jewel loaded for me."

"Honey." Jewel reached for her sister. "Why does it matter to you so much about saving Hooper?"

"He's done nothing wrong; he's a good man. He was nice to me that day in the park." Nadya's voice took on a whine, and her eyes filled with tears.

A whisper of unease rippled through Gina, and she noted how glassy Nadya's eyes were. Not just the tears, but also her pupils were dilated and a trickle of sweat ran down the girl's temple.

"Nadya?" Jewel asked. "I thought you said the drugs were out of your system?"

"They are."

"You're getting flushed and starting to sweat, sweetie. Is your fever back? How do you feel?" Jewel reached out and felt Nadya's forehead.

"The fever's not from the drugs," Nadya muttered. She

folded her arms across her chest and slouched back in her chair. "It's the change thing. The moon."

Gina's head snapped to the window, and sure enough the sky was darkening; the sun was setting. Which meant the full moon was rising.

Oh, shit. "What's going to happen to her?"

"We don't really know," Jewel snapped as she pushed her chair back and helped her sister to her feet. "Her father's dead, and no one in the clan ever had a lot of contact with shape-shifters. We're on our own with this."

Gina's heart went out to them. The girl had been so worried about the innocent Hooper. She couldn't be evil. Thinking she was evil just because she was a shape-shifter was like people thinking Gina was crazy because she had visions.

"You're not on your own," Gina said, pushing back from the table to help them to the sofa. "We're all here with you. Caleb, make some tea, and, Angel, get your headquarters on the phone and find out all you can about werewolves and shape-shifters of any kind. Anything and everything that applies to their first change. Drake, can you feel anything that might help us?"

## 17

Fear raced through Jewel as she bathed her sister's forehead with a cool cloth. She'd tried to give Nadya the rest of the healing potion, but she'd refused. What was going on with her was natural for her body; the potion wouldn't have any effect.

"What did you learn?" she asked when Devil came to kneel by them.

"Yeah," Nadya slurred. "What's happening to me? It's like everything is in slow motion."

"The HPG archives don't have much on true shape-shifters. Not like the ones you described to us before. But from what they have on werewolves, the fever is normal. Your other senses will also be extrasensitive, which is why you could hear Drake and I talking about how to kill Vetis when we were only whispering. The changes have been building gradually and should peak soon."

Fear spiked in Jewel's gut. "Peak?"

Nadya groaned and doubled forward, clutching her stomach.

"She shouldn't shift though. Werewolves shift right away, but it's because they have only one shape. We're fairly certain Nadya won't shift until she wants to."

"He's coming," Nadya sputtered through a series of groans. "I can feel Vetis; he's near. He's looking for me."

Jewel looked at Devil, panic threatening. Devil put a hand on her shoulder before he stood. "It's okay, we can deal with him. You look after Nadya."

He turned to Drake and Caleb, taking them to the far side of the room. Gina came over and sat beside Jewel. "She's going to be fine."

Hope rose. "Did you have a premonition?"

"No," Gina said, staring at the huddle of men on the other side of the room. "I have faith."

Jewel wanted desperately to be in on what the men were planning, but she wouldn't leave Nadya's side. Her groans had gotten louder and higher until, blessedly, she'd passed out.

"Will the protection spell hold while she's unconscious?" Gina asked, handing Jewel the onyx-handled dagger she'd asked Gina to retrieve from the bedroom.

"I don't know. I think it's faded already; that's why she could sense him nearby."

"That's good," Devil said as he joined them. "We want him to come to us here."

"We do?"

"Yup." He gave her a wicked grin, and her heart skipped a beat in its rapid tattoo. "You just stay by Nadya's side and do what you can for her."

"What are you going to do?"

"What I do best—kill." His grin widened as he handed Gina some things. "Well, second best, maybe."

Jewel watched him walk away and chuckled. He'd been

flirting with her! A demon that was willing to kill anyone and anything to get to her sister was almost on their doorstep, and he was flirting with her!

If she didn't know better, she'd think she could fall in love with that man. Grinning like an idiot, she met the dark gaze of the woman on the other side of her sister.

Gina had watched the byplay, smiling the whole time. She sat next to Nadya, a wicked-looking knife of her own in one hand and a deadly pistol in the other. Seeing her there, ready to fight with them all, made Jewel realize she was finally seeing a true family in action, ready to stand together.

The two hunters nodded to each other and got into position. Devil moved right up beside the front door, and Drake stayed just inside the living room. Jewel watched as Caleb planted a lusty kiss on Gina and then positioned himself at the kitchen entrance so he could see both the living room and the back door.

They were ready.

Silence descended on the house as they waited. Five minutes went by—ten minutes. Jewel was just starting to wonder if Nadya had been imagining things when the front door blew off its hinges and a blank-faced, burly goon stormed through the entrance. Devil let him pass right by as the guy headed mindlessly for them, and Jewel almost screamed at him. Then Drake stepped up, and with one smooth move, stuck the goon between the ribs and let him drop to the floor.

By then more goons were rushing in, and the sounds of flesh hitting flesh filled the house as the fighting began around her in earnest.

Adrenaline spiked, and her pulse pounded as Jewel got to her feet and stood at the ready in front of her sister. Gina was also on her feet, at the entrance to the kitchen, her eye going between the action in the kitchen with Caleb and the goons flooding the living room, circling her and Drake.

Jewel ducked as a goon with a ponytail took a swing at her; she came up with a swift uppercut. His head snapped back, but he didn't go down. She swung again and again, hitting him in the ribs, the jaw, and even kicking him in the balls, but the guy just kept coming, forcing her backward with every step. Finally he just grabbed her beneath the arms and tossed her aside.

Terror ripped threw her as she landed and saw him reach for Nadya, but a loud crack filled the room, and a hole appeared in the center of the guy's forehead. Jewel looked over and saw Gina swing her gun into the kitchen; another crack filled the house as she disappeared into the kitchen fray.

Another goon got past Drake, and Jewel jumped to her feet, dagger in hand. She wasn't going to make the same mistake twice. She took a hard hit to the head getting close to the next one, but the ringing in her ears didn't affect her aim. With a shout and a quick spin, she used the motion of her body to carry her arm through, and she slit the guy's throat. Arterial spray hit her in the face, making her blink to get it out of her eyes, but she didn't stop. She jumped on the back of the goon leaning over the sofa, his hands already on her still unconscious little sister. With a savage growl she grabbed a handful of hair and yanked his head back. A quick slice, and they both hit the ground.

Suddenly Nadya sat rigidly upright on the sofa, her arms and head thrown back as a chilling scream ripped from her throat. Jewel scrambled to get out from under the heavy body of the dead goon as she saw Drake drop to his knees and Vetis walk into the room. Jewel searched the hallway and saw Devil's body on the floor, surrounded by several of the fallen goons.

Vetis ignored Jewel, his crimson glowing eyes focused on her little sister. He raised his hands to the now awake Nadya, his mouth forming a grotesque smile. "Come to me, Nadya. Let the darkness in; feel the power of it."

"Nooo!" Fear and rage made Jewel desperate as Nadya's body started to rise from the sofa.

Nadya seemed frozen as Vetis lifted her, turning her in the air to face him, her screams cut off and her eyes searching around wildly, looking anywhere but at Vetis.

"Hey, Vetis!"

The shout came from the front entryway, and Jewel turned to see Devil standing there, bent over, blood streaming from a cut over his eye and one arm clutching his side. Her heart soared; he was alive!

Vetis ignored him, his focus on Nadya. Jewel pushed at the body trapping her legs. She stood just in time to see Nadya close her eyes, her lips moving even though no sound came out. Her body fell back to the sofa, and Vetis roared.

"Demon!" Devil called from the entrance, slowly limping forward. "Face me, you bastard."

Hooper's body spun around, and he snarled at Devil. "You think *you can stop me?*"

"I think I can kill you," Devil declared as he raised his arm and fired.

Flames burst from Hooper's chest, and an unholy howl of pain and frustration filled the house. Hooper's body crumpled to the floor, flames engulfing it. The howl continued until finally, he fell face forward on the carpet and silence descended.

# 18

"Ouch!" Angelo pulled back instinctively when Jewel poked at the stab wound in his side.

"Don't be a baby," she said, shaking her head. Gina had fetched the supplies from the bathroom, and Jewel was cleaning the edges of his wound with peroxide. "You fight off evil muscle heads and set a demon on fire with a flare gun, yet you flinch at a little first aid?"

They sat outside in Caleb's backyard, taking inventory of wounds and just being together as a family. The night air was warm, and the moonlight glinted off Jewel's hair, making his chest tight and his blood heat. Lord, how could he get a hard-on after what he'd just been through?

Gina snatched up the bottle of peroxide Jewel had just set down and patted at the scrape on Caleb's forehead with a cotton ball.

"Yeah, Angel, be glad you don't have to get stitches." She tossed the cotton ball on the picnic table and looked at her lover. "Speaking of which, I'm taking you to the emergency ward. I'm not sewing up that cut."

"I hate hospitals," Caleb muttered. Then he eyed Devil's sister and shook his head. "Mind you, with the way you shoot, I'll do whatever you say, honey."

Angelo grinned. He'd only known Caleb a short time but already his opinion of him had improved. The straight-laced guy was still there, but he wasn't so uptight. Life with Gina would keep Caleb on his toes, and Angelo was glad to see the man could adjust fittingly.

Jewel turned to Gina. "Where did you learn to shoot like that?"

"With a career military dad and an older brother determined to follow in his footsteps, I had to pick up a few skills to remain part of the family."

"Ha ha." Devil reached over and mussed up his sister's hair, love and pride making him grin like a loon. "Don't let her fool you. She was always the first one on the shooting range, and the best one."

"I can stitch your head for you, if you want," Drake said to Caleb as he emerged from the back door of the house. He glanced at Devil. *Clean-up crew is inside; the bodies will be gone within the hour.*

Unaware of the silent communication between the hunters, Caleb eyed Drake and the first-aid kit in his hands. "Really?"

"Sure, I even have a local anesthetic in here."

"Yeah, guess you guys would carry around a pretty well-stocked field kit, huh?" Caleb grimaced at Gina. "Okay, sweetheart, step aside and let the man go to work."

Jewel patted the bandage on Devil's side. "And you're next, big man."

He smiled and pulled her close in a hug, fully aware that Drake would be adding yet another surgery scar to his body soon. Despite their bumps, bruises, and cuts, all of them had survived the fight in one piece. Even Nadya, who had quickly left the group to sit quietly under a tree fifteen feet away while everyone cleaned wounds.

"Drake," Devil said quietly, nodding his head in Nadya's direction. "She okay?"

His partner met his gaze. "Feeling a little lost . . . and a little to blame."

Jewel pulled away from Angelo, but he held her back. "May I?" he asked.

"Um, sure." She nodded and sat in his spot when he stood to make his way to the teenager's side.

She didn't even look up at his approach, and he bit back a groan as he slid to the ground with his back against the same tree. "How you doing?" he asked.

He didn't look at her. She was facing north, and he was was facing west, but their shoulders touched and he felt her shrug.

"This was going to happen no matter what you did, Nadya. Don't try to take the blame on yourself."

He felt her look at him, but he stayed focused on the full moon above them. Waiting.

Finally she spoke, her accusation no less heartbreaking in its softness. "Why did you have to kill him?"

"Hooper?"

"Yeah. I get that the muscle heads were just that, big dumb bad guys willing to do anything for a buck, but Hooper was innocent. You should've let me send the demon back to hell; then Hooper would've lived."

It sucked that this tough, kindhearted sixteen-year-old had to deal with so much, but there was nothing he could do about it. Nothing but help her to understand that there was war between good and evil going on every day, and sometimes, in order for good to win the battle, bad things needed to be done.

"If we'd somehow managed to restrain Vetis long enough

for whatever change was happening to you to be over—which was *not* something you had any control over—exorcising him would've killed Hooper anyway."

"You can't know that!"

"Yes, I can. Hooper's body wouldn't have lasted once Vetis left it, because he took a knife to the jugular this morning. The demon inside him was all that was keeping Hooper alive. This way, at least somewhere inside that body, Hooper knew that when he died, Vetis did, too."

Nadya didn't speak, and the two sat silent. Angelo wanted to drop his shield and search her mind, but he couldn't do it. She'd been through enough that night; he couldn't bring himself to invade her privacy.

It turned out he didn't need to. "What are we going to do?" she whispered after a few minutes. "Where are we going to go? The clan never really wanted us; they were scared of me and happy to leave us behind, I'm sure. But they're all we've ever known."

Devil stared at the small group on the picnic table nearby, his soul at peace with everything that had happened in the last few days. He'd killed a man, but he'd done that before. He'd killed a demon, and he'd do it again. For a while, before Vetis had led them back to Pearson, he'd started to worry about his own soul—about the things he'd done. But as he sat there, he was at peace with who he was.

He was a soldier, a fighter . . . a hunter. And he'd do what needed to be done to protect those he loved.

There *was* a war going on every day, and the holier than thou couldn't fight it. Men like him were needed to protect the good. He needed to remember what he fought for. It wasn't for the rich old man who paid him to fight . . . it was for this—for the good in people.

His sister and her man were together. Nadya was alive and

strong, even if nobody really knew what she was capable of yet. His best friend was alive, and his new lover . . . well, she was something special.

"Don't worry too much about the future, Nadya. Destiny can be a funny thing, Sometimes it finds you when you least expect it." With that said, Angelo stood up and held out a hand to her. "For now, I think your sister needs to know you're safe with her."

They could've stayed at Caleb's house that night. The invitation had been there, but all Jewel really wanted to do was grab her sister and run. So she did.

They only went as far as the roadside motel on the edge of town, but it was far enough.

"What do we do now, Jewel?" Nadya asked quietly from her spot on the bed.

"We stick together." It was a simple answer, but it was the only one she had. Sure, they could track down the caravan and rejoin the clan, but they'd never truly be part of it. They were different.

The real problem wasn't where they would go, and they both knew it. Gypsy blood insured they didn't feel the need for a permanent home or a white picket fence. The real problem was, neither of them knew what was going on with Nadya's powers.

"I think Devil and Drake could help us." Nadya's words were said so softly, Jewel almost didn't hear her.

"What do you mean?"

Her sister sat up and met her gaze. "No one in the clan came with you to get me. No one cared enough to help us, but those two did. They could've done what they needed to do without getting involved with us."

"They needed me as much as they helped us, Nadya. Don't make them into heroes just yet. Plus, Kaz was a big help, too.

He couldn't be here, his grandfather needed him, but he *did* help, don't doubt it."

Nadya eyed her and heat crept up Jewel's cheeks. She was telling her sister not to make Devil into a hero, but deep down, she couldn't stop from feeling that he truly was.

A sharp knock on the door brought her eyes to the clock. Speak of the devil, literally. Not many other people would be knocking on her door at four in the morning. Heart pounding, she smiled at her sister and headed for the door. "Get some sleep, we'll make a plan in the morning."

"Hey you," she said as she stepped out of the room and closed the door behind her.

He rocked back on his heels, his arms crossed over his broad chest, face blank except the fire in his eyes. "You left without saying goodbye."

*Keep it casual, Jewel.* She swallowed the sudden knot in her throat, and shrugged. "I'm not real fond of goodbyes. Didn't think it would be your thing either."

"I wasn't planning on saying goodbye." With one step forward he had her pinned to the door, her hand pinned above her head. "You have been a pain in my ass since the first moment we met. You're stubborn and argumentative and smart and beautiful and . . . and I'm not ready to let you walk away."

Jewel's breath caught and her heart thumped against her rib cage. *He* wasn't ready to let her walk away? She swallowed hard. "As fun as it's been, what you're ready for doesn't matter right now, Devil. What matters is my sister. Nadya is changing, and my first priority is her. We need to find someone who can tell us what to expect."

He leaned in and a shiver danced down her spine when his nose nuzzled against her ear and his lips brushed her neck. Geez, he was potent! She had to fight the urge to wrap her legs around his hips and tell him to fuck her there and then.

"Devil," she groaned. She wanted to tell him she wasn't ready to walk away either. That for the first time in her life, she wanted more. She wanted . . . she didn't know *what* she wanted, but she didn't want to never see Devil again.

Chest to chest, thigh to thigh, he kept her pinned to the door as he lifted his head and looked deep into her eyes. "I'm here to offer you a job. Hunter Protection Group can use someone with your talents, and you can use their resources to help Nadya. Plus, we'll have some time to . . . get to know each other better."

Color crept over Devil's cheekbones and something fluttered in Jewels chest. "Work with you?"

"Not *with* me. Not always anyways. Drake is my field partner, and we make a good team. You have to go through some heavy field training before you can work with us in that capacity. But HPG is ready to offer that training, and a secure place for you and your sister, with people from various supernatural and paranormal backgrounds." He stepped back and gave her some space, his eyes suddenly shuddered. "What do you think?"

A job. A permanent job that offered her safety, adventure, training . . . and a chance to be close to Devil. A chance at the *more* she'd suddenly started to crave.

"Hell yeah!" She launched herself at him, arms around his neck, legs around his waist. She planted a long kiss on his mouth before nipping at his bottom lip. "Are you sure you're ready for me?"

"More than ready," he growled, holding her tight.

A Bonus Free Read From Sasha!

# MOUNTAIN RETREAT

# 1

---

Mac Goodman's palms began to sweat as soon as he turned off the gravel road that wound its way up the mountain and onto the rutted dirt one that was little more than a path between pine trees. Five miles on a road that made it impossible to go more than fifteen miles an hour had his heart beating like a trip-hammer. Nikki Marks was at the end of that road. He was sure of it.

And he was not letting her get away from him again.

For the first time since he'd woken up to an empty bed two days ago, tension eased as the trees melted away and the rustic cabin came into view. The small blue Toyota truck parked in front of it confirmed his suspicions. She was definitely there.

He parked next to the truck and strode up the steps and through the entrance beneath the moose antlers his dad had hung more than twenty years ago.

A quick glance around the main room showed that it was empty. Instinct and the absolute silence of the room told him there were no living souls in the cabin. Fear shot straight to his heart. Was he too late?

One hand on the gun at his hip, Mac ignored the adrenaline pulsing through his system and moved silently to the bedroom door. He prayed that when he opened it he'd find her sleeping on the bed and not dead. He turned the knob and eased the door open, only to find the room empty.

The breath he hadn't even been aware he was holding rushed from his mouth, and he leaned against the wall for a minute. Her truck was here—she was here.

Heartbeat slowly returning to normal, he headed out of the cabin and into the bush to the west of the cabin. If Nikki wasn't in the cabin, he knew where she was. Within seconds he could hear the running water of the nearby river. He stopped just inside the tree line and stared, the breath rushing out of his lungs in a gust.

Rising from the rushing water like a nymph, Nikki walked slowly toward the shore—naked, skin glistening in the sun. Shoulders back, chest thrust forward, her walk was confident, her steps sure, even in the rushing water.

She shook herself like a dog, water droplets spraying everywhere, and then just stood there, head tilted back, absorbing the sun's rays. She was beautiful. Small breasts perfectly tilted, nipples rigid and flushed a dark pink, begging for attention. Some would say her trim waist, flat belly, and leanly curved hips weren't womanly, but to him, she was the only woman he'd ever wanted.

Suddenly her shoulders tensed and her head turned, her gaze going immediately to where he stood. "Mac," she whispered.

He stepped out from the behind the tree, and their eyes met.

Her dark eyes were round and full of turmoil when she spoke. "I should've known you'd come after me."

*Three days earlier*

His shift was finally over, and Mac's feet were dragging as he took the steps up to his apartment. He loved his job, he really did. Truly, the only reason a person would ever be a cop is if they loved it and understood the meaning behind it; the hours were shitty, the pay worse, and the thanks nonexistent. But it gave him a sense of satisfaction.

The only thing that could make his life better would be to have someone to share it with. It was days like he'd just had that made him long for someone to come home to.

When he slowed in front of his door, the hair on the back of Mac's neck stood up as soon as he slid the key into the lock. Before his wrist turned and the lock tumbled, he *knew* that someone was on the other side of that door.

*Gotta watch what you wish for, buddy,* he chided himself mentally.

He slid one hand across his body, slowly pulled the 9mm SIG Sauer from his holster, and opened the door with the other hand. Walking into the apartment casually, as if he didn't expect anything, he let his gaze roam the room in one smooth sweep— that stopped when he saw the woman pacing restlessly alongside his sofa.

Pleasure hit him hard, but he quickly slammed the door shut on it. He hadn't seen Nikki Marks in just over fifteen years, but he still recognized her the instant he saw her.

He still wanted her as his own the instant he saw her.

Nikki had never been a particularly beautiful girl—until she smiled. When she smiled, her eyes lit up and her face transformed from simple to sensational.

She wasn't smiling then.

"Nikki?" Mac said, standing frozen in the doorway. "Is that you?"

"Hi, Mac," she said with a little wave. "How you doing?"

He just stared at her—in his living room—flesh and blood. Just like a dream come true.

With a mental head shake he flipped the safety on and returned his gun to its home under his arm. He closed the door behind him and stepped into the living room, hands loose at his side, not threatened, but ready for anything.

At one point in time Nikki had been everything to him, but he didn't know her anymore, and he needed to remember that. "What are you doing here? Are you okay?"

"What?" she asked, eyebrows raised and lips tilted in a half-assed smile that didn't reach her eyes. "I can't drop in on an old friend?"

He kept his voice neutral, his eyes scanning the apartment quickly to make sure she was alone. "It's been almost fifteen years since you disappeared from Pearson, Nikki. Somehow I doubt this is a casual visit to an old high school friend."

"I didn't disappear, Mac. We moved away; families do that sometimes."

"You left without saying good-bye."

Their eyes met, and he fought to keep his expression blank. There was no way he was going to let her know how much her actions had damaged his young heart. How often thoughts of her had kept him up at night, even as he'd gone through the motions of moving on with his life.

"Good-byes have never been my strong point," she said softly as she walked slowly toward him. "I much prefer hellos."

With that, Nikki slid her arms around his waist and curled her lithe body against his, her head fitting perfectly under his chin. Heart pounding in his chest, he stayed strong for a moment. But she felt too good, too real. With a sigh, he closed his eyes and returned the hug. "I never could stay mad at you."

They held each other for a long moment. Max breathed

deeply, inhaling her scent and reveling in the feel of the one girl he could never forget in his arms once again.

He stroked a hand up and down her back, noting the bumps of her spine and the fact that she was a lot thinner than she'd been as a teenager. Almost too thin. "You're in trouble, aren't you?"

She leaned back in his arms and smiled up at him. "What makes you say a thing like that?"

"You broke into my apartment after fifteen years without a word, just to say hi?" He couldn't bite back his snort of derision as he took a step away from her. He needed distance; he never could think straight when she was close to him. "Christ, Nikki, you must not have a very high opinion of my intelligence."

"You always were a smart-ass, Mac." She shoved her hands into the back pockets of her jeans and met his gaze head-on. "Key word used to be 'smart.' Has that changed?"

He stiffened. "Not at all, which is why I know this is more than just a friendly visit."

"You're right. I did come for more than a casual visit, but I was hoping you'd give me a bit of time before you turned all cop on me and the interrogation started."

Her posture thrust her small breasts forward, and Mac tried not to drool. Memories of how sensitive those breasts were, of Nikki's mewls of pleasure as he'd suckled at her nipples, rushed to the forefront of his brain, and he spun around on his heel.

"A cop is what I am," he said and headed into the little kitchen. As he went, he tossed aside the light jacket he wore to hide his shoulder harness and gun. Anxiousness had his muscles so tight they were twitching as he reached into the fridge for a beer. "You want a drink?"

"That would be nice, thank you."

That was his Nikki—always polite, no matter what.

Mac grabbed another beer from the fridge, twisted off the cap, and held it out to her. She took it, and the flash of her pink tongue as she took a long drink straight from the bottle had his cock twitching in his pants.

God, how he'd loved her. At seventeen, he would've done anything for her. But he'd let her disappear from his life fifteen years earlier because he hadn't known how to stop it, and now he had to keep reminding himself that he didn't really know her. Not like he'd thought he did.

He'd been a teenage boy, born and raised in Pearson with both parents and friends he'd known since grade school. She'd been a sixteen-year-old girl with a single mother who moved at the drop of a hat. For all their differences, there'd been an instant connection between them when she and her mom had moved in next door; they'd been instant friends.

It had never sat right with him, the way things had ended. After being just friends for almost a year, things had shifted. They'd been great as a couple. In his hormone-fogged seventeen-year-old brain, he'd thought things were perfect with them. So perfect that after months of making out and stopping just shy of all the way, they'd finally done it. Both of them had been virgins, but they'd declared their love and sealed their vows with their bodies.

The next day Nikki hadn't shown up at school.

He'd gone to her place after classes only to find out that she and her mom had pulled up stakes again, and they were gone. Mac had often thought about tracking her down once he became a cop, but he'd never followed through.

As if she could read his mind, she laughed softly. "Funny, isn't it? For whatever reason, you're the first person who came to my mind when I needed to feel safe."

The primitive need to protect crept over Mac, chasing away memories of the past. He forced aside all the personal feelings and questions hammering at his skull and shifted into cop mode. Then he remembered her interrogation comment.

Planting his feet shoulder-width apart, he folded his arms over his chest and waited. He wanted to help her. Scratch that— he *would* help her. He'd never turn her away, and she knew it.

It was why she'd broken into his apartment and not someone else's. But that didn't mean he had to make it easy on her.

The silence grew, and so did the tension between them. Restless energy came off her in waves as her hands twitched on the beer bottle.

Finally Nikki shook her head and offered him a small smile. "There's some weird shit in the world today, huh?"

He thought of the things he'd seen people do to hurt each other or simply to get what they wanted. "Yes, there is," he said.

More silence.

Mac bit his tongue to keep from probing. He really wanted to know what she was doing there and why it had taken so long for her to come back to him. But he wasn't ready to force it. His gut tightened, and he realized he wasn't sure he was ready for the answers.

Instead he figured he'd try a new tactic. Start out simple. "I'm starving. You hungry?"

Her eyes widened slightly, and Nikki nodded. With a small smile he opened the fridge again and started pulling out ingredients. "How does a bacon-and-egg sandwich sound?"

"Wonderful."

Mac knew his sudden change in attitude had thrown her a bit, and that's what he'd wanted. She was obviously on edge about something, and he needed her to relax.

Pretending her sudden reappearance in his life was nothing special, Mac started to gently probe. "So tell me what you've done with your life? Are you a best-selling author and I just don't know it because you use a pen name?"

Her lips twitched, and a spark of life flickered in her dark eyes. "Nope, that dream didn't last. I'm a chef."

He cocked an eyebrow at her. "And I'm making you a bacon-and-egg sandwich for dinner? What's wrong with this picture?"

That got an actual laugh and the smile he'd been waiting for. Her dark eyes twinkled, her checks flushed, and white teeth flashed between plump, kissable lips. The tightness in Mac's chest eased, and he grinned back at her.

This was Nikki. His first love.

They chatted lightly as he finished frying the eggs. Bacon came out of the microwave, and he put the sandwiches together and handed her one.

"I get only one?" She eyed his plate with three on it as they sat down at the table.

Mac remembered the feel of her spine through her T-shirt and handed over another sandwich. "I can always make more."

She told him how when they'd left Pearson it had been to move to Vancouver. Her mom had wanted to be in a bigger city, one where she could get a job and have a decent chance at finding a rich man. Nikki had gotten a job in a hotel after graduation and worked her way up in the kitchen, apprenticing under a top chef for years before she could claim the title as her own.

When she never mentioned their last night together, or their relationship, he tried not be disappointed. They went into the living room after eating, and he tried to steer the conversation toward what had brought her there.

Nikki set her beer bottle down on the coffee table and slid a slim leg over his lap to straddle him. His cock instantly stiffened, and his blood heated. She slid her hands up over his chest and around his neck as she pressed a soft kiss to his chin.

"Right now, I just want to forget about it all." Several more kisses rained along his jaw as she rubbed her body along his. Her hair tickled his nose, and the scent of wildflowers filled his head. Her fingers wove through his hair, and she tugged his head forward until their foreheads were pressed together.

She spoke softly as she looked into his eyes. "Will you just help me forget it all? Make me feel good, Mac. The way only you ever could."

Her luscious lips covered his, and Mac went for it. His arms wrapped around her, one cupping the back of her head as he lost control. His tongue speared between her lips, and her flavor overwhelmed him. She tasted so good. Better than he remembered.

Her whimper of passion echoed through the room and went straight to his groin. God, how he loved the sounds she made. Her hands clutched at his shoulders, her hips ground down against his aching cock, and her tongue dueled with his.

"Yes, Mac!" she cried when he tugged her head back and scraped his teeth across the tendon in her neck. "Make me feel good. Make me forget."

It took a minute, but her words did sink into his brain, and Mac remembered where he was. Who he was—who she was. And how he really didn't know her anymore.

His hands circled her waist, and he lifted her off him. "I'm sorry, Nikki. But I can't do that."

"Huh?"

"I can't make you forget." He rubbed his chin to hide the way his hands still trembled with the need to touch her. "Not until you tell me what it is you're trying to forget. Why you're here."

Frustration radiated from her as she jumped from the sofa. "Damnit, Mac! Can't you just—"

"No, I can't." He shook his head as he stood. He grabbed her by the shoulders and stared into her eyes. "You know you're safe with me, but until you tell me what's really going on, that's all I'm going to do for you."

A tornado of emotion swirled in her dark eyes, and her lips parted silently as she stared back at him. Hope surged inside Mac.

Then she closed her eyes; her chest rose and fell as she took a deep breath, and when she looked at him again, her eyes were calm and her expression blank.

"I should go," she said as she reached for the battered backpack next to the sofa. "I never should've come here."

"No way." He blocked her way. "You are *not* running away again, Nikki. You said you needed to feel safe. I can protect you. If only you'll tell me what you're running from."

"Mac." She shook her head, worry creeping into her gaze. "You don't know what you're getting into. This was a stupid idea. I need to leave."

"You are not leaving." He bent low, grabbed her thighs, and threw her over his shoulder.

"Mac! Put me down right now!"

Heart pounding, he strode into the bedroom and tossed her on the bed. "You are staying here, at least for tonight. You need to feel safe . . . and I need to know you're safe."

She glared at him from her position, flat on her back in the middle of his bed. His cock throbbed with the need to join her, and he stifled a groan. "We'll talk tomorrow and you *will* tell me what's going on. Because, Nikki, I'm not letting you run away again."

He closed the bedroom door behind him and leaned against it for a moment. If Nikki wanted to run, she had to get past him.

Mac stretched out for a long night on the sofa. He closed his eyes and let the memories roll over him. Hours later, he finally drifted off to sleep after he admitted to himself that even if Nikki never told him what she was hiding from, he'd do everything in his power to keep her in his life this time.

\* \* \*

"Nikki?" Mac's eyes snapped open, and he sat straight up on the sofa. The bedroom door was still closed, but the apartment was silent. Too silent.

When he opened the bedroom door, his suspicions were confirmed. Empty.

The bedsheets were mussed, like someone had tossed and turned in them all night, and the window was open. Mac strode to the window and looked out on the parking lot four floors down.

How the hell had she gotten out?

# 2

Nikki watched Mac come closer, and her insides started to tremble with fear. The small bit of softness she'd seen in him days earlier was gone, his tense body and blank expression showing only pure determination. But that wasn't what she feared.

She feared the animal inside and the urges she couldn't control when the moon was strong.

"Why did you run, Nikki?" he ground out when he came to a stop in front of her. "Why did you even bother to walk back into my life if you were only going to run right back out?"

What could she say? That she'd run to protect *him*? He'd never understand, not without a full explanation, and she couldn't give him that. She'd thought she could, but seeing him again, being with him, touching him, kissing him . . . she couldn't do it.

She'd lost so much since she'd been bitten almost four months ago, and she couldn't stand to lose him, too. Her memories of him, of their time together, had been the stuff fantasies were made of. Young love with a boy no other man in her life had ever been able to measure up to. She'd loved the boy, and she'd instinctively turned to the man. But while she might need him, he'd be better of without her.

Safer and happier without her in his life.

"You shouldn't have followed me."

"Why not?"

"Because I don't need protection." But he would if he stayed around much longer.

She'd been through only three moon cycles since she'd been turned, but she knew if Mac didn't leave, there was a good chance she'd kill him. Her hungers had overpowered her will before.

Hyperaware of her complete nudity and the moisture already gathering between her thighs just from being near him, she turned away and started up the path to the cabin.

"You don't have any clothes?" His voice behind her was blank.

The heat of his eyes on her ass as she walked made the urge to stop, bend over, and beg him to fill her up almost impossible to ignore.

Nikki gritted her teeth and spoke over her shoulder, her steps not slowing. "As you can see, I'm fine, Mac. I just needed to get away from my life for a while. I thought a little weekend fling with you might be the ticket, but you weren't interested. So I came up here to be alone."

She trotted up the steps of the cabin and turned, blocking the doorway.

Mac didn't hesitate. He continued up the steps and stopped only when he was inches from her body. His minty breath drifted across her cheek, and eyes full of blue flames bore into hers. "And the stuff you said about coming to me when you needed to feel safe? Was that a lie?"

She tried to speak, but her lips moved soundlessly. She couldn't lie to him, not when he was so close—not when she could look into his eyes and see his soul. The love he'd had for her was still there, and it made the beast inside her howl. Her heart pounded, hot blood rushed through her veins, and the hunger for raw and carnal mating surged through her.

She did need him. Not just to feel safe, but to feel . . . human. Her life had been turned upside down, and she needed to find her center again, to find a way to control the animal that would control her if she let it. Only she could do that, but she couldn't do it alone. She needed a man to help curb the hungers the animal gave her.

"Mac," she murmured. Her hands rose of their own volition and rested on his chest. His heart pounded against the palm of her hand, the rapid beat matching hers perfectly. She swallowed the saliva pooling in her mouth and glanced over his shoulder at the setting sun. The moon was rising, and the trembling inside her had increased. She couldn't hold back the change much longer without his help.

The time for him to leave was over.

"Mac, I need you to be sure. If you're going to stay, there's no holding back and no going back." She swallowed and stepped forward until the rigid tips of her breasts brushed the cotton of his shirt. "Ever."

The raw emotion in Nikki's big brown eyes and the way her full bottom lip trembled as she spoke hit him like a sucker punch to the gut, and he was a goner. Watching her in the river and then being so damn close to her naked body and not being able to touch. . . . The heat was coming off her in waves, and he could smell her arousal. He hadn't even touched her!

She raised up on tiptoe and rubbed the length of her body against his—and his control snapped.

Years of pent-up longing surged inside him, and he wrapped her tightly in his arms and slanted his mouth over hers. He shouldn't do this. He shouldn't let her manipulate him—they needed to talk, not fuck. But he couldn't stop himself. He wanted her too much.

She was what he wanted. What he'd always wanted.

They touched, and they both went up in flames. Mac slid his hands down her back, cupped her ass, and lifted her against him as his tongue speared between her lips and swept through her mouth.

Her hands tangled in his hair, pulling him closer as her legs wrapped around his waist. Soft, supple skin heated beneath his hands. He wanted to touch more—had to have more. Spinning on his heel, he perched her on the wooden rail of the deck and surged against her core, the denim of his jeans the only thing that kept him from sliding home.

Her hands slipped between them and went to work on his zipper while his hands traveled over her nakedness. He cupped her breasts while he scraped his teeth down her neck; she moaned when his lips circled one rigid nipple and sucked. Her hands ripped his jeans open, and he groaned when her greedy little hands circled his hardness.

"Now, Mac." Her legs tightened around him, and she rubbed the head of his cock between the swollen lips of her pussy. "I need you now!"

Without a thought in his head, he reacted. A sure thrust of his hips and he was deep inside her wet heat. She cried out, her hands gripping his hips as she threw her head back and rocked against him. He leaned in, watching her face as he held her tight against his chest and pumped his hips and fought for breath. He had no control, but neither did she.

Her fingers dug into him, urging him on, faster, harder.

"Yes, Mac! Make me yours again." Their eyes met, and his heart swelled to match his cock. He pumped harder, seating himself as deeply inside her as possible.

"Christ, you're hot!" he panted as his balls tingled in warning. "I'm not going to last long."

"Yes!" she cried out, and her cunt tightened around him. Her whole body tensed, her cry turning to a scream as her orgasm hit. Her insides spasmed, tightening like a vise around his cock. Mac wrapped his arms around her, and he held on tight as he followed her over the edge.

"Nikki!" he groaned as his world tilted and their connection became the only thing that mattered.

When his body emptied and the last waves of his orgasm faded, he became aware of the way she still clutched at him.

He hummed a mindless sound of pleasure and stroked her back softly. Comforting her, cuddling her, just holding her. Her head rested against his chest, his chin rested on her head, and they both caught their breath. Mac opened his eyes and looked out over the small yard and the surrounding trees. The sun was setting over the trees, and a chill was growing in the air.

He pulled back slightly and looked down at the woman in his arms, a little unsure of what had just happened. They were still connected, his semihard cock nestled inside her warmth. While it had been a fast and furious coupling, it had felt like more than just sex.

*You're dreaming, man.*

He tensed. What a fucking idiot he'd been. Literally. He'd let her manipulate him and distract him, and he still didn't know what the hell was going on. He started to pull back, and she surged forward, wrapping her arms around his neck and kissing him deeply.

When he relaxed and started to kiss her back, she pulled away gently. Her teeth nipped at his bottom lip, and she smiled. "It's good to be in your arms again."

Nikki felt Mac's cock stir and thicken inside her, and her pulse jumped. The man had lived up to every fantasy the boy

236

had inspired over the years. She knew they needed to talk. That she had to tell him her secret. But she also knew that when she did, she'd have to watch him turn away in revulsion, and she just wasn't ready for that yet.

She leaned in and kissed him, putting all her pent-up longing and desire into it. "Take me to bed, Mac," she whispered against his lips. "Please."

He shook his head at her, and for a moment, panic hit. He was going to refuse her! Then a groan rumbled out of him, and her heart swelled as he scooped her up against him. With quick, sure movements, he turned and carried her into the cabin, kicking the door closed behind them.

# 3

_____

It had been forever since she'd felt so cherished. Mac's eyes never left hers as he strode into the bedroom and laid her down on top of the patchwork quilt covering the bed. He stood and made quick work of his clothes without letting go of her gaze. But when his chest was bared, she couldn't stop herself. Her eyes began to wander, drinking in the sight of the man he'd become.

The light spattering of hair across his chest tapered into a treasure trail down his flat belly, making her mouth water. Then, in one smooth move he pushed his jeans and shorts down and off. The movement made his muscles bunch and flex beneath golden skin and Nikki's insides clenched in anticipation. When he took the extra few seconds to take off his socks, her lips twitched.

He was definitely the man for her. If there was one thing that always killed the mood, it was a man in such a rush to get busy that he came to bed with his socks still on.

The heat of his eyes running over her naked form when he straightened had her stretching out on the bed and running a hand over her own body. Hunger ripped through Nikki, her body tightening as needs battled within her. Using the sexual need to push aside the animal battling inside to get out, she trailed her fingertips over her breast, and across her ribs. With a quirk of her lips she spread her legs and touched herself for him.

A low groan rumbled from Mac and he stepped forward. His knee sunk into the mattress next to her and she grinned as Mac came down over top of her.

For a moment they just lie there, faces inches apart, gazes locked, bodies perfectly aligned. She pulled her hand out from between them, and reached for him.

Nikki's heart pounded so hard there was no way Mac couldn't feel it. She could see the same knowledge in his eyes that she felt in her heart. This was it. The promise of young love had finally bloomed between them, and they could never go back.

She didn't want to go back.

A calmness came over her, soothing the hungry beast within as everything in her world shifted and clicked into place. "Mac," she whispered. Her lips parted, but no words would come. What could she say? She'd always known he was in Pearson, she could've stayed in touch when he had no idea where her mother had taken her off too. It was her fault that they'd lost years.

"It's okay." He brushed his lips over her brow softly. First one, then the other, and down her cheek, soft kisses as he murmured reassurance to the words she couldn't speak. "We're going to be all right, Nikki. You and I . . . it's okay."

His lips met hers and his tongue slipped into her mouth, urging her body and soul to open up to him. She closed her eyes and reveled in the feel of his weight, his touch, his taste.

It was delicious. It was heaven. It was . . . *Mac.*

"Yes," she sighed, her hands sliding all over him. His back, his shoulders, the muscles dancing against the palms of her hands. As fast as her heart pounded and her blood raced, she wasn't in a rush. She didn't want her time with him to end, and as long as they were together, touching and connecting, there would be no stopping.

Wanting more, *needing* more, she cupped his firm butt in her hands and pulled him against her. His cock slid between her folds and the head nudged her clit. A whimper escaped as she curled her body, wrapping her legs around his hips and digging her nails into him. "Mac, don't tease me. Not now. I need you."

His cheeks flushed and he groaned. He quickly reached between them, the tantalizing rub of his knuckles against her clit as he rubbed the head of his cock up and down her slit had her back arching and a growl of pleasure easing from her lips. "Mac!"

A rough chuckle filled the room. "You just feel so damn good, Nikki." Then he breached her entrance and they both stilled. "So good," he said softly, and slid home.

His hands cradled her head, the rough pad of his thumb drifting across her cheek as their gazes locked and he began to move. Suddenly, something inside Nikki shifted and her arousal softened, turning to . . . contentment. A unique pleasure as her muscles relaxed and her body moved to match Mac's rhythm naturally.

All her thoughts and worries and panic about the past, and the future, faded as it became clear to her that this was what she'd been looking for—this connection where nothing mattered but him. Satisfaction rolled over as she watched Mac's cheeks flush red, and his features tighten as he loved her.

She kept her hands on his hips, urging him on. Their bodies danced with nothing between them, not even air. Her heart pounded and hot blood raced through her veins as Mac's eyes widened and his breathing became harsh. "Yes," she said. "Yes, Mac. Come now. Come for me, baby."

"Nikki?"

The question was in his eyes, even as his hips worked faster, his moves becoming urgent and a little rough. He was waiting for her.

She shook her head, and in an instinctive move, slipped a finger between his ass cheeks and tickled the sensitive entrance there. "No, Mac. For you. Please. This is for you."

His whole body tensed and he shoved his cock deep inside her as his surprised shout of satisfaction echoed through the room. Warmth flooded her insides as his cock throbbed and twitched against her sensitive inner walls and a small orgasm rippled through her.

But that wasn't the real joy for Nikki. The real joy came from the feel of Mac collapsing on top of her, his breath rushing against her neck and his arms clutching her to him.

And when a few moments later, Mac rolled to his side still holding as if he'd never let go, tears welled in Nikki's eyes.

"I need to sleep," he muttered, his heartbeat slowing beneath her ear.

"Yes." She snuggled close to him, weaving her fingers into the light hairs on his chest. "Sleep now, Mac. I'm here."

A sighed eased from him. "Please be here when I wake up. Don't run from me again, Nikki."

She bit her lip before placing a soft kiss over his heart. "I'll be here. I promise."

And she would be. She was done running.

# 4

Pain sliced through Nikki as she slid silently from the bed. Less than an hour had passed since Mac had fallen asleep, and the last thing she wanted was for him to wake up and see her change into a wolf.

She stumbled from the bedroom, barely managing to pull the door closed behind her before dropping to all fours. The pull of the moon was too much for her to resist. She'd been able to fight it while Mac had been inside her, fucking her furiously and taking the edge off her need in another way.

Fighting the pull caused more pain, so she gave in. Her bones cracked, and her skin stretched. Fur popped out, and her limbs became legs, her hands and feet paws. Seconds later, her vision changed, the world becoming shades of gray and green but in sharper detail. Her ears swiveled on her head, and her nose twitched at the additional strength of her senses.

She raced around the cabin, jumping over the sofa and onto the sturdy counter in the kitchen, off the counter and in circles around the small space as her mind raced. What to do? What to do? She couldn't get out of the cabin unless she jumped through a window. Breaking the glass would surely wake Mac.

She didn't want to wake him. She wanted to tell him about her new . . . condition before he actually had a chance to see it. She knocked over a chair in her panicked frenzy and froze. The bedsheets rustled in the other room but then stilled.

Her heartbeat slowed, and she calmed. She needed to think. Just because the moon stole control over her shape every month, it didn't mean it stole her mind, too. She'd managed to hold off the change until past midnight. Full dark. That was better than the month before.

She padded over to the corner of the room and curled up in a ball. While a large part of her yearned to be outside the cabin, running free through the trees, she was actually pretty calm. More calm than she'd ever felt when forced to change by the moon.

It was a good sign.

She lay in the corner, listening to the sounds of nature and wondering if she'd ever feel natural in her alternate shape. She'd been told that she could learn to change at will. That as her body became more accustomed to the virus in her bloodstream, her strength would grow and she'd be able to draw on her wolf senses at any time. Even without changing form. But she'd never be able to refuse the call of the full moon.

For the night before and the night after the full moon, the pull wasn't as powerful. As she grew stronger, she'd be able to control those nights better, but the one night of the full moon, she'd never be able to resist. For one night every month, she *had* to change.

And Mac just had to show up on one of those nights.

As if her thoughts called to him, her ears twitched at the sound of stirrings in the bedroom. Her head came up, and her muscles tensed as his quiet curse filtered through the walls. He was awake, and his footsteps were headed for the door.

She sat up on her haunches, alert to every sound and fully aware she had nowhere to hide. The doorknob turned, and the bedroom door opened to reveal Mac barefoot and bare-chested with his jeans zipped but not snapped as he strode into the room.

He stopped dead in his tracks just inside the room when he spotted her. Not a muscle twitched when their eyes met for a brief second before Mac's gaze slid away. He slowly walked backward, his hands out in front of him, his gaze centered on her but not challenging her.

Despite the adrenaline making her heart pound, her mouth opened and her tongue lolled out. He looked pretty damn hot wearing only his jeans, and he was obviously smart. No sudden movements, no direct stares to challenge the animal instincts she had so little control over. She shifted her weight from paw to paw and then stood on all fours when he disappeared back into the bedroom but didn't shut the door.

She could hear him move toward the bed and then back toward the door. When he stepped around the corner again, his gun was in his hand.

"Good dog," he crooned, his eyes on her as he moved to the window and glanced outside. "Damnit, Nikki. Where are you?"

Nikki stepped forward, her tail starting to wag. At her movement, Mac raised his gun and aimed it at her in one smooth motion.

She didn't think. The muscles in her hindquarters bunched, and she instinctively launched herself at him. She hit his chest, and his arm flung wide, the gun going off as he fell onto his back with her on top of him. She had her jaws wide and her teeth at his throat, when his scrabbling and clawing hand got hold of her throat. He pushed her away, and she realized what she'd almost done.

Their gazes locked, her above him, and she fought for control of her animal instincts. Remorse welled, and she opened her mouth and began to lick his face. Pathetic whines of apology escaped, and she bent down, lying on top of Mac, her belly against his as she tried to communicate with him.

Mac almost pissed himself when the wolf had jumped and knocked him flat on his back. He faced some scary shit in his life, in his job, but the sight of a wild animal lunging for him beat drugged-out psychos by far.

When the animal suddenly stopped its attack and started licking him, he had no idea what to think. He just lay there, holding his breath and thanking God. After a minute of the tongue bath, he sat up and pushed the wolf aside.

He took a better look it. "You are a wolf, right?" Maybe it was just a big dog.

It?

He leaned over to pet it carefully and saw the soft gleam in its intelligent eyes. "Yeah, you're a wolf. A girl, too, aren't you? Such a pretty girl." He scratched her behind the ear, and she leaned heavily against his leg, head tilted up, big brown eyes adoring him.

"Okay, that's enough," he said as he bent to pick up his gun. He snapped his jeans shut and tucked the gun into the waistband at the small of his back. "We need to find Nikki."

A quick trip to the bedroom and he pulled his shirt over his head only to trip over the wolf when he turned around. How the hell had she gotten in the cabin, anyway? Was she a pet of Nikki's? Nikki had to be around somewhere—her truck was still there.

He strode to the door and opened it. He waved his arm out the door. "Go find Nikki. Show me where Nikki is, girl."

The wolf sat down and stared at him.

"Come on. Nikki, the woman who let you into the cabin. Go find her."

They stared at each other until Mac shook his head. "It was worth a try." He stepped out onto the deck and stared at the space around him.

The night was silent except for the sounds of nature he rarely heard in his day-to-day life. Moonbeams filtered through the trees, the cool mountain air bringing a rush of goose bumps to his skin. With a shiver he stared out at the shadowed landscape and remembered the one and only time he'd brought Nikki there.

Her mom had had a new boyfriend, and Mac was torn between his alone time with his dad and being there for his friend when she was feeling alone and left out. The problem was solved when his dad had said she could come to the cabin with them.

Nikki had fit right in. She'd gone target shooting with them and fishing in the river. She'd even gutted her own catches and learned to start a campfire on her own.

Mac's dad had been impressed. Mac had fallen hard.

He'd kissed Nikki for the very first time while they'd sat on the steps of the cabin. The cabin had been special to him before that night but was even more so after. And she'd known it. She had to have known he'd follow her there.

Fear laced his insides, but he knew it was hopeless to go looking for her before the sun came up. He couldn't track her at night, no matter how well the moon lit up the ground. Once he was in the trees, he'd be blind.

"Damnit, Nikki," he muttered and headed back inside.

Mac paced the interior of the cabin, the wolf at his heels with every step. Fear, concern, and anger . . . they were all wound up tight in a knot in his gut as he wondered where Nikki was. Had whatever she was running from caught up to them? If so, how could he have slept through an attack?

And that certainly didn't explain the wolf. The only explanation was that Nikki'd been up to the cabin before. That the wolf was somehow a pet, and she'd left it there to guard him while she . . . while she what? What the hell could she possibly be doing out in the forest on a mountain in the middle of the night? Scratch that—in the predawn hours?

He'd been awake for over two hours, and she still hadn't come back. God, he was such a fucking idiot! A complete brainless knucklehead who'd let his dick lead him into a position he hated. One in which he had no idea what was going on or what to do next.

A helpless position.

"Fuck!" He slammed his fist down on the kitchen counter.

He stared out the window over the counter, berating himself as he watched the sky grow lighter. Dawn would be soon, and he could go looking for Nikki. His mental planning and the silence of the cabin was broken by a plaintive whine and a sharp female cry.

"Nikki!" He spun away from the window to see that the cabin was empty. A soft thud came from the bedroom, and he raced into it with his heart in his throat. When he rounded the corner, the first thing he saw was Nikki, naked and curled up in a ball on the floor by the bed.

"Nikki, my god!" He rushed to her side and knelt down. "What happened? Where were you?"

She lifted her head and met his gaze, her eyes full of trepidation and lingering pain. Mac's heart kicked in his chest, and he cupped her cheek. "Are you okay?"

Her hand came up and covered his, the warmth of it seeping

into his skin as her lips moved but no sound came out. Her eyes, so dark and stormy. . . . She was trying to tell him something.

His brain clicked into gear, and Mac suddenly became aware that they were alone—completely alone. As in, no more wolf.

His mind raced, and his heart pounded as he stared down at the woman in his arms. The woman with the same big, dark, and intelligent eyes that had watched him pace the cabin for the past couple hours. Eyes that were now pleading for understanding.

"What the . . ." He stood and took a step back, shaking his head.

Pain and regret were clear on Nikki's face as she scrambled up from the floor. "Mac, it's me, Nikki. I'm still the same—"

"You're the wolf!"

She flinched. "Sometimes, yes. I can explain!"

He just stared at her, stunned, until she reached out to him again.

"No," he said and stepped back quickly. As fucked up as it was, with his head working hard to absorb what he'd seen, his body was reacting wholeheartedly to her naked nearness. "No." He shook his head. "First you're going to put some fucking clothes on, and then you're going to tell me everything—*everything,* Nikki. From the beginning. No secrets, no lies, and no more holding back!"

He spun on his heel and went to wait in the other room.

# 5

Oh, was Mac pissed!

The hurt and anger and confusion she'd seen when he'd looked at her had stolen her breath. But . . . he was *mad!* He wasn't disgusted or repulsed, he was pissed off!

Hope surged inside her, and Nikki scrambled around the room for her jeans and a T-shirt. She didn't bother with underwear or a bra; she was in too much of a rush to get into the other room and talk to Mac.

Hurried steps brought her within a foot of him. He stood in the kitchen, leaning against the counter with his arms folded over his chest. "Why didn't you ever tell me?"

He thought she'd kept it secret since they were kids!

"Oh, no, Mac! This is a new thing. I'd never have kept this a secret from you when we were together. As it is, you're the first person I've told."

Pain flashed across his face. "But you didn't *tell* me, Nikki. If I hadn't followed you up here, what would you have done? Do you plan on living up here forever? Hiding?"

"No. I was going to come back to you next week. Honestly!

But the moon was too strong. I could feel its pull while I was at your house, and I could see the distrust in you still. It was stupid of me to think I could just barge back into your life and have you be there for me. I didn't want to lose control and change while I was in your apartment."

"Is that why you ran again?"

Heart pounding, Nikki stepped a bit closer to him. "Yes. There are three nights a month that the moon pull is stronger. And when I get upset or angry, the wolf gets closer to the surface. You locked me in your bedroom, and I was scared that if I didn't get out, you'd open the door and get attacked—by me. Do you believe me?"

He looked away, and Nikki watched the muscle of his jaw clench and unclench while he worked through what she'd said. The roaring in her ears quieted as she calmed herself, waiting for his answer. And it was an important answer because they both knew that if he didn't believe she had been planning to go back to him after the moon phase, there was no use talking about anything else.

# 6

---

Mac finally turned his gaze back to her. "Is this your only secret? You're not running from a stalker—just yourself?"

"Is that what you thought? That some ex-boyfriend or something was chasing me?"

"What was I supposed to think?" He unfolded his arms and started to pace. "You break into my apartment and tell me you need to feel safe before you disappear again. Which I guess makes sense now. . . . A superstrong werewolf could probably make the jump from a fourth-floor apartment no problem." He stopped pacing and glared at her. "I checked you out. You have no record, you have no debts, and you weren't a witness of record on anything, so I had to think it was a man you were running from."

"I'm sorry." She stepped closer and put her hand on his arm. The muscles flexed beneath her palm, but he didn't pull away. "It didn't occur to me that you would think that. I was too wrapped up in my own shit to think about a lot of things. All I knew was that going to you felt right. I needed to be with someone I trusted. Someone I knew cared about me . . . and I went to you. I didn't think about how you would feel until after you walked in the room again."

Mac stared at her. "And then what did you think?"

She didn't hesitate. "That I wanted you."

His eyes shuttered, and Nikki realized what he'd thought. "No, not like that! Well, I'll always want you like *that*, but I meant . . . that I wanted you . . . in my life . . . forever. That I wanted to do this right, so you'd accept me and maybe learn to love me again."

Heat flared in his eyes, and he stepped right up to her. His calloused fingertips brushed against her cheek, and her heart fluttered at the same time the rest of her insides melted.

"I never stopped loving you." His head lowered, and she met him halfway.

Lips touched, mouths opened, and tongues tangled. Sweet, sweet joy flooded Nikki, and she hung on to Mac as if she would never let him go. When they came up for air, Mac smiled at her. "We have a lot of catching up to do."

They went out onto the deck and sat on the steps and talked. The sun had risen, and the day was warmed quickly as Nikki told the story of how she'd been bitten.

"About six months ago I started dating this guy, Daniel. It was nothing special, just a casual dinner and dancing every now and then. Three months ago, one night while we were—um . . ."

He raised an eyebrow. "Fucking?"

She blushed.

"Yes, while we were having sex, he bit me." It was strange to talk so openly with someone, anyone. Nikki worked hard in her day-to-day life, and she didn't have a lot of friends—none, really. She'd mostly been content on her own, with some casual boyfriends. Yet at the same time, there was a comfort level here with Mac she'd never felt with anyone before. One that warmed her insides and filled her with contentment.

"It hurt, but at the time I was a little distracted and didn't really pay attention. The next morning, when Daniel told me what he'd done, I didn't believe him." Memories of that night, that moment in time, flashed through her mind. Her heart raced, and her palms began to sweat. She'd thought Daniel was some sort of psychopath or belonged in a mental facility. Mac put his hand on her leg, giving her comfort without actually saying anything, so she continued.

"I dumped him, of course, and he respected it. He was all remorseful for biting me, and I really just thought he was crazy. Then, as the full moon got closer, I started to change. I was hungry all the time, and for meat—the rarer the better. My sex drive went nuts, and I started to get strange flashes of loud hearing and shifts in my vision. I saw a doctor, but everything was fine. Then . . . the day before the full moon, things got bad. I called in to work sick and stayed at home because every bone in my body ached. Daniel showed up at my door and helped me through my first change, but . . ."

"But what?" he prodded carefully.

Fear and shame rose within Nikki. She didn't want to tell him—she didn't want to ever remember what had happened that night—but forgetting would be worse. "Because I fought it so hard, and because I hadn't understood the needs and urges my body had been putting on me for the week building up to that night, when the change did come, I had no control over myself. The animal instincts overcame me, the terror and confusion of it all . . ."

"Nikki?"

A shudder ripped through Nikki. She didn't want to remember her first change. She didn't want to remember anything about that night or the next two nights after that. But Mac had a right to know.

"I attacked Daniel's sister, who'd come with him to help me

through it. I almost killed her, Mac. If she hadn't been a were-wolf herself, she would have been dead."

Mac looked into Nikki's tormented eyes and saw that this was what she'd been running from. More than anything, she was scared of not being able to control the wolf. He wrapped an arm around her shoulders and hugged her to his side. This tiny woman was stronger than she knew. "But you didn't kill her, Nikki. And they knew what they were getting into by going there. They had a job to do, to help you, and they did it, as they *should* have. He did this to you; if anyone is to blame, it's Daniel."

She leaned against him, her chin tucked against her chest, eyes avoiding his. Love swelled in his chest, and he curled a finger under her chin, making her look at him as silent tears rolled gently down her cheek. "You did nothing wrong. It was instinct, and everyone survived it. You're obviously learning control because instead of ripping open my throat when I had a gun on you last night, you gave me a tongue bath."

She sniffled, and they chuckled. He pressed a soft kiss to her lips and smiled. "Right?"

Pride mingled with the love he felt when she straightened her shoulders and smiled at him. It wasn't her full megawatt smile, but a soft one that touched his heart and made it hard to breathe.

"Right," she said. "The moon call is strong for the day before the full moon, the day of, and the day after. I've learned quickly that I have more control on the night before and after. I'm learning to control the call and the power that comes with being a . . ."

Mac's lips twisted. "A what? A wolf?"

"A werewolf."

They stared at one another, and Nikki's head tilted to the

side, her gaze sharpening. "How come you didn't totally freak and run in the other direction when you figured it out?"

Mac thought about Gina Devlin and some of the things he'd seen. "I have a friend who has a few special talents of her own. Magical or supernatural or mystical—whatever you want to call them. But she's sort of opened up my mind to the fact that there is way more out there than most people are aware of. Plus, I've seen some really strange things as a cop. Deaths, bodies disappearing . . . unexplainable things. I guess I've sort of always known, deep down, that some legends might be more than just legends."

Nikki pulled away from him slowly, and the air around them cooled just a bit. Concerned, he pulled her back to his side.

"What's bothering you now?" he asked.

"A friend?" she said quietly, glancing at him from beneath her lashes.

Mac bit back a grin. "Yes. A friend. Gina has her own man problems at the moment, and I've never been one of them."

She nodded and sat silently. Mac watched as her fingers twisted in her lap and she chewed on her bottom lip. She was so . . . cute in her uncertainty, but he couldn't stand it anymore. With a low growl he pushed her back on the deck and covered her body with his own. "You are the only woman who's ever owned my heart, Nikki. You being a werewolf doesn't change that. In fact, as I see it, there might be some bonuses in it for me."

"Oh, yeah? Like what?" She wrapped her arms around his neck and grinned up at him, her happiness clear.

"Didn't you mention your sex drive going nuts?" He kissed one corner and then the other of her smiling mouth. "I can help you with that, you know."

"Oh, really?"

"On one condition."

"And that is?" She tilted her hips and wrapped her legs around his hips.

He framed her face with his hands and gazed into her eyes. The love he felt was reflected back, and he knew everything was finally the way it was meant to be. "Marry me."

Tears welled in her eyes, and her bottom lip trembled. "Are you sure, Mac? We don't even know each other anymore."

"I've always known you, Nikki. We've always been meant to be. . . . I believe that. Do you?"

"Yes." She pulled his head down and kissed him passionately. When he pulled back a little for air, she heaved and twisted and flipped him onto his back. Stretched out on top of him—the heat of her sex pressing against the hardness beneath his zipper, her breasts crushed against his chest—she smiled wickedly. "Wolves mate for life ya know. There's no going back now."

Then she tugged up his shirt and started to give him a whole new kind of tongue bath, and he was in heaven.

"Who wants to go back?" he said with a pleasurable moan. "Forward all the way, baby!"

Please turn the page for an exciting sneak peek
at Sydney Molare's "Matinee" from
SATISFY ME AGAIN,
coming next month from Aphrodisia!

# 1

Mina Sinclair had had her share of crazy ideas, but as she gazed at the dilapidated building with peeling paint, a broken and taped glass door, and rotten shingles hanging precariously from the angle of the roof, she knew this had to be her craziest.

*If only I'd chosen another night to grocery shop, life would be different.*

Two weeks ago, Mina was gathering the contents of her dropped purse off the ground when an SUV squealed its brakes across the parking lot, followed by the unmistakable sound of gunshots. Instead of staying low, Mina had made a really bad decision: she rose up and screamed. Of course, the men in the SUV zeroed in on her stricken face. Panicked, she'd somehow fallen into her car, stabbed her keys into the ignition and zoomed out of the parking lot, losing them in rush hour traffic. But, she'd left her purse—containing all her information—on the ground.

The "visit" came not one day later. The stranger was waiting quietly in her apartment when she returned from work, or rather faking work. Her nerves had been too shot to do more than go through the motions. This stranger sitting in her living room—just like in the movies—validated all her fears.

The man was short, stocky and had a definite accent. *Italian*, Mina thought. Not that she'd been around many Italians. In all likelihood, it was probably a subliminal Hollywood influence which made her draw that conclusion.

The conversation was succinct: Forget what she'd seen, don't go to the police, and a suggestion that leaving town was in her best interest. He'd shoved a case sitting at his feet toward her, making his point. It contained one hundred thousand dollars. The point was taken: "They"—whoever they were—needed no complications and if that much money was being slung around so easily, Mina was dispensable.

Mina spent a frazzled, sleepless night, peeking out of windows, pacing the floor, and jumping at the slightest sound before she formulated a plan. The next morning, Mina stuffed the money in a duffel bag along with a change of clothes. She'd left for work like normal, ridden the elevator to her floor, changed into a jogging suit, then taken the stairs back down and out the back. Mina caught a taxi to the nearest bus station and jumped on the first bus out of town. She'd switched to trains then taxis then back to buses—anything cash with no ID—to ferry her further and further south to a new life.

When the bus had pulled into St. Paulus, Mina, sick of running and watching over her shoulders, had felt a peace descend on her. Without a thought, she'd exited and checked into the small St. Paulus Inn. After purchasing a used car from St. Paulus Motors—a cheap Ford Focus—Mina had spent the rest of the night thinking of another plan. She was still praying it worked.

With a hearty sigh, Mina opened her car door and stood on the sidewalk. The realtor, Charlotte Charles, had proclaimed the building a "fixer-upper" as she'd thrown the keys onto her desk before urging Mina, "Open it up. See if you like it." But as Mina caught sight of squirrels frolicking on an upper window-sill, the TH, and the crooked, broken remaining RE of the the-atre, she wondered if there could be any fixing up for this one. Still, she had seen few choices meeting her building renovation and living expenses budget.

*Keep your mind open and find someplace you can both work and live,* her mind chided. After looking at a dozen buildings—loving the ones she couldn't afford and cringing as the list dwindled to this last one—her initial optimism was fading fast, but not gone completely. With a survivor's resolve, she lifted her chin and unlocked the fragile glass door.

*Here goes everything.*

They heard the car stop in front of the building at the same time. Cal pricked up his ears momentarily before mentally turn-ing over the playing card. "My book, old friend." He slapped his hands together.

"Just lucky, you old goat," John grumbled as the cards slid across the table.

A door shut.

"Wonder who it is this time? That realtor lady again?" John couldn't stand the realtor showing his beloved property. In his opinion, Charlotte Charles had misrepresented, misspoke, and just missed the beauty of the place altogether. Just hearing her voice grated on his nerves. John floated a card in the air before flipping it over and dropping it to the table. King of spades. "Beat that, chump!"

Cal rubbed his hand across his whiskers as he studied the levitating cards before shooting one on top of the table. "You forgot we were playing joker, joker, deuce, ace, *then* king of spades?"

John mumbled something incoherent, brown eyes flicking between his suspended cards and the table.

Steps were heard coming up the stairs.

Cal let out a sigh. "Guess we need to postpone this one."

"Yeah. Let me get the chains together. I'll bet we can get rid of this one within ten minutes." John's eyes twinkled.

Cal chuckled and countered with, "I say six and a half, tops."

"You're on!" They gave an airy high five, and then dissolved.

The cards dropped to the table, some to the floor, as the door squealed on its hinges as it was pushed open.

A step into the room.

"Hello?"

The voice was feminine, husky, and definitely *not* the realtor lady. Cal and John held their chains silent as the body hesitantly followed the voice into the room. A shapely, hose-covered leg attached to wide hips, and, as their eyes traveled upwards, a nipped waist and ample chest. The face was feline, the black hair curling and spiking in total contradiction to the business suit she wore. But in short, the woman was breathtaking.

Mina was surprised and elated the first floor of the building was in pretty good shape. The old seats had long ago been ferreted away, leaving a nice-sized, cavernous space. Yes, there were mountains of trash to be removed, but Mina could tell the building still had "good bones."

She had second thoughts as she stepped into the room at the top of the stairs. The realtor had said the place needed serious work, but as she surveyed the interior, she wondered if she wanted this large of a challenge. Old posters lay curling, disarrayed, covered in layers of dust. It was obvious no one had set foot in here in years. Her eyes shifted to a table in the comer. There appeared to be cards scattered on and around it. She walked closer, her footprints leaving a trail in the layers of powder. Undusty cards.

Mina shivered as thoughts of who else might inhabit the building flitted into her head. She pulled her canister of Mace from her purse and held it in front of her. It might just be a harmless vagrant, but then again, it might not.

She pushed the thought down as she noticed the walls. Mina ran her hands over them—real knotty-pine wood paneling. She sniffed. The scent was faint but still present.

*Why would they have a knotty-pine paneled room in a theater?*

The thought was pushed down as a smile played over her face and refurbishing ideas popped in her mind. This could be a library. A knotty-pine paneled library. The smile widened, making it appear that the cat had definitely swallowed the canary.

"Damn, that is a fine-looking woman right there," John stated, eyes focused on Mina's bosom. Today, yesterday, and tomorrow, she was definitely his type.

Cal had to agree with him. He felt a woody forming as her perfume wafted over to him. How long had it been since he'd been only a ghostly voyeur versus an active participant in sex? Nearly thirty years. Thirty years of watching others ... and getting ghostly blue balls. "Think we should do the chain rattling anyway?"

"Hell no! Did you see how she rubbed the walls? Walls we put up panel by panel ourselves? She knows good details when she sees it. Beats the hell out of that realtor—"

"I know." Cal interrupted John's familiar tirade. "Why don't you just figure out a way to give realtor lady some of your 'good loving' and get that stick out of her butt in the meantime?"

John frowned at the entire concept. "There is no way I would waste my time on a stuck up, non-factual woman like that realtor, alive or dead. She is *not* my type, or anybody else's type I know. That's why she is single."

"Sounds like you've been peeking in her windows to know that," Cal smirked.

John waved the comment away. "Whatever. Let's just focus on this little lady right now."

"She definitely has potential," Cal commented as he watched Mina rubbing her hands over and over on the paneling.

"Shoot, she has more than potential. I can feel it. She's The One."

"Might be. Don't put your chain away just yet." Cal watched Mina's every move.

The air seemed to freshen just from opening the curtain. The late sunlight revealed there was dust everywhere, but it didn't seem as oppressive as it had previously.

As Mina continued to run her hands over the knotted wood and looked at the size of the room, she wondered if the previous occupants had . . . *lived* over the theatre. Joy infused her soul as the thought banged around her cranium. Had she already found a place to work and live? Two birds finally killed with one meager stone? She jumped in joy, causing a dirty poster to fall over onto the dusty floor.

Mina sneezed as she lifted the poster from the dust. The title screamed in red ink, "Love on the Run." A buxom blond sat astride a Harley, blouse partially opened and covered by the dark hands of a leather-clad biker. Hmmm. Interesting. The realtor had said it was once a movie theatre, but looking at the playbill, she wondered what kind. Mina lifted another poster. This one blatantly proclaimed, "Sex Goddess from Venus." The brunette on this poster wore a sheer white toga-like garment, and, as she looked closer, Mina realized the shadows she'd taken for smudges were actually the woman's nipples. She shook her head. She'd never heard of either of the movies.

As she leaned to pick up another poster, she felt the unmistakable touch of hands on her butt. She yelped, turned, eyes wide. Nothing but air and the dust she had disrupted as she jumped, swirled in front of her.

*That felt just too real.*

Hands cupping the underside of her buttocks, brushing lightly up the sides. She'd had a few men touch her like that so she was sure. But no one else was in the room.

*Snap out of it!*

Mina retrieved the can of Mace before turning back to the poster she had been reaching for. Just as she leaned over again, the hands returned, this time squeezing her waist. She yelped, hands clapped onto her midsection, and met her own body, nothing else.

*Get it together!*

But she couldn't as the hand sensation skimmed up past her ribs and rested beneath her bust, clenching and releasing. The sensation, now circular rubbing, seemed to ooze beneath her bra to encompass her full breasts. Breasts that bad been denied any other contact but her own hands and a bath towel for too long. A moan escaped as she felt her nipples thickening and elongating, yearning—no, aching—for a touch.

It came.

The impression of fingers tugging at the encased nipples made them turgid, straining to be released into the air. The Mace fell unnoticed to the floor as her hands wrapped around the swollen breasts. Mina couldn't stop her fingers from unbuttoning her blouse, unclasping her bra, and baring her fat nipples in the air.

Phantom hands caressed and pulled at the aureoles; stroked

and cupped her heavy orbs. Mina pinched her nipples in response; opened her mouth in a gasp as the wetness seemed to enclose around the left nipple, and then the right. Bliss.

Mina unconsciously spread her legs and leaned backwards as the wetness turned into wet suction. Suckling. Her clit lurched and her panties dampened. Her fingers were beneath her skirt, searching for her stiff button when the phantom lips mirrored her train of thought; flicked across her sensitized nub. She gasped and then screamed as the throes of a monstrous orgasm buckled her knees.

"We shouldn't have done that," John said, hands still stroking the swollen nipples bared to the world. It was those wide squeeze-me-please hips that drove him to touch her again and again.

"Ahuh, but we did," Cal replied, blowing on the panty-clad mons. The sight of those bare nipples had forced him to join in. He hadn't meant to, but seeing John's lips puckered around those dusty berries made him want to suckle also . . . then more.

"We should stop." John kept stroking.

"In a moment." Cal kept blowing.

"We'll drive her away."

Cal looked at Mina's glazed-over eyes and watched her heartbeat thump in her chest. "No. She will definitely be back," he responded with a confidence borne of knowing he knew how to please a woman when he was alive. From the look of things, nothing had changed.

# 2

"So did you like the building?" Charlotte Charles asked Mina as she retrieved the keys from her outstretched hand.

Mina gave the matronly woman a hesitant nod. To be honest, she wasn't paying much attention to what Charlotte was saying since she was still so confused by her body's reaction in the building. What in the world possessed her to get herself off in an empty dilapidated building? What if someone else had been there and caught her in the middle of her self-loving?

Her mind zoomed back to the previous hour. Hands stroking and loving her up and down. Twin mouths on her nipples. The culmination of sensations at her clit. She had to admit, it had been the best orgasm she'd had in years.

Smiling, Mina pulled her mind away from the self-tryst and tried to focus on the conversation. Charlotte was now frowning and silent.

"What?" Mina had no idea of what she had missed. She prayed she hadn't voiced her thoughts aloud. Now that *would* be embarrassing as hell.

Charlotte cleared her throat. "Did something *happen* at the building?"

*Goodness, could she tell?* "Ah . . . no."

"You sure?" Charlotte leaned forward, gray eyes piercing Mina's soul.

Mina felt the hairs rising on the back of her neck as she stared at Charlotte. If she had actually voiced her thoughts, Charlotte would have looked shocked, not this in-depth analysis she was doing now. Something else was up. "No. But seems like you think something should have, so spill."

The realtor busied herself with retying the bow on her polkadot, outdated blouse before speaking. "Sometimes people hear chains clanking, see paper flying about, just unusual things."

Well, getting horny and masturbating in an abandoned building was very unusual for Mina, but she didn't plan to reveal that. "No. No paper flying about, just dust. Definitely no chains clanking," Mina assured her with a shake of her head.

"Good," Charlotte replied, relief evident on her face.

Mina remembered the posters on the floor. "I do have a question, though."

The frowns were back in Charlotte's face. "Go ahead."

"There were movie posters all around and they were *suggestive.* I was wondering what type of movie theater was there before?"

A glimmer of a smile played on Charlotte's lips before she answered. "It was a triple-X–rated theater."

*Did she say triple-X?* That would explain the pornographic posters. "When did it close down?"

"Oh around twenty-five, thirty years ago. These young guys, I believe their names were John Whitmore and Cal Tolero or Toledo, I forget, anyway, it was run by these two guys. But they disappeared one night and no one has seen them since."

"They were murdered in the building?" No way was she interested in buying Amityville-gone-theater.

Charlotte shrugged. "No one's found either's body, so it's safe to say, if they were murdered, it probably wasn't in the building."

This was interesting indeed. "Any family?"

"That's what's so fascinating about this case. They showed up one day out of the blue, buy the building and open an X-rated movie house. The town was in an uproar, but they had the correct licenses and truth be told, not enough people protested to have them shut down." Charlotte snorted. "Honestly, I heard that many of our 'upstanding citizens' frequented the place. I know it was rumored they were making a mint. Had to be something to keep them in this small town."

There was much truth in that statement. St. Paulus had one factory that was on its last leg and the rest of the community depended on logging of the forests to survive. According to what the realtor had told her previously, nothing much had changed in forty years. There was a huge warehouse distribution plant being built that was supposed to open within a year. But right now, life was as it had been for many decades, minus an X-rated theater.

"So who owns it now?" Mina inquired.

"The town. No family came forward to claim it after the men left, and then it was condemned and reverted to the town twenty or so years ago."

No family. What kind of men had no family looking for them? Did they return to their families and just forget the town? Or was there something more sinister in the making? Mina's massive curiosity made her suddenly blurt, "I'll take it."

Charlotte didn't blink as she pulled a contract from her desk. "It won't take us but a moment to fill this out. How much are you offering?"

\*  \*  \*

John was having a hard time pushing the lush vision of Mina from his mind. It didn't help that his cock was still hard and throbbing. He wished for the millionth time he could have sex one last time. One last glorious, fulfilling moment of pressing his shaft between warm thighs, tangling between wet bush hairs, and releasing his seed into a deep, dripping cavern of love. Why didn't he follow his first mind thirty years ago?

Cal was having just as rough of a time as John. He absently ran his hands over and through his dirty blond strands, still smelling her oh-so-female scent in his mind. God, she was ripe. And he was dead.

"You think we should follow her?" John finally asked a pensive Cal.

"And be what? Her guardian angels or something?" Yes, they'd visited every home in town and could tell all of their secrets, but this time, it just didn't feel *right.*

"No, just keep an eye on her. She might be upset and not want the building." *And we couldn't enjoy her again.*

Cal heard the thought and echoed the sentiment, but he wouldn't interfere. If it was meant to be, it would be. "Naw, why don't we just let her make up her own mind about the building? Then, whatever happens, happens."

"Think they'll tell her about us?" John knew they'd made too many faces whiten in fear for the townspeople not to gossip about the haunted theater house. That didn't keep the vagrants and druggies out, though. The addicts just thought they were some of their drug-induced hallucinations for the most part.

"Probably."

John knew he was right. No way would they withhold something that juicy from her. If that irritating realtor didn't spill the enchiladas, you could bet the townies would. Resigned to whatever the future held, he asked, "Ready to get back to our game?"

"In a minute," Cal responded, the vision of fat, dusky nipples still on his mind.

# 3

Mina stood in front of *her* building, the deed clenched in her fist. She couldn't believe the negotiation and sale had taken all of four days. That had to set a record for a commercial real estate closing.

She smiled as she turned the key and opened the door again. The dusty, mildew smell assaulted her nostrils, but she ignored it as she trotted up the stairs to her library.

Try as she might, Mina couldn't get her reaction in the room out of her mind; couldn't understand why this room had made her feel so *sexy*. Twenty years of having sex and she managed to give herself her best orgasm ever. Go figure. The funny part was, she'd tried to duplicate the orgasm; tried to repeat her finger-loving performance again in her hotel room. She'd failed miserably. But she wanted that overwhelming rush of hormones; wanted the gush of juice running down her legs again.

Mina strode into the room, expecting her body to jump to attention. She twirled around, making the dust motes dance, as she traced a finger along a wall and pulled a tattered drapery from a window. She finally stopped and grinned at the dirty room. Her new home. That's when she noticed the tall cabinet doors.

The doors reached to the ceiling along the far wall. There were no knobs or handle to use as pulls, so Mina removed a nail file from her purse and wedged one open. She jumped back as it creaked wide. Mina didn't know if an army of rats would pour out or—she shivered slightly—a dead body. She was more than relieved when neither happened. Instead, inside were round metal canisters from floor to ceiling: celluloid movies. She hadn't seen one in decades.

Excited now, Mina forgot her previous reservations and wedged open the remaining doors, revealing more of the same. As she brushed the grime away and read the titles, an addendum to her plan formed in her head. By her estimate, there were nearly three hundred movies present. And judging from the titles she quickly skimmed, a goldmine of old erotica.

Her head was spinning with more ideas, adrenaline pumping, when she spotted a closed door she'd previously missed. Mina strode over and turned the knob. It squealed on its hinges as it opened little by little. The faint light through an opaque window revealed an old-fashioned bathroom, complete with a claw-foot tub and a wide pedestal basin sink. The spiders had taken up residence and Mina heard the skitter of small feet behind the wall.

What did she expect?

Mina crossed the floor and stood at the head of the tub. It was stained and the fixtures rusty. She turned the handle, surprised that it moved easily. Of course, no water flowed. She was sure it had been off for decades.

Her hands traveled across the basin sink where spider webs covered the faucet head and fixtures. She quickly tangled her hand in the web and pulled them away. An ornate mirror hung above the sink, its silver grimed over. She rubbed some of the grime away and smiled at her image. Winking at her own face, she tugged her shirt from her waistband and opened it wide. Then she perched one hip on the edge of the basin. She was prepared to act on any signals her loins gave her.

Cal groaned as Mina's shirt flapped wide. She wore a scrap of a bra that was so sheer, her nipples were visible through it. He wished he could read her mind; wished he knew if her pulling her shirt open was an act of desire or just hot weather.

John had been elated to see Mina return. His cock rose and saluted as soon as they'd heard the car door shut. It was now a flagstaff waiting for someone to climb upon it. Never one to be a follower while alive, he stayed true to himself in the afterlife as he floated over and hovered in front of Mina.

"John, I don't think we should—" Cal fell silent as John waved him off.

"Hush, man. I just want to feel her again."

"I know. I just don't want us to overwhelm her and she rescinds her transaction."

John chuckled a bit. "You and I both know there isn't a woman alive that would run from a great orgasm, no matter the source."

"True." Cal nodded, eyes peeled to the berries staring back at him. "Do your thing then. I'll just watch."

"Man, you've been a voyeur for three decades. I can't speak for anybody else, but I plan to see how far I can go with this thing—" John's voice faltered as Mina suddenly shifted, placing her breast in the full sunlight. He licked his thick lips, felt his cock grow as he gazed at the golden skin and the fine hairs coating it. They glowed in the warm rays.

John wanted to bite and bruise the tender flesh in pleasure–pain. Wanted to drag his tongue around and around the "outtie" navel above her waistband. Wanted to turn her around, sink his rod to the hilt and pinch those hanging tatas as they thrashed into the air. He couldn't help himself; he ran a finger between the exposed spheres.

Cal sighed behind him.

John turned his head to look back at him. "Still gonna watch?"

"I'm thinking," Cal responded, his hand now wrapped around his own stiff cock.

Mina didn't jump as she felt the warmth in the center of her chest. In fact, she welcomed it. Inhaling deeply, she let her head loll backward as the heat radiated beneath, and then around her globes. Her nipples hardened and saluted through her sheer bra. Mina ran her finger around her back and unclasped the sheer harness. Her breasts dropped beneath the fabric and into the cool air.

An ethereal touch to the stiff knobs made her moan. She clenched the now throbbing mounds; held them out for more. A wispy touch flicked back and forth across the tips, setting them on fire and sending sparks downward. Her clit lurched, pulsed. Honey pushed past her pussy lips and wet her thin panties.

Mina lifted from the basin and stood as she pulled her skirt over her ass. She turned and placed one foot on the edge of the tub, her hands headed for her clit.

John stood behind Mina, cupping her breasts in his hands. He knew she'd felt his touch when she'd moaned as he flicked her puckered nipples between his fingers. He pressed his body more fully into her, seating his cock between her thighs. He felt fleeting moments of warmth, nothing more.

Needing more, he closed his eyes, tried his damnedest to telepath his thoughts into Mina's brain. Craved for her to want *him*.

\* \* \*

The image burst into Mina's head—brown skin, cut muscles, hazel eyes and succulent lips. Mina had had her share of lovers, but one thing she definitely knew: this man had never been one of them.

*Let me love you,* the man whispered as his hands rubbed up and across her belly, leaving a fiery trail behind.

Mina exhaled noisily as teeth seemed to nip the back of her neck, a tongue following suit. The tongue slowly flicked her earlobe then swirled into her outer canal. Her entire body tensed as the wet appendage brushed deeper, and then warm, sweet breath was blown around her hot spots. The tongue teased and made promises as it nipped across her shoulders. Oh, the sensations! She was burning at her core. Her body quaked with desire and need as she felt a thick probe seat between her legs.

*Feel me.*

Her moan was prolonged and guttural. Wisps of heat burned upwards as she felt hands move and spread her thighs further. Mina ached with desire; clit throbbed with need as unseen fingers tap-danced inward. Her fingers refused to wait; indeed, mashed and circled her erect clit with abandon.

John pressed himself onto her back, lightly bending her forward. Mina gasped as fingers dipped into her heat, swirled and pumped as she rained honey.

*Let me love you.*

Mina arched her back in consent; spread her pussy lips in anticipation. The touch was at first fleeting, and then firm as the cock pressed between her lips inch by delicious inch. The thick cock's descent stopped only when her hips were tickled by the man's bush. Then the movement was reversed just as slowly, before the cock was thrust to the hilt.

*Damn!* Mina's pussy groped and Kegeled around the massive cock. Her fingers slid beneath her pussy to cup a heavy sac.

She squeezed and was rewarded with a double pump. Emboldened, she spread her legs wider, arched her back more, pushed backwards and pistoned rapidly, reaching for Nirvana.

Mina didn't have to wait long. She felt the pinpricks shoot up her legs and she clenched her inner walls as hard as she could. Her clit exploded before she slumped to the floor.